REBELS IN PISA

NICO ARGENTI
BOOK 5

KEN TENTARELLI

ISBN: 979-8-9856624-2-9 (ebook)

ISBN: 979-8-9856624-3-6 (paperback)

ISBN: 979-8-9856624-4-3 (hardcover)

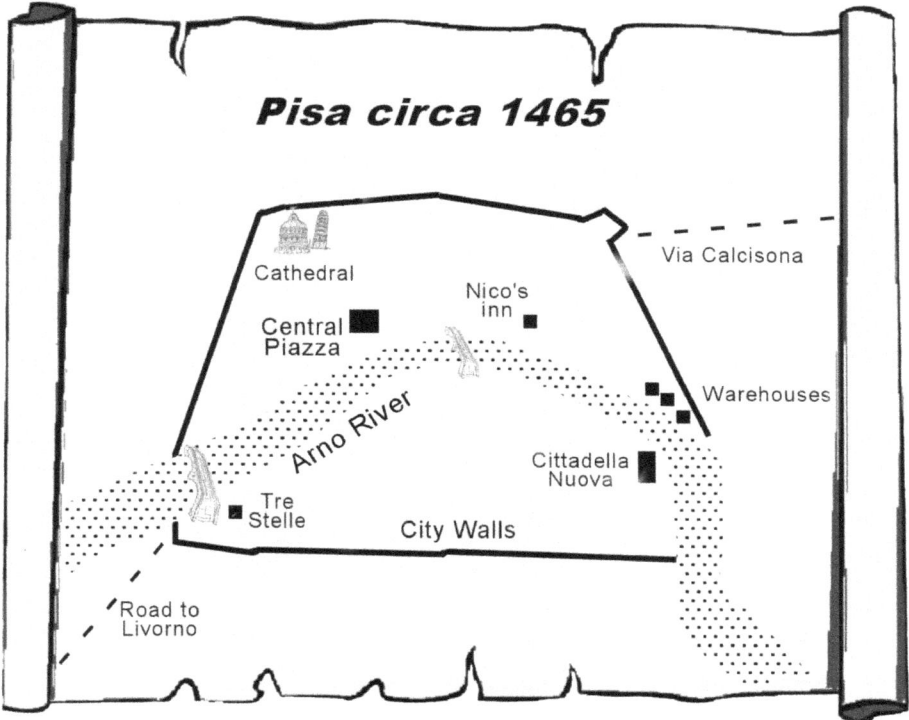

Pisa circa 1465

Cathedral

Central Piazza

Nico's inn

Via Calcisona

Warehouses

Arno River

Cittadella Nuova

Tre Stelle

City Walls

Road to Livorno

REBELS IN PISA

NICO ARGENTI
BOOK 5

KEN TENTARELLI

ISBN: 979-8-9856624-2-9 (ebook)

ISBN: 979-8-9856624-3-6 (paperback)

ISBN: 979-8-9856624-4-3 (hardcover)

Pisa circa 1465

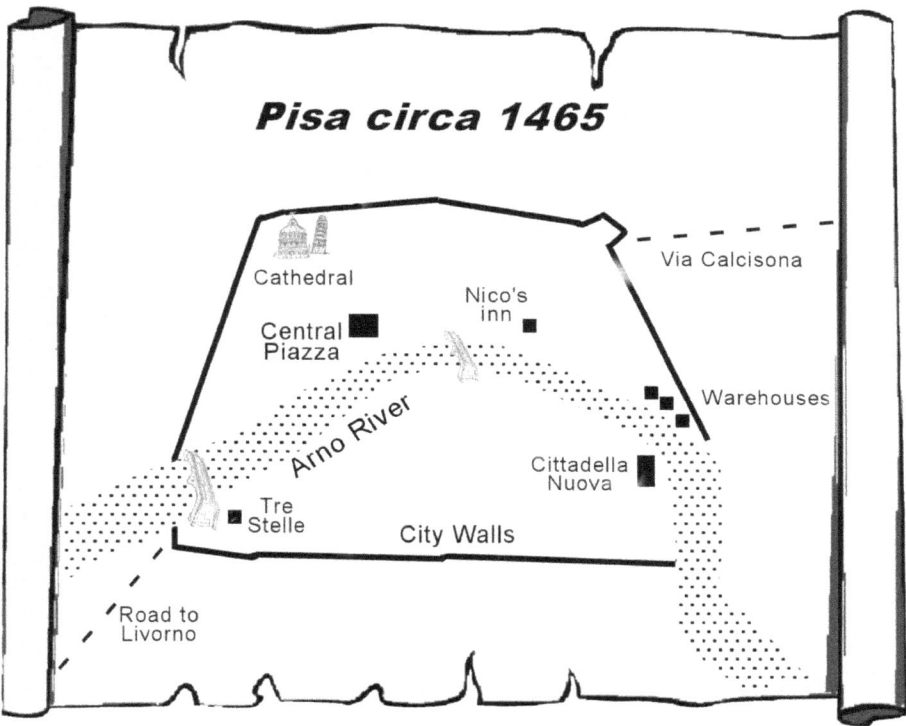

Cathedral

Central Piazza

Nico's inn

Via Calcisona

Warehouses

Arno River

Cittadella Nuova

Tre Stelle

City Walls

Road to Livorno

1

FLORENCE, AUGUST 30, 1465

First Chair of the Ten of War, Andrea Mozzi, the government official responsible for overseeing the Florentine army, stood gazing out a window across the piazza when Chancellor Scala entered the room. Scala passed between the conference table and massive desk that nearly filled Mozzi's office, prized space because the windows faced across the piazza to Palazzo della Signoria, the government office building.

"What draws your attention, Andrea?" Scala asked his friend.

"The Signoria's session ended moments ago. I find it telling to observe which members exit the building together." He pointed to a pair of men in animated conversation. "There is a cordial relationship I hadn't expected."

Scala raised an eyebrow. "In addition to being members of the Signoria, they're both members of the wool guild. At guild meetings they represent themselves as fierce competitors, but there's no indication of a bitter rivalry today." Scala swept his gaze across the piazza. "Here comes Moretti." A thin man wearing a dark green doublet scurried from the Palazzo della Signoria across the piazza toward Mozzi's office. He clung tightly with both hands to a portfolio of papers. Moretti would not be late for his meeting with two of Florence's most powerful officials.

Moretti stopped in the doorway, awaiting Mozzi's signal for him to enter. Mozzi raised a hand and beckoned his visitor. "Come in. Sit with us," he said.

Moretti stepped into the room then paused, uncertain where to sit, near the others or at the far end of the table. He chose a position midway along the side opposite Scala, and set his folio down carefully, as though fearful that it might scratch the highly polished tabletop.

As First Chair of the Ten of War, Andrea Mozzi was one of the most powerful and feared men in the Florentine Republic. He alone could commit the republic to wage war or to avert one. Some judged him as brusque because he never opened meetings with pleasantries. Only his confidants, like Chancellor Scala, knew his genial side. Mozzi faced Scala and declared. "Chancellor, you have a matter that bears discussion." The formality was for Moretti's benefit, as Scala had already briefed his friend when they had met earlier in the day.

To indulge Moretti's ego, Scala replied, "Signor Moretti brought the matter to my attention, so it would be best if he described his concern to you, Signor Mozzi." Scala and Mozzi used their given names only with close associates and Moretti was not among them.

Moretti reached for his folio, then reconsidered and folded his hands. "I often travel to Pisa to buy wool for my mill. Whenever I'm in Pisa, I join my cousin for dinner. He owns a brick yard. On my latest visit, he chose a small trattoria, one frequented by locals. While we were eating, I overheard snippets of a conversation at a nearby table."

Moretti's hands quivered as he opened his folio and removed a sheet. "Six men were at that table. One of them mentioned that he was arranging to purchase a quantity of weapons." He glanced down again at the sheet. "Yes, those were the words he used 'a quantity of weapons.'" Looking up, Moretti added, "A short time later, the man mentioned that he would be training loyal men to use the weapons."

"Did your cousin hear the conversation as well?" Mozzi asked.

"No. I was seated close to the men who were speaking. My cousin was across the table. It was a small trattoria, but it was noisy. The man's casual reference to weapons disturbed me. Later, I asked my cousin if he knew the men. He dismissed their remarks as braggadocio, but he did say there are many in Pisa who seriously resent Florentine rule. Even my cousin had complaints about the governor."

"What was the name of the trattoria?" Mozzi asked.

Moretti beamed, proud that he remembered. "Tre Stelle. It's across the river from the center of the city. As I said, it's a small place frequented by the locals. My cousin picked it because they serve excellent fresh seafood."

Scala rubbed his chin and reflected, "It's been four decades since Florence annexed Pisa, yet there are still malcontents in Pisa who hope for independence."

Mozzi turned toward Moretti. "Will you be returning to Pisa?"

"I have other business contacts in Pisa, so I'll be returning there, but I don't know when. Next week I'll be in Siena."

With a thin smile, Mozzi said, "You've done well by bringing this issue to our attention. Pisa has more than its share of agitators. Yours isn't the first such concern brought to our attention, and we must be on guard for those who advocate violence. Your vigilance is commendable."

Scala smiled inwardly, knowing that Mozzi had complimented Moretti the way one might praise a dog to encourage good behavior. Scala was also skilled in cultivating information sources, so he followed Mozzi's lead, saying, "Signor Moretti perceived a possible problem and came to me as soon as he returned from Pisa. As a result, I've already alerted the members of the Security Commission that they may need to go to Pisa to investigate these rumors."

"The Signoria met earlier. How did its members react when you told them about the situation in Pisa?" Mozzi asked.

Moretti recoiled, surprised by the question. "I didn't tell them. Today's meeting was about taxes. A few of the members who own vineyards want to raise taxes on imported wines." Moretti regained his composure and added, "And I thought you should be the first to know about the situation in Pisa."

Scala and Mozzi pledged to keep Moretti informed of any information uncovered by the Security Commission. After Moretti left the room, Mozzi leaned forward, resting his elbows on the table. "This is the second report of unrest in Pisa. We can't allow it to fester. What have you told the commission members about the mission? How will they proceed when they arrive in Pisa?"

"It's not clear how they should proceed. They'll use discretion as they have in their prior assignments."

"Will they contact the Provincial Governor?"

"The Governor is a trustworthy Florentine, but I can't say the same for the members of his staff. Some are Pisans who may have divided loyalties."

Scala paused a moment then added, "Also, I've received reports stating that Pisans have been displeased by the governor's rulings. If those reports are accurate, his attitude may be exacerbating the situation, so I think it best if the commissioners keep their mission secret initially."

Mozzi nodded. "I too have heard that the governor treats Pisa as though it were his own duchy. He has even resisted directives from the Signoria, so he might not be pleased to have members of the Security Commission in his territory. However, there is one person the Security Commission members can look to as a reliable contact if they find themselves in need of assistance. Captain Tano Carfi heads the army delegation at Pisa. In the past, he reported to a military officer in Florence, but after the last period of unrest in Pisa, the Signoria decided that Carfi should report directly to me so I can keep my associates on the Ten of War apprised of any problems. I've known Tano for many years and have complete faith in him."

"I'll pass the captain's name to Nico along with the name of the trattoria that Moretti mentioned, the one where he overheard the conversation that got him excited. Those bits will at least give the commissioners a place to start."

Mozzi leaned forward and rested his big hands on the table. "I'm extremely pleased with our new Security Commission. In the few months that it has been in existence, Nico, Massimo, and Vittorio have accomplished more than we could have anticipated. They stopped Milan from overwhelming our wool industry and they defused a threat from mercenaries in Bologna."

"I agree," Scala said. "When we formed the commission, I had reservations about whether those three could work together effectively since they have very different backgrounds and personalities. After seeing the results they achieved in Milan and Bologna, I've become convinced that their differences let them complement each other, and I expect that collaboration will again prove successful in Pisa."

2

FLORENCE, SEPTEMBER 2

From his position in the gallery at the rear of the courtroom, Nico eyed the prosecutor shifting uneasily in this chair. The edgy behavior surprised Nico because he knew Luca Sasso as one of Florence's most confident litigators. Nico had first met Luca a decade past on an athletic field when Luca's Santa Novella team challenged Nico's Santa Croce team for the city pallone championship, and over the years, the two men had become fast friends. Today, though, Nico found Luca's normally high confidence to be lacking.

Luca began his accusation against defendant Bruno Fiorello, an ironworker with a history of violent behavior and robbery. This time Fiorello found himself charged with assault. Reluctantly, Luca called upon the sole witness who claimed to have seen the altercation, even though he knew the man lacked credibility. The stigma became clear when Fiorello's lawyer had his turn to question the witness. He undermined Luca's case by showing that the man had been drinking heavily when he claimed to have seen the crime and that he had lied under oath when testifying at a prior trial.

After both lawyers completed their presentations, the magistrate, following normal practice, announced, "I must take time to deliberate. Expect my decision tomorrow." He gathered up his notes and exited the chamber. Others followed until Luca Sasso and Nico were the only two remaining in the room.

Luca remained seated at the prosecution table, gazing at the empty witness stand, his shoulders slumped. He sensed Nico approaching, rose, and hugged his friend. Nico said, "Even before the trial began, I could tell you were troubled."

Luca shrugged. "I know Fiorello is guilty, and I knew that I didn't have enough evidence to prove it. If it were my choice, I wouldn't have taken this case to a tribunal because the Guardia hasn't been able to gather sufficient evidence, but the schedule wasn't under my control."

Nico put his hand on Luca's shoulder and said in a sympathetic tone, "I used to have faith that our legal system would always produce a just outcome. I've learned painfully that the system sometimes struggles."

With his face showing mild amusement, Luca said, "If the trial were being held twenty years past, Fiorello could have been tortured until he confessed. It was a brutal system, but it produced results in situations like this. Cosimo de Medici made many changes that helped our republic, but at times like this, I think that eliminating torture wasn't one of the improvements." Nico did not respond, certain that his friend's comment was made in jest.

Bruno Fiorello stepped outside into the sunlight and inhaled deeply. The air no longer held the oppressive heat and humidity of summer. A gentle breeze foretold the cooler autumn days ahead. Bruno snickered as he watched his lawyer moving briskly across Piazza della Signoria on short legs, scurrying like a frightened duck. Bruno had to admit his initial misgivings about the lawyer had been unfounded. This was the third time that the little man had defended him, and in each case he had done well. Bruno could tell from the magistrate's scowl that the lawyer had effectively rebutted the eyewitness's testimony, and the delay to allow the magistrate to deliberate was a purely perfunctory act. He knew that he would soon be acquitted.

Bruno Fiorello was fortunate to have the best defense lawyer in the city. His boss, the manager of the iron smelter, had seen to that. On most days he, along with a crew of other men at the smelter, shuttled iron ingots from the dock to a warehouse outside the city. As laborers, none of those men were individually valuable to the company. Any of them could be replaced by peasants eager for work. Florence always had more peasants than jobs, but Fiorello's willingness to perform other tasks without question set him apart from his fellow ironworkers. The boss would be at a disadvantage if his underling were to waste away in a prison cell, so he happily paid the lawyer's fee to have Fiorello available to do his bidding.

Nico and Luca saw the self-satisfied defendant standing in the piazza when they exited the court chamber. Luca gnashed his teeth with contempt for the scoundrel who had skirted justice. The lawyers crossed the piazza to a small trattoria that served simple traditional meals. Its tasty food and prompt service made it a favorite of lawyers and notaries who frequented the establishment throughout the day, as their schedules allowed.

The server, a young woman with a pretty face and a welcoming smile, followed the men to Luca's favorite table near the kitchen. She carried two mugs of beer and set them down even before the men were seated. She knew the preferred lunch time drinks of all the regular patrons. If they had arrived later in the day, she would have brought wine instead of beer, a Chianti for Luca and a Brunello for Nico.

Luca ran a finger over the rim of the mug. "Ah, Giulia, someday I'm going to marry you." Her smile broadened. She dismissed playful teasing from other patrons, but she carried a faint hope that Luca's might be more than a casual flirtation. Like other women of her social standing, she often dreamed of marrying a handsome and wealthy lawyer. That Luca was also pleasant and thoughtful set him above the trattoria's other patrons. The men didn't ask for a menu because the chef prepared only one lunch offering each day and it was always delicious.

The trattoria was unusually quiet compared to others in Florence because lawyers spoke softly, never sure whether a lawyer or notary at a nearby table might be employed by their competition. They could not risk having a detail mentioned casually in noontime conversation compromise one of their court cases. Nico took a sip of beer and said in a low voice, almost a whisper, "The defense lawyer seemed self-assured... and capable. His questions were direct. He didn't waste time with trivialities."

Luca took a large swig before responding. "He's one of the best, and very expensive. A laborer like Fiorello couldn't possibly afford his fees."

"Someone else arranged for him to represent Fiorello?" Nico speculated.

"I'm certain of that," Luca replied. "Fiorello works at the Bastine iron smelter. When old man Bastine was in control, he hired only reputable men. Now his son, Rinaldo, is in charge, and he has no reservations against hiring known criminals and lowlifes. Fiorello is no stranger to the courtroom. Two months past, I prosecuted the case where Fiorello was charged with assaulting the owner of a rival smelter. I suspect he was ordered to do so by Rinaldo, but there is no way I could prove that connection."

"Was Fiorello found guilty?" Nico asked.

"No," Luca replied with a sneer. "The Guardia had not been able to find any witnesses to that crime, but Fiorello's lawyer produced someone at the trial who testified that Fiorello wasn't the assailant. The goddess Fortuna has been smiling on Fiorello and she may see him acquitted again, but eventually the lady will turn her back on the reprobate and when she does, I'll be there to see that he spends his days in prison."

The server set generously filled plates of shellfish and pasta in cream sauce in front of the men. The fare was exactly what Nico had expected. Ever since he was a child, he had challenged himself to guess the featured entrée solely from its aroma. After years of honing the skill at his cousin Donato's restaurant, he was rarely wrong. The server's eyes locked on Luca as she announced, "The chef selected the clams himself when the barge arrived from Pisa this morning." Nico knew immediately that the shellfish were mussels, not clams, but he saw no benefit in correcting her.

Luca watched the server until she passed into the kitchen out of view, then he took another swig of beer and leaned back in his chair. Nico noted his friend's eyes following the girl and quipped, "Are you drawn to this trattoria by the food or that lovely young woman?"

Grinning broadly, Luca retorted, "Must it be one or the other? Am I not allowed to favor both?" In a serious tone, he said, "Nico, I was surprised to see you in the gallery. I've rarely seen you since you were appointed to the Florentine Security Commission."

"My business at the Chancery ended early today, and I heard you were prosecuting a trial nearby."

"Regrettably, you didn't see my best today. Come again next week. I'll be filing charges against a stonemason who used inferior materials in a bridge he built for the city. That case might not have all the intrigue of your adventures, but I'm confident of a win."

"I'd enjoy watching you score another win, but I might not be in Florence next week."

"Are you being sent away again?" Luca asked.

"Yes. My last two assignments took me to Milan and Bologna. This time I will be going to Pisa. When I took the position on the Security Commission, I didn't realize I would be spending so much time away from Florence."

Luca leaned forward, his elbows on the table. "Are you unhappy?"

"No, not at all. As you said, the assignments are exciting and our commission has foiled some serious threats against the republic, but I do regret the time away from family and friends."

Luca grinned. "By friends, I assume you mean Bianca."

Nico's eyes sparkled. "She's coming to Florence in a few days to call on customers."

"Surely she doesn't travel alone."

"No, her uncle, a former member of the Siena Guardia, always accompanies her. When they arrive in Florence, she and I intend to meet with my friend Sandro Botticelli. Do you know him?"

"I've heard the name. If I recall correctly, he's an artist."

"Yes, he is. He wants to meet with Bianca to talk about dresses and a painting. A strange combination. I'm not sure what is on his mind."

Luca laughed. "It can be impossible to guess what creative ideas are conjured in the minds of artists. You've told me that Bianca has her own dressmaking business. Does she have any clients in Pisa? If so, perhaps she can join you there."

"Her home and business are in Siena. She comes to Florence often because she has many customers here. She has a few customers in Faenza, and she has had inquiries from Milan, but none from Pisa. Her customers are wealthy women." Nico laughed. "I don't know whether there are any wealthy women in Pisa."

Luca downed another mussel, took a swig of beer, and asked, "Are you free to say what is happening in Pisa that demands your attention?"

"A member of the Signoria, who is a lodestone for gossip, heard a rumor about agitators who want to gain Pisa's freedom from Florentine rule. He spread the hearsay to other members of the Signoria, and now they're pressing to have the matter investigated. Some excitable members of the Signoria see Satan everywhere, so now they fear there may be an uprising in Pisa." Nico waved a hand in a dismissive gesture and said, "It could be nothing, but trouble often makes its first appearance in a rumor."

Luca raised an eyebrow. "Better you should find nothing than to face Satan. When do you depart for Pisa?"

"It hasn't been decided yet." Nico's lips turned up in a smile. "I hope to spend a few days with Bianca before I must leave. I think my fellow commissioners, Massimo and Vittorio, could be ready to leave tomorrow. Vittorio rarely has commitments that keep him in

Florence, and Massimo has only to pull himself free from the arms of his latest lovely."

Luca raised his mug in a toast. "May your endeavor be successful and if Satan is stirring Pisa, may he never hear your approaching footsteps."

3

FLORENCE, SEPTEMBER 5

Cool air followed the river's course as Nico crossed the Ponte Vecchio bridge to Florence's Oltrarno district. A flock of ducks glided over the bridge and settled onto the Arno River. Nico kept the birds in view as he walked along the riverbank, but he thought only of his heart's treasure, Bianca Cellini, and the precious little time he would have to spend with her before leaving for Pisa. He turned away from the river and continued a short distance to Palazzo Corsini. The palazzo was the residence of Signor Corsini, who owned a large woolen mill that made him one of Florence's wealthiest citizens. His wife was one of Bianca's devoted customers.

A servant answered Nico's knock. Nico introduced himself and stated that he was there to meet with Signorina Cellini. As the servant led Nico to an anteroom, he said, "The signorina is with Signora Corsini. You may wait here until she is free."

Nico crossed the room to a bookcase that lined one wall and withdrew a book titled *De Docta, Ignorantica,* Learned Ignorance, by a German philosopher. Nico had heard of the book with the strangely contradictory title, but he had never seen a copy. He recalled philosophy professors debating the subject when he was a student at the

University of Bologna. Some professors subscribed to the bizarre precepts while others ridiculed them. Nico settled into a chair and tried to read, but he found his eyes glazing over and his thoughts wandering after reading only a few pages. His mind was on Bianca, not on philosophy. A few minutes later, although seemingly an hour to Nico, Bianca appeared in the doorway to rescue him. He startled upon hearing her call his name and looked up abruptly, nearly dropping the book he had been holding. He rose, took her hand, always warmer than his own, and kissed her gently.

From Palazzo Corsini Nico and Bianca headed across the river to the Uccello, his cousin Donato's restaurant. "You seem pleased," Nico said. "Was your visit with the signora fruitful?"

"Better than I had anticipated. Signora Corsini asked me to design a dress for her to wear at an upcoming event of the Wool Guild. We had planned to meet to discuss style ideas for the dress. I hadn't known that her younger sister would be joining us. The girl became so excited at hearing my design ideas that we spent most of the time discussing dresses for her. Now, instead of having an order for one dress, I have orders for three new dresses."

"And the number might grow further when you hear what Sandro has in mind," Nico said. "He's going to meet us at the Uccello. He gave only a fragmented explanation of his reason for wanting to meet with you, but he did mention the need for a dress. Perhaps a gift for a woman friend," Nico speculated.

"I didn't know that Sandro had a special woman."

"One can never tell with Sandro. His life changes direction from day to day."

The Uccello's outstanding food offerings — 'incomparable' was the word often used to describe them — earned it the reputation as Florence's finest restaurant. In reality, it was a private club where men could relax, dispense with social rigor, and, as one patron said, 'escape from wifely pressure.' Only on Sunday afternoons and certain holidays were women permitted in the main dining room; however, the Uccello also had separate rooms for private parties where women were always welcome. Nico and Bianca entered through an entrance that led directly to one of the private rooms.

Five place settings on the dining table suggested that Donato and his wife Joanna would be joining Bianca, Sandro, and Nico for dinner. A side table held three bottles of Venaccia, a white wine from Siena selected by Donato in Bianca's honor. Across the room near the kitchen, Sandro was waving his arms wildly as he regaled a server with one of his many tales about incompetent government officials. Suddenly, Sandro raised both arms and slapped his hands together above his head. Both men burst into laughter and the server nearly dropped the tray of *stuzzichini* he was holding. Sandro's carefully choreographed arm movements cued Nico that he had already heard that story, although he couldn't recall which government functionary it belittled.

When Sandro saw Nico and Bianca, he scampered across the room, took one of Bianca's hands, and looked at it as one might gaze upon a precious jewel. "If you had been at Troy, Paris surely would have selected you as the fairest over those squabbling goddesses Athena and Aphrodite, and Homer's epic would record a different outcome of the Trojan War. I would not believe it to be possible, but every time I see you, you are more lovely."

Bianca smiled politely, while Nico merely shook his head. Both were accustomed to Sandro's hyperbole. Nico quipped, "I can't help but wonder whether that fabrication wins you success with the prostitutes at *il Pennello*."

After recoiling in feigned offense at Nico's comment, Sandro laughed, kissed Bianca lightly on the cheek, and embraced Nico. Nico led the trio to the table and poured three glasses of wine. Sandro read the markings on the bottle, then raised his glass. "To the vintners and the lovely women of Siena."

After joining Sandro's toast, Nico said, "I'm eager to hear your reason for wanting to meet with Bianca."

Sandro took another sip of the golden wine, set down his class, and said, "You've seen one of my paintings that depicts a scene from Greek mythology."

"Actually, I've seen two of them," Nico replied. "One at Palazzo Pitti and one in the main hall at the hospital in Siena. Bianca has seen both as well."

Sandro's eyes widened in surprise. He turned to Bianca. "You saw my painting of Venus and Apollo at Palazzo Pitti?"

"Yes," Bianca replied. "I visit with Francesca Pitti every time I come to Florence. She's always keen to see my newest dress designs. She also showed me the portrait you made of her."

"I didn't paint the portrait. As a student of the maestro, I merely added the background."

"Francesca said that you also added shading to the portrait."

Sandro startled and raised a finger to caution silence. "You must never repeat that. She should not have told you. The maestro would be horrified if he heard that. Filippo Libbi's an extraordinary artist, but he's in great demand with more commissions than time allows. If the portrait could have had his full attention, he would have done the shading properly. My brushwork only compensates for his lack of time, not for any failing of his skill."

Sandro paused, took a sip of wine, leaned forward, and said, "Tell me honestly your impression of the painting at the hospital, the one of the muses."

"It's my favorite of those on display," Bianca replied. "The bright colors make it stand out from all the others. It's..." She paused to find the right word. "Cheerful. And the scene is so realistic. Looking at it, I feel as though I'm looking through a window to the past."

Sandro beamed with pride. "I am one of six young artists sponsored by the Medici. We are given complete freedom to exercise our artistic creativity. It's truly an exceptional opportunity. Once each week we artists join together in the courtyard at Palazzo Medici to paint, share ideas, and view each other's work.

"At our last meeting, I was working on a scene depicting the goddess Artemis. I sensed someone standing behind me. I turned and found myself facing young Lorenzo de'Medici. He looked intently at the rendering, hardly more than a sketch. He studied it for several minutes, then he commented using the very same word you chose. He said it made him feel cheerful.

"When Lorenzo took a step back, he said, 'This painting is small and perhaps that best fits this subject. Can you imagine a subject that lends itself to being done larger... full size?' I was struck dumb by his attention to my work, so I merely nodded. Since then, I've been thinking about his suggestion, and I have an idea. It's not fully formed, just a concept: the transformation of the goddess Flora."

"Flora, the Roman goddess of springtime," Nico said aloud as he recalled her story. "She was originally Chloris, a nymph, who was transformed into a goddess by the god of the west wind."

"Ah, you do your tutor proud that you remember the story," Sandro said. "That is indeed the myth's essence."

"What has this to do with Bianca?" Nico asked.

"To bring my mind's images to life, I must see them before me. I must behold the cascade of Flora's hair, the draping of fabric and the folds in her gown." Sandro set his gaze on Bianca. "I need gowns for the nymph Chloris and for Flora, the goddess of *Primavera*."

Bianca pursed her lips thoughtfully. "I've been experimenting with printing patterns on different kinds of fabric, and recently Nico's friend Armando sent me a measure of soft silk from his mill. The fabric is brilliant white with a bright luster. Printed with colorful springtime flowers, it could be perfect for your Flora. I'll need to take measurements of the woman who will be wearing it."

Sandro stroked his chin. "Normally I use the women at *il Pennello* as models, but they all have dark hair, and in my vision, Flora has light hair and fair skin." He kept his gaze targeted on Bianca. "Even in this dim light, the golden highlights of your hair are radiant. The color is unusual for Italians."

Bianca ran a finger through the hair cascading onto her shoulder. "My light hair is from my father. He came from the Kingdom of Denmark to study at the Salerno medical school. He met my mother there and never returned to Denmark. I understand that light hair is common in Denmark."

"I have a thought," Sandro suggested slyly. "If you would consent to be the model for my Flora, you could fit the dress to yourself."

"I've made many gowns, but never for myself, only for others." Bianca reached down and smoothed the front of her dress as she considered Sandro's idea. "I've only made simple clothes for myself."

Turning to Nico, Sandro asked, "Do you have an objection to Bianca being my Flora?"

Nico laughed. "It's not my position to object. Bianca makes her own decisions."

Bianca tacitly agreed to Sandro's proposal saying, "It will take time for me to print the flower patterns."

Sandro raised his wine glass to his lips and leaned back in his chair, satisfied that he would have not only gowns for his painting but also a lovely woman to portray Flora. "Time is not a concern," he said. "I have yet to conjure a complete vision for the painting and doing so will take time. It always takes time."

Donato and Joanna entered the room, followed by servers carrying trays of antipasti. After telling the newcomers about Sandro's endeavor, the conversation moved to a discussion of Nico's assignment.

"You must take better care of yourself in Pisa than you did in Bologna," Joanna cautioned.

"Massimo will be with me. He can protect me from the Pisan rabble," Nico joked.

"You make light of the danger, but you still bear scars from the beating you received in Bologna," Bianca admonished.

Nico and Donato shared a look. Both men knew that Pisa, like every other city, had a district where criminals and lowlifes roosted, but neither man wanted the women to worry. Donato came to Nico's aid, saying, "I've traveled to Pisa many times to make arrangements with fishermen so the Uccello can have seafood on our menu, even when other restaurants in Florence cannot. In my time there, I've never seen violence. I would say Pisa is a tranquil city."

Joanna countered, "You would say the same for Milan or Bologna, yet wherever Nico ventures, trouble finds him. He needs to be more wary." She placed a hand on top of her husband's, which he understood to mean that she would not welcome further objection from him.

After an awkward silence, Sandro asked, "Are you permitted to divulge the purpose of your mission to Pisa?"

"I know only that a member of the Signoria heard that dissidents in Pisa are once again talking of independence. The report may be only a rumor. Vittorio, Massimo, and I will visit places where agitators might gather so we can learn whether there is a real threat or only petty grumbling. Our intent is to listen. We don't plan to confront any troublemakers."

This time it was Joanna and Bianca who shared a look and a thought. *They never intend to confront trouble at the outset; yet it always seems to find them.*

Conversation dwindled as the antipasti platters were passed around the table. Shortly after dinner, Sandro, Donato, and Joanna found reasons to leave. They knew this was the last opportunity for Nico and Bianca to be together until he returned from Pisa.

4

PISA SEPTEMBER 6

The three Security Commission members traveled separately from Florence to Pisa. Massimo had arranged passage on one of the many barges that traverse the river between the two cities. He told Nico, "The barge is slower than horseback because it stops at wharves in towns along the way, but it's a more pleasant, smoother ride." Smiling, he added, "I can relax and watch the lovelies on shore as I float by." Vittorio hadn't spoken with Nico before he departed for Pisa, so Nico did not know his mode of transport.

Since Nico was the last of the three to leave Florence, he opted to travel by the fastest means, on horseback. He set out after breakfast, stopped midway to eat a lunch packed for him by his sister Alessa, and arrived at Pisa in mid-afternoon. He took a room at an inn that Chancellor Scala had suggested along the Arno River, near the center of the city.

Nico had not been able to think clearly enough to plan his next steps when he was bouncing along on horseback. Now, alone in his room, as he washed away a layer of road dust, he pondered how he was going to find the agitators in a city where he knew no one. He wondered how Massimo and Vittorio intended to proceed. Vittorio would certainly have a plan; he always had a plan. Massimo did not need one. The goddess Fortuna favored Massimo, so success always found the handsome, outgoing soldier. Nico chuckled as he thought, "If history is a guide, Massimo is already in a tavern somewhere charming a comely serving girl."

Nico opted to orient himself to the city while considering how he might hunt for agitators. Like Florence, Pisa was divided by the Arno River. Nico walked along the riverfront until he saw the cathedral's bell tower in the distance to his right. He turned away from the river and followed the road to the cathedral. Unlike Florence, the cathedral was not in the city center. It was in a far corner close to the city wall.

He stood for a moment admiring the unique structure, a mixture of several architectural styles. He marveled at the differences between Pisa's cathedral and Florence's Santa Maria del Fiore. How is it possible, he wondered, that construction on both began about the same time; yet Pisa's cathedral was completed nearly two centuries earlier.

From the cathedral, he walked a short distance to the campanile. Nico had to admit to himself that the bell tower, with its arcades of columns, was more beautiful than the bell tower in Florence, but at least Florence's tower stood up straight. Like Venice, Pisa prospered through trade with North Africa and the Levant, but it had none of Venice's worldliness. It was a small city like Milan, but it lacked the wealth and ducal court of Milan's Sforza family.

Nico continued his exploration of the city, thinking he might recognize other sites, but none looked familiar. He had visited Pisa once before when he was a youngster. He remembered fondly the time he spent there with his parents. His father had been an army officer who traveled with Florentine diplomats on official missions. Those assignments often took his father away for weeks at a time, leaving Nico and his mother behind in Florence. The visit to Pisa was an exception; it was a holiday excursion that the family shared. He recalled playing near a pond in a field of tall grasses, but on this walk he saw neither a field nor a pond. Could the city have changed that much in little more than a decade?

Nico wound his way through the city center and back to his inn. He had no sooner entered his room when a knock on the door interrupted his thoughts. After being attacked by thugs when he had answered a knock on his door in Milan, he was reluctant to open the door. "Who?" he asked brusquely.

"A courier from the Florentine Chancery with a message from the Chancellor," came the answer.

Nico released the latch, pulled the door open, and faced a young man who was covered with a heavier layer of road dust than the one Nico had just washed away. The courier held out a note and as soon as Nico took the paper, the courier turned to leave.

"Wait," Nico called out. "Would you like to come in? There's a basin of water where you can wash and there's water to drink."

"Thank you, Messer Argenti, but the chancery maintains facilities where I can wash..." He looked down at his doublet, its deep red fabric hidden under tan road dust and added, "and don fresh clothes."

Nico unfolded the note and read the two concise lines penned by Chancellor Scala's hand. 'Meet Trattoria Tre Stelle. Inquire Father Mazzei at Santa Caterina.' During the time Nico had been a member of the Security Commission, little more than a year, he had learned to decipher the Chancellor's cryptic notes. The first line told him to rendezvous with Vittorio and Massimo at Trattoria Tre Stelle. The second line suggested that he begin his search for information about the possible agitators by speaking with a priest named Father Mazzei at the church of Santa Caterina.

Scala's note did not say when Nico should meet his colleagues at the trattoria, so he decided to go there and wait until the others appeared. At the inn's common room, he found the innkeeper asleep in a chair when he went to ask for directions. Both the innkeeper and the gray striped cat sleeping on the man's lap emitted rhythmic wheezing sounds. Nico's approach awakened the cat, who scrambled up onto the man's shoulder. "Whaa.." the man shrieked as one of the cat's claws raked his cheek. He shook himself awake, spotted Nico, and grimaced as though expecting Nico to lodge a complaint about his room.

"*Scusa Signore*, can you direct me to Trattoria Tre Stelle?" Nico asked.

The innkeeper rubbed his eyes and repeated, "Tre Stelle." He squinted and furrowed his brow as he regained his senses. "Follow the river as it flows until you come to the bridge. Across the river, you will see the church in Piazza San Paolo. The trattoria is behind the church." He rubbed his eyes again, stared up at Nico, and added as a caution, "Tre Stelle? Are you certain? It's not popular among visitors. The food may be acceptable, but it's not the finest in the city."

Nico shrugged. "I'm meeting someone."

"After you cross the river on the Ponte della Cittadella, walk along the river. You will see Tre Stelle on a side street, but look carefully because it has only a small sign," the innkeeper added.

Nico followed the innkeeper's precise directions. As the innkeeper had said, Tre Stelle was small, with only four tables lined along one wall. It was too early for dinner, so Nico was not surprised that the tables were empty. A telltale scent of fish drifted in from the kitchen. With the Ligurian Sea being close, the fish certainly would be fresh, so if the chef were competent, the food should be more than acceptable.

Massimo stood with a beer mug in hand, talking to a woman who was assembling a plate of antipasti on a side table. They were the only two people in the room, although noises from the kitchen suggested that the chef, probably the woman's husband, was preparing the dinner fare. The woman's hair, black streaked with gray, was wound into a knot atop her head. She wore a spotless white apron over a simple blue dress. Her hands moved deftly as she arranged alternating slices of cheese, fruit, and smoked meat. Without turning to look at Nico, she said to Massimo, "The man who just entered must be one of those you are expecting." After filling the antipasti plate, she went to fetch a mug of beer for Nico.

Nico and Massimo moved to the table at the rear of the room and took seats facing the entrance so they would see Vittorio when he arrived. The woman followed them to the table, where she set the antipasti in the center of the table and a mug of beer in front of Nico.

Massimo said, "I didn't see you at the inn, Nico. The Chancery arranged a room for me at the inn near the Santa Cristina church. Are you at the same inn?"

"No, Chancellor Scala must have us scattered throughout the city. My room is across the river, near the city center. I took a walk earlier to the cathedral, and I passed several churches, but not Santa Cristina."

"The church and the inn where I'm staying are on this side of the river."

Vittorio pulled the door open enough to peer into the trattoria and scanned the room. When his eyes adjusted to the darkened interior, he saw his colleagues and joined them at their table. The woman, cued by a small bell that sounded when the door had opened, followed Vittorio to the table. She set another plate of antipasti on the table and asked Vittorio, "Beer?"

Seeing that Nico's and Massimo's glasses were nearly empty, Vittorio replied, "A pitcher."

"Dinner tonight is sea bass with leeks. Our son works on one of the fishing boats. He always brings us the best of the day's catch," the woman said proudly. "With one fish, I can usually serve four or five sailors." She looked directly at Massimo as she added, "but if you haven't eaten since making the journey from Florence, maybe one fish will be right for three hungry travelers." The innkeeper might be wrong about Tre Stelle not having the finest fare in Pisa, Nico thought.

Massimo looked at Vittorio and asked, "The Chancery arranged for Nico and me to have rooms in different parts of the city. What arrangement did they make for you?"

"I had suggested to Chancellor Scala that we could better observe the people of Pisa if we were separated. I am lodging in Livorno, not Pisa."

"The seaport?" Nico retorted with surprise.

"Yes," Vittorio replied. "I've been to Pisa before, so I'm familiar with the city. In Roman times, it was a port city. At that time, the sea came right to the city walls, but in the past millennium, soil washed down from the hills filled the harbor. At first it became a swamp and now it's completely filled and has been made into farms. Pisa is a long distance from the sea, so a new port for seagoing vessels was built at Livorno."

Nico said, "The two towns complement each other, with Livorno being the seaport and Pisa being the commercial center. Goods from Livorno are moved to warehouses in Pisa where they are stored, before being transferred by barges to towns and cities along the Arno River."

Vittorio continued, "I chose to stay in Livorno because sailors are constant complainers. Complaining is like a religion with them. I want to know whether there is a growing resentment of Florence among the sailors in Livorno. If I find none, I'll find a room in Pisa." Looking to Massimo, Vittorio asked, "Are you going to make contact with the Florentine army contingent in Pisa?"

"No. The Chancery hasn't been notified of soldiers hearing anything about troublemakers planning hostile actions, so I plan to start by frequenting places popular with lowlifes and criminals, places where a glass of beer can loosen a tongue."

Nico laughed. "While Vittorio is nosing around foul-smelling ships, you'll be spending time in taverns and brothels."

Massimo grinned. "We each must make sacrifices in our own way." He raised a hand, gesturing toward Nico. "And what will you be doing, lawyer? From your dress, it appears that you intend to spend your time in courtrooms."

For the first time, Nico noticed that Vittorio and Massimo were wearing simple smocks of the kind worn by workmen, while he wore a fine tunic. He didn't voice his observation, although he decided to be more conscious of his clothing choices in the future. "I received a note from Chancellor Scala suggesting that I contact a priest at the church of Santa Caterina. The note didn't say what information the priest might have, and the Chancellor didn't mention the priest when I was in Florence."

The woman was serving customers at the only other occupied table when the chef brought a platter containing a large sea bass to the table. He filleted the fish at the table and served each man a generous portion. Conversation slowed during dinner. Afterwards, the men agreed that the food was delicious, and the venue afforded privacy, so they would meet again at Tre Stelle in two days.

5

FLORENCE SEPTEMBER 6

The patriarch of the Bastine family ambled into the room with the bearing of a lost soul. "Where's the driver? He's supposed to take your mother to church this morning. She wants to make a novena. Yesterday, I told him to bring the carriage early this morning."

Across the room, his son Rinaldo glanced up from the papers he had been reading and grumbled, "I've told you before, father, he can't be relied upon. Every day after work, he goes to a tavern and meets with laggards who spend their days gambling. He probably had so much to drink last night that he's still sleeping in an alley somewhere."

The father waved a hand dismissively. "Be a good son. Get a carriage for your mother."

Rinaldo turned so his father could not see his scowl. "I have work at the smelter. I'll get a stableboy to bring the carriage for her."

"It doesn't matter who drives as long as she gets there. If she misses the novena, she'll complain all day, and I can't spend another day with her nagging me." The old man cocked his head. "Maybe I should come to the smelter with you. You said that a new shipment of ore is arriving today."

"Yesterday. The shipment came yesterday." *Lord help me*, Rinaldo thought, *his memory gets worse every day.* "I have matters to discuss with Fiorello. You don't want to be bothered."

The senior Bastine slumped down onto a chair. "I'll wait here for the carriage. Maybe the driver is just late and he'll bring it soon."

You can wait until the angel of death comes for you, but you won't see that weasel again if Fiorello did what I told him to do.

Whenever his schedule permitted, Rinaldo ate a hearty breakfast before going out to manage operations at the smelter, but he wouldn't have that pleasure today. His father spoke the truth: if a carriage did not arrive in time to take his mother to the morning novena, she would spend the entire day whining. However, it wasn't his father's suffering that concerned Rinaldo, it was fear that the old man might leave the house and go to the smelter. Rinaldo believed that old men like his father should play cards and read books. They should not meddle in business affairs.

Rinaldo passed through the kitchen on his way out of the house. With one hand, he grabbed a date-filled sweet roll and with the other, he grabbed the cook's daughter's curvy backside. The poor girl, afraid to protest, or even to tell her mother, could do nothing but tolerate his repeated abuse. She had friends who endured worse.

Neither the girl nor Rinaldo saw Rinaldo's sister Gemma enter the kitchen and witness the incident. Her memory returned to a similar episode years past when she had found another girl pinned against a wall by her brother. One of Rinaldo's hands had cupped the girl's breast and his other hand had slipped up under her dress. On that occasion, Gemma had reached for the nearest object, a shovel, gripped its shaft tightly with both hands, and swung the blade, slamming it against Rinaldo's head. He crashed to the ground, dazed. He never again touched the poor girl, and he still carried the scar where the blade's edge cut into his cheek.

When his father had learned of that incident, he had banned Rinaldo from the house for a week. The boy took his meals outside, some in the rain, and he slept on the damp ground. At week's end, his father had said, "If the Devil has finally left you, you may return to my house." Now Rinaldo was no longer a boy who could be cast out by his father, so Gemma vowed that she must be the one to vanquish this new devil. As she watched her brother leave the kitchen, she puzzled over the ways she might discipline her brother.

Rinaldo walked to a stable outside the city walls where he arranged for a carriage to take his mother to the church, and he hired a horse for himself. Bright sun and a gentle breeze from the hills north of the city made for a pleasant day. Had he not had an appointment with a customer later in the day, he would have walked the additional mile or so to the smelter.

The smelter sat on a bluff where Torrente Mugnone, a stream flowing down from the hills near Fiesole, joined the Arno River. Rinaldo scanned the horizon to the north, looking for any storm clouds. The smelter was close to the stream so waterpower could operate the bellows that forced air into the blast furnaces. Seasonal autumn rains always swelled the stream, sometimes pushing over its banks. Two years past, water from the raging stream inundated the smelter, causing operations to be suspended for a week. On this morning though, Rinaldo saw only blue sky.

He tied the horse to a post, walked to the small office building attached to the smelter, and looked through the building's only window but saw no one. He went around to the smelter entrance, where he flushed red when hot air engulfed him as he reached the open doorway. He scanned the space, reluctant to enter the stifling, noisy work area. He spotted several men, sweating and covered with ash, who were tending the two blast furnaces, but he didn't see Fiorello.

He turned toward the dock where barges came to unload their cargo of iron ore and spotted a supervisor. "Where is Fiorello?" he shouted.

The supervisor finished coiling the rope he had been holding and walked toward Rinaldo. "You didn't hear?"

"What? What didn't I hear?"

"Fiorello was arrested. They say the Guardia caught him beating up someone in an alley."

"Merda!" Rinaldo bellowed. He stomped a foot and ground his boot heel into the dirt. "Where is he now? Where did they take him?"

"I don't know," the supervisor replied sheepishly. "The Guardia have him, so I suppose he's in a prison cell."

"What happened to the man Fiorello was beating on?"

The supervisor shrugged and stepped back, not wanting to be within striking distance of his frenzied boss. "I don't know. I didn't hear anything about him."

Fiorello was supposed to finish the weasel. If he's still alive, it could lead back to me. Someone must know what happened to Fiorello, Rinaldo told himself.

Rinaldo rode to the stable, dismounted, dropped the reins, and yelled to the stable boy, "Take him." Fuming with every step, he walked from the stable to the office of his lawyer in the center of the city where he burst into the office and demanded, "Is he in?" The clerk, accustomed to Rinaldo's insolence, responded with a weak smile. He rose from his desk intending to knock on the lawyer's door and announce Rinaldo's arrival, but Rinaldo held up a hand to freeze the clerk in place and pushed his way into the inner office.

The lawyer was standing alongside his desk practicing an opening statement he had prepared for an upcoming case when Rinaldo burst into the room. He set the papers he had been holding down on his desk, settled into a chair, and motioned for Rinaldo to be seated. He disliked interruptions, and he disliked Rinaldo, but the prospect of a bountiful payment softened his objections. Work done for Rinaldo was always lucrative.

"You are troubled, Signor Bastine. How can I help to ease your burden?" Before Rinaldo could speak, the lawyer called to his clerk. "Bring something for Signor Bastine." From Rinaldo's prior visits to the law office, the clerk knew the man had a fondness for pastries. He rushed out to the neighborhood *pasticceria.* It was early, so he knew the shop would still have an ample selection of sweets.

The lawyer had informants in all the Guardia district offices to keep him apprised of any crime that might call for a defense lawyer. He looked at Rinaldo with a knowing smile, and said, "There was an assault last evening in the Santa Maria Novella district. Might your concern be related to that incident?"

"I heard that Fiorello has been arrested."

"Again?" the lawyer said to emphasize Fiorello's repeated transgressions.

Rinaldo ignored the question. "I must know the condition of the victim. Is he alive? Has he been identified?"

The lawyer folded his hands together on his desk. "Sadly, the victim did not survive the beating, and he has not been identified."

Some might have been upset by the victim's demise, but not Rinaldo. Death meant the victim could not be connected to him. His muscles relaxed. Since he was not at risk, he could concern himself with his minion. He took a deep breath, exhaled, and said, "The book of Luke says, 'if a brother is in need, God will love those who help him,' so we must do what we can for Fiorello. Loyalty is important and Fiorello is loyal."

The lawyer's stomach turned. *How can Rinaldo say those words without choking on them? It's been a long time since Rinaldo touched a Bible. If he read the Holy Words, he would know that his misstated quote is from John, not Luke.*

He leaned forward and rested his elbows on the desk. "You must understand, this is a serious matter. It is not like Fiorello's habitual brawls. The victim is dead. Fiorello may be charged with murder. And there are witnesses."

Rinaldo did not ask about the circumstances of the crime, and Fiorello's guilt did not matter to him. He waved a hand dismissively and said, "You've always been able to find flaws in the prosecution's case. I'm confident that you can do so again."

Although the lawyer knew that countless criminals walked the streets of Florence thanks to loopholes he uncovered, it hurt to be reminded of that bitter fact. "I will look into the matter."

Rinaldo left all thoughts of Fiorello at the law office. As soon as he stepped into the street, his attention turned to business. He was already halfway across the city, so rather that retrieving the horse from the stable, he opted to walk the rest of the way to meet with his customer. A short distance beyond the Porta la Croce gate, he came to the shop of Florence's most productive armorer. The sound of hammers striking metal blanks drummed in his ears well before he reached the shop. "How can anyone tolerate this infernal noise?" he said to himself.

Inside, three shirtless smiths pounded forge hammers against metal bars repeatedly, carefully shaping the blanks into daggers, swords, and other fierce killing instruments. Two of the men did the initial modeling; the third man, a craftsman and member of the armorers' guild, honed each piece precisely into its final form.

The shop owner spotted Rinaldo and signaled the smiths to take a break, otherwise conversation would have been impossible with the constant pounding of metal upon metal. The owner wore a heavy leather apron, although he never did any smithing himself. He pulled sound-deadening cloth wads from his ears. "Rinaldo, I trust you've been well." Rinaldo muttered an incomprehensible reply. "The men are finishing the last of your goods. They will all be ready for delivery tomorrow, as we agreed." From the shelf behind him, he lifted a sword having a wide blade and a spatulate tip and handed it to Rinaldo. "We matched every sword we produced to this one, as you requested. What did you call it?"

"A Kaskara," Rinaldo replied.

"Yes. Kaskara." The owner didn't ask who would be the recipient of the unusual blades.

"I have additional needs," Rinaldo stated.

"Certainly. Whatever you desire. More Kaskara?" The armorer had already supplied Rinaldo with a dozen of the oddly shaped weapons. He thought it strange that the owner of the smelter that supplied his metal blanks was now a customer, but he knew better than to question the windfall.

"No. A more conventional design will be sufficient this time. I have learned that the men who will use them are neither trained nor experienced in combat."

"Ah, our one-handed sword would serve that purpose well. And how many do you require?"

"I don't have a final count. I need to show this customer that I can deliver quickly and at a fair price. We have to prove to him that Florence can satisfy him, otherwise he might look to armorers in Milan or weapons imported into Genoa."

The owner boasted, "Our blades are the highest quality, superior to anything produced in Milan."

"Quality will not win this customer. He doesn't know metals. Only cost and speed of delivery will matter to him."

The armorer rubbed his chin. "Any measures I take to lower cost will compromise quality. It has taken years and much effort to build my reputation. I cannot have it known that I make inferior products."

"I understand. I won't reveal my source to the customer. You have my word."

The armorer laughed inwardly. Was there any value in Rinaldo's word? He thought for a moment, then said, "There are steps I can take, but you also have ways at your smelter to lower the cost of the blanks you send me."

"That's true," Rinaldo mused. "We can shorten the firing time. It will change the carbon content of the blanks, but this customer won't notice.

"When can you deliver ten blades? Ten should be enough to entice the customer."

The armorer walked to his desk and scanned a sheet of work orders. "I can defer other work." He thought for a moment, then said, "Two days. I can have them ready two days after you deliver the blanks."

Rinaldo nodded. "Two days. Good. You'll have the blanks tomorrow." As he turned to leave, he added, "And one more thing, it might be best if the blades did not carry your mark."

6

PISA SEPTEMBER 7

A barking dog jarred Nico from a dream of sitting with Bianca on the Monte alle Croce overlook enjoying the sweeping vista of Florence, the dream so vivid that he even smelled the fragrance of alpine lilies. Nico pulled the coverlet over his ears, wishing he could return to the fantasy, but the incessant barking kept him in the real world. He rose and stepped to the window, intending to reckon time from the sun's position. Unfortunately, the view from his room looked out onto a narrow courtyard cast into shadow by a nearby building. When he pushed the window open, city noises flowing into the room along with the crisp morning air confirmed that he had slept longer than he had intended. Still satiated by the previous evening's dinner, Nico decided to compensate for oversleeping by foregoing breakfast.

He opened his duffel and looked through the clothes he had packed. Massimo had been correct in saying that his clothes were those of a Florentine lawyer. If he didn't want to draw attention in Pisa, he would need to wear simple tunics. Later, he would seek out one of the vendors who sold clothes to the city's laborers. In the meantime, he brushed dust from his only plain tunic, the one he had worn while riding on horseback from Florence to Pisa. It would be adequate for his visit to Father Mazzei.

Nico opened the door to his room, took one step into the hallway, and nearly collided with a boy of about ten years, who struggled under the weight of the heavy sack on his shoulder. Nico followed the boy downstairs to the innkeeper's small office. The innkeeper pointed to a sack on the floor propped against a wall and said to the boy, "Leave the one you are carrying and take this one to the laundry." The youngster dropped the heavy sack and hoisted the smaller one. "My nephew," the innkeeper said to Nico. "He's a hard worker." The boy, suddenly aware that Nico was behind him, stepped aside.

Nico glanced at the boy as he asked the innkeeper, "Can you give me directions to the church of Santa Caterina?"

The innkeeper raised a finger to point and opened his mouth to speak, but instead, he gestured toward the boy and said, "He knows the church. He can show you."

"Come," the boy said, his face beaming with pride at have been given the important task of guiding the newcomer. "Santa Caterina is beyond the laundry. I can leave these bed coverings at the laundry and then take you to the church."

The boy walked briskly. His self-esteem kept him from showing that carrying the sack was an effort. Nico introduced himself. Rather than calling himself Signor Argenti or Messer Argenti, he chose to say simply, "I am Nico."

"Finito," the boy replied.

Puzzled by the boy's statement, Nico asked, "Finito? Is that what you are called?"

The boy chuckled. "Yes, Finito is my name. It surprises everyone. I have two older brothers and three older sisters. When I was born, my mother held me and said 'Finito.'"

After depositing the laundry, Finito led Nico across the city and stopped in front of a gleaming white church. "This is Santa Caterina," he announced. He stood for a moment, admiring the beautiful structure. The church outshone all the surrounding buildings. It must

have been cleaned recently, Nico thought, because thin layers of soot
from heating fires made other buildings, even those of light-colored
marble, lose their luster and take on the patina of gray sandstone.

Nico read the name on a small plaque. *Santa Caterina d'Allesandria*.
He pointed to the sign and asked, "Do you know of the place Allesan-
dria?" Finito shook his head. "It's a city in Egypt," Nico explained.
The boy continued to stare up at Nico with a blank expression. Nico
considered telling the boy that Egypt was a destination in Africa and
some ships that sailed from Livorno went to Egypt, but he wasn't sure
Finito had heard of Africa, and he wasn't certain whether ships from
Livorno did sail to ports in the Eastern Mediterranean.

Nico thanked Finito for his help and entered the gothic church,
unaware that Finito had trailed him. He was immediately struck by
the sight of a large altarpiece brightly illuminated by the morning
light. He walked the length of the nave to where he could admire the
artwork. Each of its seven panels depicted a saint painted nearly half
life size. The central panel, slightly larger than the others, showed the
Madonna with Child. Nico felt chagrined that he could identify only
two of the other six images: Mary Magdalene and John the Baptist.
Even more impressive were the rows of smaller images above and
below the primaries. Thirty or more saints, Nico guessed. He doubted
that his parish priest, or even the Archbishop of Florence, could identify them all.

Nico leaned forward to peer at the image of John the Baptist, the
patron saint of Florence, when he heard the creaking sound of a side
door opening. A frail, white-haired priest stopped in the doorway to
cross himself before entering. "*In nomine Patris. In nomine Filii. In
nomine Spiritus Sancti.*" The old priest's eyes widened at seeing Nico as
though he expected the church to be empty. He carried candles in
each hand and shuffled to a side chapel. His fingers trembled as he
placed the candles in holders. Nico approached him and asked,
"Father Mazzei?"

The priest turned by degrees to face his questioner, who said, "I
am Nico Argenti. Chancellor Scala sent me to speak with you."

The priest looked puzzled at first, then said, "Bartolomeo?"

"Yes," Nico replied. "Bartolomeo Scala."

The mention of Scala's name caused the priest's eyes to brighten and his step to quicken. "Let's talk outside," the priest said, and led Nico out through the side door to a cloister surrounding a courtyard with a fountain at its center. The fragrance of fresh cut foliage reached Nico before he spotted a woman pruning flowering shrubs on a path that encircled the fountain.

"I haven't seen Bartolomeo since... since I was a priest in Milan when he was a student studying law, and now he is the Chancellor of Florence. I'm not surprised. Even as a young man, Bartolomeo showed signs that someday he would rise to hold an important position. You said that Bartolomeo sent you to speak with me?" the priest asked.

"Yes, the Chancellor thought you might be able to help me. Reports have reached Florence of unrest in Pisa. Officials in Florence worry that discontent might lead to hostile actions. Chancellor Scala thought you might have insight into the cause of the discontent."

Mazzei ran a hand down his pale cheek. The alertness he exhibited only moments ago had faded. His movements slowed and his voice softened. Nico had seen other men of Mazzei's age display similar losses of clarity, so he repeated his request. "Bartolomeo Scala said you might be able to tell me about unrest among the people of Pisa."

This time, the mention of Chancellor Scala did not spur the priest as it had done previously. With an unsteady voice, he said, "Many in Pisa are unhappy with Florence. They say Pisa is treated like an unwelcome child. I hear people say this to each other, although no one speaks about such things to an old priest. I'm sorry, but I cannot help you." Mazzei paused a minute, said, "Tell..." — he struggled to recall the Chancellor's name — "Bartolomeo that I will pray for him," then turned and walked away.

Nico's shoulders slumped. His only lead had just proven to be worthless. He had hoped that Father Mazzei could give him information about the activists, but now he had no idea how to proceed. He heard soft footfalls approaching from behind, and from the corner of his eye, he saw Finito move close beside him and look up at him expectantly.

The woman who had been pruning shrubs approached Nico. "Three years past, Father Mazzei suffered a seizure," she explained. "He has not been the same since that terrible episode. Saints forgive me, but I cannot understand why such a thing should happen to a man of God."

"The curse of age falls equally on all men, good and evil," Nico said, surprising even himself with his cogent rationale.

"Pardon me for overhearing, Signore, but this courtyard does not muffle voices. You are looking for troublemakers who might cause problems for Florence." As if to explain her reason for caring, she added, "I was born in Florence in the Santa Croce quarter. My sister still lives there." Her lips curled up in a smile upon recalling a family memory.

"Do you have information about troublemakers?" Nico asked, using her word.

"No, not me," she said, shaking her head, "but there is someone who will have information you seek, the miller."

"The miller?" Nico repeated, surprised to hear that a tradesman would have knowledge of a conspiracy.

"His mill is outside the city, but he knows everything that happens in Pisa. He has two sons. One is an official in the city government; the other one manages a warehouse. They make sure that their father is well informed."

Finito said, eagerly, "I know the grain mill. I can take you there."

Nico ran a hand through the boy's hair. "You seem to know everything in Pisa, my young friend."

Finito's response, "I've lived here my entire life," made Nico laugh.

Walking away from the mill, Nico said, "Taking bed coverings to the laundry is a big help to your uncle. When I was your age, I used to help my uncle, too."

"Did your uncle own an inn?" Finito asked.

"No. My uncle owned a restaurant. In the mornings before meeting with my tutor, I would go to the restaurant and sweep the floor."

"Does your uncle still own the restaurant?"

"His son, my cousin, owns it now. It's one of the finest restaurants in Florence. If you ever go to Florence, I'll take you there." The youngster's eyes lit up and his step quickened at the thought that one day he might visit Florence.

Finito led Nico out of the city through the Porta Monetaria gate toward the foothills to the north. A cool breeze sweeping across the flat river valley carried the faint salty smell of the nearby sea. After walking about one-half mile, Finito pointed to a building in the distance. "That's the grain mill." In another half mile, they reached a sturdy building alongside a gently flowing stream. A water wheel splashed rhythmically as its paddles dipped into the moving water.

A burly man carrying a flour sack on his shoulder walked from the mill to a nearby wagon. "Are you the miller?" Nico asked.

"He's inside," the man grunted as he lowered his load into the wagon bed.

Nico ducked his head to pass through the mill's low doorway. He paused briefly to let his eyes adjust to the dim dust-laden interior. "Are you the miller?" Nico asked a man who was drawing flour from a hopper.

"I am. I'll be with you when I finish here." Nico waited while the miller filled two sacks and his associate carried them to the wagon.

The miller brushed flour from his hands then said, "Outside." After watching his associate climb aboard the wagon and drive away, he asked, "Can I help you?"

"I was told you know everything that happens in Pisa."

The miller snickered. "Only the Lord knows everything."

Nico decided to be circumspect with the miller. "I heard there is to be a protest."

"A protest?" the miller asked, suspicion obvious in his tone.

"Against Florence."

Now wary, the miller scanned Nico from head to toe. "Who are you? Are you from the Guardia? Or that *serpe* governor?"

"Neither the Guardia nor the governor. I am from the Chancery in Florence," Nico said, only a slight distortion of the truth. "A report reached the Chancery that some in Pisa may have complaints. If there is a problem, we would like to address it."

The miller tensed and his face reddened in anger, then just as quickly, his tension dissipated. "I find it difficult to believe that the Florentine Signoria suddenly cares about Pisa. Pisans have been complaining for decades. What made Florence finally take notice that they would send an emissary? When did you arrive in Pisa?"

"I arrived yesterday."

The miller snorted. "No one can come here for one day and expect to understand us, but let me tell you this. Pisa was once a great sea power. Now our city is like a sick old woman and every year the sickness grows worse." The miller swept an arm in a broad gesture. "My grandfather built this mill before Pisa was sold to Florence by the degenerate Duke of Milan. By what law of God can one man sell a city and its people? And do you know the price?" He answered his own question. "80,000 florins. 80,000! The Medici spend that much for a wedding celebration."

Nico knew the claim was an exaggeration, but he chose not to challenge the assertion. Instead, he countered, saying, "The Medici are building a fortress..."

Before Nico could complete his statement, the miller raised a hand to interrupt. "The Medici are building their fortress at Livorno, not Pisa. They're building it to protect their shipping interests. It will do nothing for Pisa. Once Pisa was alive with businesses. Now, many merchants have gone elsewhere and those who remain see their businesses withering. Good men cannot find work to support their families."

Having vented his ire, the miller walked to the stream where he gazed at the shimmering water to regain his composure. For several minutes, he watched a bird searching for food along the stream bank. When the bird finally pulled a morsel from the soft mud and flew away, the miller turned around and returned to Nico. In a calm voice, he said, "You asked about Pisans with animosity toward Florence. Yes, there are men who say Pisa should reclaim its independence. You have only to listen to the business owners and the men who cannot find work to hear their resentment. They don't hide their beliefs. They voice their complaints openly."

Nico knew better than to ask for names. Instead, he asked, "Can you tell me where to begin?" hoping the miller might volunteer a name.

The miller folded his arms across his chest. "Ask any shop owner about his business and he'll speak of his troubles. Now, I must tend to my business." He turned back toward the mill, began walking away, and called over his shoulder, "Ask at the Medici bank. The manager is one of yours. He should be willing to speak with a fellow Florentine."

As Nico and Finito retraced their route back to the city, Finito asked hesitantly, "You were sent from Florence? From the Guardia?"

Nico thought that it might be difficult for the boy to understand the concept of a Security Commission, so he replied, "No, I'm not a member of the Guardia. I am a lawyer sent by the Signoria in Florence. The Signoria heard that some men in Pisa have concerns and I was sent to help resolve their issues before anyone resorts to violence. No one wants violence."

They walked a distance while Finito mulled over Nico's explanation. "The miller said you should listen to business owners. How will you do that?"

"I'm not sure," Nico answered offhandedly. Despite the miller's assertion, Nico questioned whether shop owners would reveal anything more than superficial concerns to a stranger. He had gained little by talking with the priest and the mill owner. The only promising suggestion was that he talk with the manager of the Medici bank.

"My uncle, the innkeeper, knows many people who own businesses. Maybe he can help you," Finito offered brightly, enjoying his role as a guide to this important visitor to his city.

From the grain mill, Nico and Finito followed the stream as it meandered closer to the city. Nico noticed the foliage change from dark green-gray scrub to light green reeds. Whether imagination or not, he couldn't be sure, but it felt that the soil underfoot was softer, spongier. "Does this area flood?" he asked.

"Maybe in the spring," Finito replied. "They say that a long time past this area was swamp when the sea came close to the city."

When the city wall became visible in the distance, Nico and Finito left the stream bank and headed directly toward the Porta a Lucca gate where they entered the city. As they neared the inn, Finito ran on ahead. He waited impatiently outside the office while the innkeeper served one of the guests. The moment that the innkeeper was free, Finito burst into the office. "Uncle, Nico...I mean, Signor Argenti was sent from Florence to fix all the problems in Pisa. I told him that you know the men in Pisa who are unhappy with Florence." The innkeeper looked at his exuberant nephew dubiously.

When Nico reached the inn, he saw the innkeeper cautioning his nephew against making promises to strangers. "Sometimes my nephew speaks when he should be holding his tongue," the innkeeper said.

Nico tried to clarify his purpose. "I can't promise to fix problems myself, but if I can understand the concerns of the men of Pisa, I can bring the issues to the Signoria in Florence."

Reluctant to become involved, the innkeeper searched for the right words. "Finito is correct in saying that there are men who are bitter about Pisa's treatment by Florence. They gripe constantly to each other, but they won't speak to a Florentine." He leaned back against a counter. "To them, the governor represents Florence. Whenever people brought injustices to him, he showed no interest in correcting the problems." He bit his lip, thinking that, like his nephew, he had said too much.

"There must be some who would speak to me," Nico said with a hint of desperation in his voice. "We visited a miller who suggested that I speak with the manager of the Medici bank."

The innkeeper paced across the room and gazed out a window. A building in the distance caught his attention. He turned back to face Nico. "That is a reasonable suggestion." Nico waited patiently until the innkeeper continued. "The manager of the Medici bank in Pisa is one of your own, a Florentine. He must deal with irate businessmen regularly, so he should know their troubles and complaints."

"Do you know him?" Nico asked.

The innkeeper chuckled. "No, I have no need for a large bank like the Medici. My business is with a small Pisan bank."

"I told you my uncle could help you," Finito said as he moved toward the door. "I can lead you to the Medici bank."

Nico tousled the boy's hair and said, "I appreciate your help, Finito, but I've already kept you too long from your chores."

As Nico turned toward the door, the innkeeper said, "The banks are not open at this hour. You'll have to wait until morning."

"It is not late. The banks in Florence are open at this hour," Nico said reflexively.

The innkeeper's glance drifted down at the floor and then back up at Nico. "There isn't enough business in Pisa to fill a day. Many businesses are forced to limit their hours."

Nico used the afternoon to find a vendor of simple smocks that would let Nico fit the persona of a common worker. At the central market, he visited two stalls and both proprietors took offense that someone would ask them for peasant clothes. The second vendor directed Nico to a nearby convent that collected clothing for the city's needy. For a generous donation, Nico came away with two smocks. Although used, they showed little wear and would suit his purpose.

Mindful of his sister Alessa's reproach, Nico used his time in the evening to pen a letter to Bianca. Alessa was right in urging him to be more attentive to Bianca. He closed his eyes and visualized Bianca's golden hair and lovely smile. He could imagine her designing a beautiful, printed fabric for a dress that she would model for Sandro's painting. When Nico was with Bianca, conversation always came easily, but he struggled to find news worthy of inclusion in a letter. He did not want to dwell on his disappointment at having made little progress thus far in finding any agitators, and he had not seen enough of Pisa to describe the city. Finally, he settled on telling her about his amusing companion for the day, Finito.

7

LIVORNO, SEPTEMBER 7

It was Vittorio's outstanding performance as a Guardia investigator that had earned him an appointment to the Florentine Security Commission. Years of experience had taught him the best way to become acquainted with new places and people took patience, enough to observe their behavior from daybreak to dark. He rose early to begin his familiarity with Livorno by walking the length of its waterfront.

He donned a heavy cloak for protection against the cold mist that had blown in from the sea overnight. From his inn, one block from the water's edge, he could hear waves slapping against a breakwater, but the thick fog blocked his view of the fishing boats and ships moored at the wharf. Every day, fishing boats hunted bluefin tuna and swordfish in the bountiful Ligurian Sea. Larger vessels loaded with Florentine wool and Milanese silk sailed from Livorno to ports in Sicily and northern Africa where they exchanged fabrics for fruit and spices.

When Vittorio reached the wharf, he heard voices coming from his right. Following the sounds led him to a ship where a man standing outside the wheelhouse, most likely the captain, was berating the crew. "Where is Stefano? Were you all drunk again last night?"

One of the crewmen replied, "We didn't get drunk. All we had were a few beers at The Rusty Anchor, and Stefano wasn't with us." Vittorio noted that the statement drew strange looks from the other crewmen, but none challenged him.

The captain turned to the cabin boy behind him. "Go to Stefano's house. Tell him to move his ass. We've got to sail with the tide. We can't wait for him. Go! Go!"

The boy jumped from the deck, ran toward the town, and quickly vanished into the fog that swallowed both his form and the sound of his feet slapping against the wet ground. As Vittorio and the others watched the gray vapor for the boy's return, an almost imperceptible shift in the wind drew the fog away from the town and out onto the water. As that fog thinned, a cluster of houses became visible in the distance, one with its door ajar. The cabin boy stood outside, speaking to someone in the house.

Seconds later, the boy turned away from the house and raced back to the ship. Gasping for breath, the boy said, "He's not there. His wife said he didn't come home last night. He's missing."

"Merda," the captain bristled. "We can't wait. The rest of you will do his job on this voyage. Unhook the lines and ready the sails."

Vittorio watched the ship ease itself away from the pier and read the name *Nereid* painted on the stern as the vessel silently slid into the mist. Two fishing boats cast off from their moorings at a nearby dock and followed in the wake of the large vessel. The captain might be correct in his assumption that Stefano was off somewhere recovering from a night of excessive drinking. Vittorio had no reason to believe otherwise, but Vittorio never settled for assumptions. Although Stefano's disappearance bore no relationship to Vittorio's assignment of uncovering dissidents who might be planning hostile actions against the Florentine Republic, the experienced investigator felt compelled to pursue the matter.

A young woman answered Vittorio's rap on the door. A colorful ribbon held her long dark hair back from her face. Her plain gray smock may have been clean when she dressed; now it showed food stains from the infant she held close. Vittorio registered surprise at her having opened the door to a stranger. No Florentine woman would have done so. Without introducing himself, Vittorio said, "I'm looking for Stefano."

The woman took a quick glance toward the waterfront, wondering whether this man might also be from the fishing boat. "He's not here. I don't know where he is."

"When did you last see him?"

"Yesterday afternoon. He went to the cobbler shop, and he never returned."

"Has he ever disappeared like this before?"

"No," she answered quickly, then began to wonder about the man asking questions. "Who are you? Are you from the Guardia?"

Although Vittorio had a letter issued by the Florentine Signoria introducing him as a member of the Florentine Security Council, he felt sure that showing the letter to the woman would only add to her confusion and concern. Instead, he replied, "I'm a visitor from Florence." Before the woman could ask why a Florentine had interest in her Stefano, Vittorio said, "Can you think where he might be? Is there someone he might be with?"

"No. There's no one." Her anxiety growing, she tensed and said, "I couldn't sleep last night." She shifted the infant from one hip to the other. "Stefano knew he would be leaving this morning for Tunisia, and he would be gone for weeks. He had a shoe that needed fixing and he wanted to have it repaired before he sailed." The infant, sensing her discomfort, began whimpering.

"Did you ask about him at the cobbler's shop?"

"Not yet. After I feed the baby, I'll go there."

"Stay with your child. I'll speak to the cobbler," Vittorio said in an authoritative voice that kept the woman from disagreeing.

Vittorio had noticed the small cobbler shop earlier when he rode from Pisa to Livorno. The shopkeeper was just opening his shop when Vittorio arrived and followed him inside. Vittorio did not know Stefano's family name, but he knew that would not be an obstacle. He said, "Stefano brought a shoe yesterday for you to repair."

With a quick glance, the cobbler saw that the man before him was a stranger, but he had no reason to withhold information. He walked to his workbench, picked up a shoe. "Stefano left this to be repaired. He said it had to be done yesterday because his ship was sailing this morning. It just needed the leather to be restitched." He held the shoe so Vittorio could see it and pointed to the new stitching. "I told him it would be ready in about an hour, but Stefano never came back. Did he send you to get the shoe?"

Vittorio waved a hand dismissively. "I didn't come for the shoe. I'm looking for Stefano. He's missing."

"Missing?" the cobbler repeated.

"His wife said he didn't come home last night, and he hadn't returned by the time his ship sailed this morning. Did he say anything to you? Did he say where he was going after he left your shop?"

The cobbler set the shoe back down on the workbench. He leaned back against the bench and ran a hand through his thick white hair. "He was going to see someone at the shipping company. He didn't tell me a name." The cobbler bit his lower lip. "He seemed troubled."

"What do you mean, troubled?"

"He kept squirming like a child who knows a secret or knows that something is wrong but is afraid to talk about it."

"You said he was going to the shipping company. Are you sure he said the shipping company and not the ship?"

"Yes, that's what he said, the shipping company."

"His ship is the Nereid. Do you know the company that owns it?"

The cobbler gave a resigned shrug. "His wife must know," Vittorio said to himself.

This time, when she answered the door, Vittorio recognized the woman's changed mood immediately. On the surface, she displayed relief at her husband's return, but the experienced investigator detected her underlying fear. "Stefano is back," she said excitedly. "He returned home shortly after you left here."

"I'd like to speak with him."

"He's in bed. He's not feeling well."

Her quivering voice keyed Vittorio to press further. "Is he sick?" The woman opened her mouth to speak, but she couldn't find the right words. Her faltering confirmed Vittorio's suspicion. "I want to speak with him," he said forcefully. He pressed the door open wide and stepped into the house. "Where is he?"

The frightened woman stepped aside and pointed. Vittorio swept past her into the bedroom. A single candle on a side table illuminated a figure in the bed. Even in the dim light, Vittorio could see Stefano's swollen eye and the welt on his forehead. "What happened?"

Stefano turned away to avoid facing his questioner, but Vittorio walked around the bed to get a better look at the victim. Darkened bruises covered both of Stefano's arms and a gash on his chin still oozed blood. "Who did this to you?"

"I don't know. I didn't see them. They grabbed me from behind," Stefano groaned. With all the strength he could muster, Stefano asked, "Who are you? Why are you questioning me?"

"I'm a member of the Florentine Security Commission. Now tell me, the people who hurt you, what did they want? They must have said something."

"No, they didn't say anything."

"They just grabbed you and started beating you for no reason?" Vittorio said incredulously.

Stefano cast his eyes down and said nothing.

Vittorio bent slightly to look directly at the injured man. "You didn't get those bruises on your face from men behind you. You must have seen them."

In a raised voice Stefano said, "I don't want to talk about it. I want to rest."

Vittorio pressed further. "You went to speak with someone at the shipping company. Whom did you speak to? What is the name of the company?"

Stefano grimaced as he raised his head and bellowed, "Get out! Leave me alone! I won't say anything more." He turned away and buried his face in a pillow. The expression on Stefano's wife's face told Vittorio that nothing would be gained from interrogating her. He left the house and headed to the waterfront.

The wharf was empty except for two old fishermen when Vittorio reached the waterfront. A lone cargo ship peeked above the distant horizon. Only time would tell whether it was coming to Livorno or heading for another port. The fishing fleet out in the prime fishing grounds was too distant to be seen. Vittorio watched the two men for only a minute before approaching them. Unlike Massimo and Nico, Vittorio never fabricated stories or excuses. He always spoke directly. "A ship named Nereid left port this morning. Do you know it?"

When one man responded with a grunt, Vittorio asked, "Do you know what company owns the Nereid?"

The two men exchanged glances before one replied, "*Transporto Rapido.*"

"Can you tell me where to find the company's office?"

The man pointed toward a side street. "Go past the livery. The company office is where the road curves." Before Vittorio could ask another question, the man added, "If you're looking for the owner, he is not there. I saw him leave earlier for Pisa. Maybe try tomorrow."

8

PISA, SEPTEMBER 7

Massimo washed his face but didn't brush his hair. He rooted through his duffel to find his shabbiest tunic, frayed at the neck and worn through at one elbow. He had packed a variety of clothes so he could adopt the persona of a scruffy peasant or the dinner guest of a princess as the situation demanded. Outside the inn, he found a patch of bare ground, bent down, and scuffed his boots with a coating of dirt. Satisfied that he could blend in with the local laborers, he headed for the district where warehouses fronted the Arno River.

He took a position facing the flowing water with his head turned enough to let him observe the arriving workers. Some had ghostly blank expressions. Others were buoyed by pleasant thoughts: recent flirtations with a buxom barmaid, a winning night of gambling, or maybe just a tasty breakfast. None seemed eager to spend another day lugging crates.

Four large warehouses lined the riverfront, with two smaller structures set behind them on a side street. Barges tied to docks in front of two of the buildings floated high in the water. Shortly after the last worker disappeared into one of the buildings, doors swung open and workers began carrying terracotta crocks out to a barge.

Massimo guessed they were filled with spices destined for Florence or Empoli, where they would be transferred to wagons headed for Siena.

Massimo moved closer to peer in through the open doors. One man directed the others, telling them which items to take and in which order they should be loaded onto the barge. When the loading was complete, ropes were unfastened from the dock and secured to the harnesses of horses, ready to pull the barge upriver.

Massimo entered the building and approached the supervisor. "I need work." He tried affecting a Neapolitan dialect using the brash staccato he had learned when his army unit was stationed in Naples. He knew he couldn't pass as a Neapolitan among their own, but he hoped his feigned dialect would keep the supervisor from identifying him as a Florentine.

The supervisor replied, "I just took on two men yesterday. I have a full crew." Massimo nodded his understanding and turned to leave when the supervisor added, "Ask Giuseppe." He gestured in the direction of the next warehouse. "He always needs help. No one stays with him for long."

Despite the ominous comment, Massimo walked to the next building where men pulled a cart laden with chunks of iron ore from the warehouse to the dock, then began loading the ore onto a barge. They grimaced as they lifted the heavy metal from the cart and hunched as they carried it to the barge. Massimo had hoped to find a less arduous way to fit in with local workmen. "I'd better gain their confidence quickly," he told himself.

Inside the building, a man with thick black hair and a beard stubble stood to one side watching the others. Massimo approached him and again, and said in his fake Neapolitan dialect, "I'm looking for work."

Giuseppe noted Massimo's broad shoulders and muscular arms. "I can always use another man. What's your name?" Massimo saw no reason not to give his real name. Giuseppe said, "See that pile, Massimo? It all needs to be loaded onto the barge."

Massimo walked to where men were moving ore from the pile. He hefted a large chunk and tossed it into a nearby cart. The other men said nothing, but they made space for the newcomer, happy to have another strong back to share their burden. When the cart was full, Massimo helped the other men drag the cart from the warehouse to the dock, where they transferred the load to a waiting barge. Massimo lost count of how many times they had filled and then emptied the cart before the barge was filled to capacity.

Sweat beaded on Massimo's forehead and dripped from his chin when he dropped the last ore chunk onto the barge. He stood motionless on the dock, letting himself be cooled by the breeze drifting over the river until one of the men beckoned in a tired voice, "Come. Drink." He followed the man past the remaining pile of iron ore and urns filled with a white powder to a table in the rear corner of the warehouse that held mugs and a large jug of lemon water. One of the men handed Massimo a mug, and another man filled it. None spoke until each had downed a mug of the refreshing liquid.

Gradually, as they recovered from the arduous work, the men became talkative and eager to learn about the newcomer. "What devil cursed you?" asked a man who called himself Nomade. He put a hand on Massimo's shoulder and smiled. "Why else would you be here if you are not cursed?"

Massimo laughed. "If I am cursed, it must have been the cute dumpling in Naples who hexed me. When she mentioned marriage, I knew it was time to leave. And what of you? Are you all cursed?"

"Whenever there is iron to move, it feels like a curse," Nomade replied.

Massimo looked out at the pile of iron still covering a portion of the warehouse floor and asked, "Is there iron every day?"

"Not every day. You picked a bad day to start. This load came yesterday on a ship from the mines on Elba. The barge we loaded is going to a smelter in Florence. Wagons will be here soon to bring the rest of the iron to a smelter near Milan, so enjoy the break because we're not done yet."

"The sign above the door says, 'Best of Africa imports,' so why is there iron from Elba?" Massimo asked.

Nomade wiped sweat from his forehead before answering. "Giuseppe said business is slow and we should be thankful for any work."

Massimo spent the rest of the workday loading iron onto wagons and then unloading bales from a barge that brought wool cloth from mills in Florence. As they left the warehouse at the end of the day, Nomade approached Massimo. "We usually meet at the tavern after work. Come with us if you're still able to stand."

The tavern was not large, but long tables that could seat a dozen or more men accommodated a large group in the available space. Two baristas handed flasks of beer to the arriving stream of tired and thirsty workers while the barkeep collected payment.

Massimo was surprised to see the supervisor having a beer with the workers. Giuseppe came to the table where Nomade was introducing Massimo to men who worked at one of the other warehouses. When Giuseppe found a break in the conversation, he said to Massimo, "You survived the day. Will you be back tomorrow?"

"I need work, so I have no choice. I'll be back. In Naples, I heard there were good jobs in Pisa, but that's not what I found. Here, everyone says that life in Pisa was better in the past." Massimo noticed that his comment caused Giuseppe to raise an eyebrow. It could have been a coincidence, but Massimo decided to see if he could provoke another reaction by continuing his fiction. "Life was good in Naples until that damned French duke, John of Anjou, tried to have his way. The loyal *compaesani* took up arms, and with the Lord's help, we sent the foreign pig and his army back to France." The other workers found Massimo's banter amusing. Giuseppe stared at him intently, his expression serious.

During his tenure in the army, Massimo had often served in clandestine assignments. On one occasion, he had cast himself as a slave trader, smuggling young women into Tuscany from central Asia. Another time, he portrayed an Austrian Count. Success came from thoroughly studying the background for each role. For his current persona, he had familiarized himself with the history of Naples, its current rulers, its culture, and even its geography. Massimo knew the danger of pressing a role too quickly, so he said just enough to elicit a reaction from Giuseppe.

~

Massimo began the next workday loading bales of wool fabric onto wagons that would take them to the seaport at Livorno. From there, the bales would be put on a ship headed for Tunisia. After a short break, he and the other men loaded urns of white power onto a barge going upriver. "The powder is phosphate," Nomade explained. "Farms and vineyards use it for fertilizer."

The men sat outside on benches to eat lunch. Nomade said that he, like Massimo, was not a native of Pisa. "I don't know where I was born. As far back as I can remember, my mother and I traveled from place to place. She never spoke about my father. It was hard for a woman alone to cope with a ruffian like me. I was always in trouble... nothing serious, but enough to cause her grief.

"Finally, she met a man, a blacksmith, who promised to give her a home. I could tell that he didn't want me around, so I kept traveling on my own. I was in Genoa before I came to Pisa."

"Do you plan to stay in Pisa?" Massimo asked.

"No. As soon as I've saved enough silver, I'll move on. I've never been to Rome, and I understand your home city of Naples is an untamed place."

"Your understanding is true," Massimo said. "The music and dancing outlast the sun and often even the moon. The women are pliable but beware their claws. Their thoughts are only of marriage."

Nomade threw his head back and laughed. "Those women aren't found only in Naples, *mio amico*. In my travels, I too have escaped from nymphs with sharp claws. I left a scrappy redhead on the dock in Genoa when I sailed away. She suggested that we visit her parish priest, so I knew it was time to say *addio*."

As the men ambled back into the warehouse after lunch, Giuseppe called Massimo aside. "Yesterday, you spoke about forcing the French to leave Naples. Do you know how the French were defeated?"

"We had some victories in battle, but the French defeat didn't come in open combat. We made it costly for them to remain in Naples. Eventually, the cost became intolerable, so they withdrew."

Giuseppe's eyes brightened. "I have an acquaintance who would be interested in learning how you succeeded... how you made the cost intolerable to the foreigners. I am having dinner with him tonight. Are you able to join us?"

Massimo smiled inwardly. "I can do that." He would send a message to Nico and Vittorio, saying that he would not be joining them at Tre Stelle.

9

PISA SEPTEMBER 8

Few people were on the streets in the early morning when Nico left his inn. Most of the shops he passed on his way to the main business district had not yet opened. To his good fortune, the *pasticceria* in the central piazza was one of the few open shops. As he munched on a cream-filled pastry, Nico gazed across the piazza at the Medici bank. Unlike the impressive structure of its main office in Florence, the Medici bank branch in Pisa was a simple storefront. Surprisingly, the Medici bank also appeared to be open and, even more surprising, two Florentine soldiers stood outside the bank, positioned like sentinels on either side of the doorway. Several other soldiers were meandering through the piazza.

The appearance of Florentine soldiers had drawn several wary shopkeepers outside, but they were the only Pisans in the piazza. Others who approached the piazza from side streets saw the contingent of soldiers and immediately turned around. Even a pair of normally curious boys halted when they spotted the soldiers.

During his time with Finito, Nico had gleaned enough of the Pisan dialect that he could speak without being readily identified as a Florentine. He felt that his imitative speech and his newly acquired clothes would let him converse with the locals without arousing suspicion. He moved toward a jeweler who was standing outside his shop with his hands on his hips, eyeing the soldiers.

Another man reached the jeweler before Nico and the two men began chatting. Nico moved close enough to listen. "Did something happen at the bank?" the jeweler asked.

"Someone said there was a robbery," the other man said in a gruff voice, then he spit into the street. "Florentines only care for their own. They wouldn't send soldiers to investigate if my shop were robbed."

The jeweler waved a hand in the air in disgust. "Robbery should be a matter for the Guardia, not the army. This is more proof that Florence doesn't respect us. They don't even trust the Guardia to do its job."

The other man balled his hands into fists and snorted. "The day may come soon when all the insolent bullies are driven back to Florence." He turned and walked back to his shop.

When the jeweler turned to enter his own shop, he saw Nico standing nearby and looking in his direction. He eyed the stranger dubiously, but said nothing. The jeweler's stare made Nico feel conspicuous, so he returned to the pasticceria and bought a lemon tart. He stood at a counter in the shop where he could view the bank across the piazza. He ate slowly.

The scene at the bank and in the piazza had not changed by the time Nico had finished the tart: soldiers still milled about in the piazza and the two sentinels at the bank held their positions. Nico debated whether to buy another tart — this one he would give to Finito — or to go back to the inn and return to visit the bank later, after the soldiers had left. He ordered a second tart and as he waited for the server to deliver it to him, an army officer came out of the bank. The officer was too far away for Nico to see his rank insignia, but his appearance made the two sentinels snap to attention.

The officer swept his hand in a circular motion above his head, which drew the other soldiers to him. Nico counted eight men surrounding the officer like chicks around a mother hen. He gave a brief command to his men, and the entire detachment marched out of the piazza, except for one who remained stationed outside the bank.

Nico wrapped the second tart in paper, stuffed it into the pouch hanging from his belt, and walked directly across the piazza to the bank. He walked with purpose and avoided eye contact with the soldier, who made no attempt to intercept him. Inside, a clerk sat at a desk to Nico's left. The clerk had both hands palms down on the desk. He gazed at papers spread across the desk but he did not move, as though he were in a daze and couldn't decide what he should be doing.

To Nico's right was the tiny office of the bank manager. Nico peered through the doorway and observed a gaunt man rubbing his hands together nervously. Color had drained from the man's face and his eyebrows twitched. He stared down at the blank top of his desk and did not look up when Nico entered the office. Nico sat in a chair facing the manager, reached out, and slapped his hand down on the manager's desk. The sudden sound snapped the manager from his trance. Too upset to object to an interloper entering his office, he looked across at Nico but said nothing. Nico held out his letter of introduction as a member of the Florentine Security Commission.

The manager reached out slowly to take the letter. After allowing time for him to read the letter, Nico asked, "What happened?"

"I just told the captain." The manager replied in a quavering voice.

"Tell me," Nico said, his voice firm.

The manager's voice steadied as he regained his composure. "Once each week, a courier takes the records of new contracts and loans from this bank to the bank in Florence. I gave the document pouch to the courier yesterday afternoon after the bank had closed and he set out for Florence. The captain said that the courier's body was found this morning on the road near Cascina. He said it appeared that the courier had been slashed by a sword, and that a paper stuffed into the courier's mouth read 'Florentines have no place in Pisa.'" The manager shivered involuntarily as he visualized the incident.

Nico had been dispatched to Pisa based on hearsay and the fear of hostile agitators. The fear had now become real. He continued his interrogation. "Did the captain know who attacked the courier?"

"I don't know. He didn't say. I should have asked, but..." His voice trailed off. "This is terrible," the manager muttered. "He worked for the bank here in Pisa longer than I have. He was a good man. The soldiers said they will tell his wife. I must see her too, but I don't know what to say."

Having never been in the manager's position, Nico could only console the manager by listening as the man expressed his pain. After several minutes, the manager regained his composure and Nico asked, "Were the documents recovered?"

"No, they weren't. I did ask about that because the pouch contained the original documents. We note all transactions in our ledgers, but without the original documents, we have no way of proving that anyone borrowed money."

"Has anything like this happened before? Have any threats been made against the bank?" he asked.

The manager put his elbows on the desk and leaned forward to rest his head in his hands. He took a couple of deep breaths before sitting up again. "There have been no direct threats against the bank, but a few of our clients have been pressured to move their accounts to a Pisan bank. And I've heard gossip. People say the Medici bank is the symbol of Florentine aggression. My wife heard merchants in the marketplace complaining that Florentine rule is hurting their businesses. The merchants were so upset that now my wife won't let it be known that she's a Florentine."

Nico raised an eyebrow. "Who is pressuring your clients?"

"I don't know. Yesterday, another client moved his accounts to another bank, a Pisan bank."

"Who is the client?"

"The bank doesn't allow me to reveal the names of our clients."

Nico still held his letter of introduction in his hand. He extended it toward the manager. "Would you like to read this again? One person has already been killed. I am certain the Signoria would not be pleased if you withheld information that could prevent further violence."

The manager's eyes darted down to the letter and then back up to Nico. Almost in a whisper, he said, "His name is Domenico Carlucci. He owns a company that imports wool from England." He paused for a moment before asking, "Are you going to speak with him?"

Incensed by the manager's indifferent attitude, Nico snapped, "Yes, and I'm also going to find out who attacked the courier."

Nico scanned the piazza. With the detachment of soldiers gone, activity had returned to normal. Only the single sentry remained outside the bank. A stream of customers flowed into and out of the pasticceria where he had bought the lemon tarts, and business had resumed in other shops as well. People passing the bank walked briskly and looked straight ahead to avoid eye contact with the lone soldier who was leaning against the building facade. Nico walked diagonally across the piazza to the *farmacia*, the shop owned by the man who had expressed his dislike of Florentines to the jeweler.

He stepped inside and waited near the entrance while the *farmacista* prepared a formulation for a woman. The woman had one arm around the waist of a young girl who held tightly to the woman. The girl's shoulders drooped, her head bent forward, and she whimpered softly. The farmacista combined several powders and poured the mixture into a paper cone that he handed to the women. He took a spoonful of the mixture, bent down, and said to the girl, "This will make you feel better."

The girl looked up to her mother for encouragement before she swallowed the medication. She scrunched up her nose at the unpleasant taste, but she did not complain. To the woman, the farmacista said, "Give her a spoonful every four hours. If she if not better tomorrow, bring her to a *medico*."

Nico moved aside to let the woman and the girl pass, then he moved to the counter. The farmacista returned his herbs and chemicals to their storage cabinet, then looked at the stranger expectantly. Nico said, "I was outside earlier, when you were speaking with the jeweler. I heard you say that the Medici bank had been robbed. I just came from the bank. The bank wasn't robbed. A clerk said that the bank's courier was attacked on the road near Cascina. The courier was killed and the documents he was carrying were stolen."

"Bah," the farmacista grumbled as he scrutinized Nico. "You don't look like a person who does business with the Medici bank."

Thankful that he now wore the clothes of a Pisan laborer, Nico laughed. "Certainly not. It's a good day when I have two silver coins to press together." Thinking quickly, Nico created a story. "I do errands for a lawyer. He is the one who does business with the Medici bank. That is, he did before, but no longer. He sent me to the bank to tell them that he will be closing his account. He's decided that true Pisans should do business with Pisan banks."

"And you?" the farmacista asked. "What do you believe?"

"People say that Pisa is like a horse and Florence is like the rider pulling the reins, forcing Pisa to go this way and that. I think it would be better if Pisans were allowed to roam free." Nico found it farcical that his persona had him disparaging Florence. Maybe he could include this amusing anecdote in his next letter to Bianca.

"Words come easily and mean little," the farmacista said. "Are you willing to work for Pisa's freedom?"

"I've worked for things that matter less," Nico replied.

The farmacista eyed the stranger, trying to determine whether he spoke truthfully and whether he could contribute to the cause, but it was not for him to judge. "There are others who hold similar views. Come back on..." He glanced down at a notepad on the counter. "Friday afternoon if you wish to meet one of them."

Nico smiled inwardly at having another lead toward finding the agitators.

10

LIVORNO SEPTEMBER 8

Vittorio followed the fisherman's directions to the shipping company's office. Immediately past the livery, the road made a sweeping curve to the right. Outside a tall wooden building, women were repairing the stitching on sails hanging on drying racks. Inside, men were threading new ropes through pulley blocks. Beside them lay a pile of old rope, weathered and worn from its service on shipboard hoists. Vittorio approached one of the women and asked, "Is this the office of Transporto Rapido?"

"This is their building, but it's not the office. That's the office," she said, pointing to a smaller building nearby.

Inside the smaller building, a man hunched over a desk mumbled to himself as he studied a paper and made notes in a thick ledger. He looked up and rubbed his eyes when Vittorio entered. Without any preamble, Vittorio said, "One of your sailors was beaten yesterday."

The man raised his eyebrows upon hearing the information. "Who?"

"His name is Stefano. Before he was beaten, he came here to speak with someone," Vittorio continued.

That statement did surprise the man, who shook his head. "He didn't come in the morning. I was here in the morning, so if he came then, I'd have seen him. Maybe he came in the afternoon. The office was closed then because the manager and I went to Pisa."

"He wanted to speak with someone at the office. You?"

The man spread his hands wide over the ledger. "I'm just a clerk. I only do these accounts and tally the freight. He would have no reason to speak with me."

Vittorio moved closer and asked, "Who else was here yesterday?"

The man cocked his head toward a door behind him. "Signor Grassi is the only other person who works in this building. He's the manager."

Vittorio gave a single rap on the door before pushing it open. The manager was already looking up when Vittorio entered the inner office. He had the leathery skin and calluses of someone who had worked with his hands before becoming a manager. Before Vittorio could state his purpose, the manager said, "The walls are thin. I heard you asking about Stefano."

"Can you think of a reason why he might have come here to speak with you?"

"Stefano is my wife's cousin, but he has no reason to speak with me. He is a crew member on the Nereid. If he had a concern about the ship, he would take it to one of the ship's officers."

Vittorio sensed that Grassi had more to tell. He folded his arms across his chest and stood firm, waiting for the manager to continue, but his aggressive posture provoked a similar response from Grassi, who rose, leaned forward, and placed both hands palms down on the desk. "Who are you?" Grassi growled.

Vittorio realized it would take a show of authority for Grassi to become cooperative. He held out the letter that introduced him as a member of the Florentine Security Commission. Grassi's eyebrows rose as he read the letter. "I don't understand. Sailors are always getting into brawls. Why is this one of interest to the Florentine..." He looked down at the paper and read, "the Florentine Security Commission?"

Vittorio had no good answer, so he deflected the question. "I can't say." He had used that phrase often during his tenure as a Florentine Guardia investigator to avoid answering questions.

Grassi picked up a netball from his desk and began squeezing it. Tension drained from his body with each compression. A few moments later, he put the ball down and said, "I just learned about Stefano this morning. Since he is my wife's cousin, I had planned to go to his house later to offer my support." He scanned the papers on his desk. "These can wait. I can go now. You can come with me."

As they passed through the outer office, Vittorio noticed paintings of two ships hanging on a wall and asked, "Your company has two ships?"

Grassi replied, "The company owns three galleons, the Nereid, the Pallas, and the Triton, that sail between Livorno and Tunisia. The Nereid left Livorno yesterday, and the Triton is scheduled to arrive tomorrow. The company also owns two smaller cargo carriers that travel to Rome and Naples." He laughed and said, "But it is not my company. I am merely the person who takes the blame whenever there are problems. The company is owned by a consortium of businessmen in Pisa."

When they arrived at the house, the door was ajar. Grassi pushed it open, stepped inside, and called, "Stefano!"

From behind Grassi, Vittorio noticed an overturned chair with a broken leg in the middle of the room. Near it, a glass lay on its side, its contents spilled onto the wood floor. A shadow on the wall drew Vittorio to the kitchen, where he found Stefano's wife sitting at the table sobbing, clutching her whimpering baby. Her dress was torn and her hair tousled. Tears flowed down a purple welt on her cheek.

"Dio mio!" Grassi exclaimed. He slid into the chair next to the woman and put an arm around her shoulder.

Vittorio moved to the bedroom doorway. A blood-stained bed cover lay on the floor. "He's gone," Vittorio announced.

Grassi looked at Vittorio, then back to the woman. "What happened, *cara mia*?"

She wiped her eyes, then said, "Two men came. They pushed their way into the house. I tried to stop them, but I couldn't. They hit me." She ran a hand over her cheek. "They pushed me against the wall." She shuddered involuntarily. "They took Stefano. They shoved a rag into his mouth so he couldn't scream and dragged him away."

Vittorio filled a glass from a water pitcher on the counter. He pulled a chair to the table, sat down facing the woman, and set the glass in front of her. In a calm, soothing voice, he said, "What did the men look like?"

She closed her eyes for an instant. "Both of them were big. Bigger than Stefano." She took a sip of water, then added, "One of them had a crooked nose... like the butcher."

For Vittorio's benefit, Grassi interjected, "The butcher's nose is bent to one side. He says it got broken in a fight."

Vittorio continued questioning the woman. "What did the men say when they were taking Stefano? They must have said something. Did they say where they were taking him?"

She thought for a moment, drew in a breath, then said, "One of them said 'we need to be sure you won't tell anyone.'" She paused another moment, then said, "No, that's not right. He didn't say 'we need,' he said 'he needs. He needs to be sure you won't tell anyone.' Those were his words."

Vittorio and Grassi exchanged glances. Two men doing the bidding of a third man told Vittorio that this was more than a street fight, but to avoid alarming the woman, he did not voice his conclusion. "Did they say anything else?" he asked.

She thought only for a moment. "No. That's all they said. I'm sure."

Vittorio asked, "Has Stefano ever mentioned anyone who would wish him harm? Anyone he had a disagreement with?"

Vittorio's questions surprised the woman. She looked at him with a puzzled expression. "No. Stefano is a gentle man. He never gets into fights or arguments. I can think of no one who would want to hurt him."

Vittorio turned to Grassi. "The Guardia don't concern themselves with brawls, but an abduction is a serious crime. You need to alert them. I'll stay here until you return. Go now. The Guardia needs to start looking for Stefano as soon as possible."

Both men stood, and Grassi moved toward the door. From behind them, the woman called. "One of them had a mark." The men turned around. She said, "A mark on his neck shaped like a foot."

"Foot?" Vittorio echoed.

She looked down toward the floor and wiggled one of her feet. Vittorio gave a quick nod and said, "Ah, a foot. A distinguishing mark like that will help to identify him."

Vittorio stood in the doorway, looking into the road while Grassi was at Guardia's headquarters. As soon as he saw Grassi in the distance returning with two officers, he slipped outside and ducked around the back of a neighbor's house. Sunlight striking the face of the approaching men kept them from seeing Vittorio's feint. He wasn't ready for the local Guardia to know that a member of the Florentine Security Commission was in Livorno.

11

FLORENCE SEPTEMBER 8

Gemma Bastine attended mass on Sundays and Holy Days, and she believed in the power of prayer, but her resolve did not extend to making novenas with her mother twice each week. She questioned whether it was faith that drew her mother to the novenas and mid-week masses, or whether it was the companionship of the other women who congregated in the courtyard before and after the services that enticed her mother. The church services were also often a prelude to her mother's shopping excursions. Prayers and shopping were the common regimen of matrons who had little else to fill their days. On this occasion, Gemma had promised to accompany her mother after church to purchase new dinner plates from a local potter.

As the older women gathered in the courtyard to share stories, Gemma stood aside, watching a butterfly dancing among the late-summer flowers when a heavyset woman approached her. "You're a Bastine, the woman declared."

Clearly, the woman did not remember Gemma's name, nor did Gemma know the woman's name, but Gemma did recall that the woman's son was a member of the Guardia. "Yes, I'm Gemma Bastine," she confirmed.

"I thought so," the woman said, proudly, pleased to have made a proper identification. "Bruno Fiorello works at your smelter."

The statement puzzled Gemma, who replied hesitantly, "My brother manages the smelter. He knows the men who work there. I'm not involved in the business, so I don't know the workers."

Undeterred by Gemma's lack of knowledge and interest, the woman continued, almost gloating, "Fiorello was arrested last night. He was arrested for beating someone to death."

Gemma recoiled at hearing of the violence. "That's terrible," she said softly.

Smiling broadly, the woman said, "My son was the one who made the arrest. He took Fiorello to prison." The woman's smile transformed into a scowl. "And Fiorello isn't the first worker at your smelter to be arrested." Satisfied that she had sufficiently demeaned the Bastine name, the woman turned away and went to join the other women, who were beginning to enter the church.

Gemma watched the woman leave, unsure what reaction the woman expected from her. She had intended to visit with a friend and then return to the church after the novena to meet her mother, but the woman's comment gave her pause. She moved to a stone bench at the far end of the courtyard and sat, her gaze on a clump of flowers and her thoughts on her brother, Rinaldo.

The woman's insinuation was not the only example of abhorrent behavior by workers since Rinaldo took control of the smelter. He had gradually changed the character of the family business by purchasing raw material from questionable sources, courting unsavory customers, and hiring lowlifes and thugs to work at the smelter. Many of the honest, hard-working men who had worked at the smelter when her father had managed the business left to find other work rather than do Rinaldo's bidding. Rinaldo's personal demeanor was also sinking further into depravity.

A shadow cast onto the flowers broke Gemma's concentration. She raised her head to see a priest in a black Benedictine robe walking toward her. The church was not of the Benedictine order, so she surmised that he was a visiting monk. His smooth skin and cherubic face marked him as young, a fact which he tried to hide with a short, well-trimmed beard. His aquiline nose suggested he was a Roman. He wore an unusual ring of intertwined gold and silver strands. The ring caught Gemma's attention because few monks wore any ornamentation other than a crucifix.

The monk lowered himself onto a nearby bench. She had never been this close to a priest. A sudden feeling of guilt swept over her, making her feel that she should have a deep secret sin to confess. "You seem troubled," he said softly, his eyes on some men entering the church. "Most find it easiest to unburden themselves inside God's house, but He can also listen to you out here in this lovely garden. He may have sent this humble servant to share your hardship if you will let me."

Gemma had vowed to stop her brother from molesting the young women servants. She had struggled, without success, to find the means to keep that oath. Perhaps she did need spiritual guidance. The young priest's quiet demeanor overcame Gemma's reluctance to speak openly about a delicate matter. She kept her gaze on the flowers, to avoid meeting the priest's eyes. "My brother has taken to..." It took a moment for her to find a suitable word. "...fondling our young women servants. One of them is only thirteen years and Rinaldo is older than I. He did this once before and Father punished him, but that was years past and now father is old, too old to discipline Rinaldo. I am the only one... the only one who can protect those girls."

"Lust drives powerful urges, but civilized men must learn to control their actions."

Gemma continued, so deep in thought that the priest's comment did not register. "He has other failings as well. I just learned that a man hired by my brother has been arrested for beating someone to death. I don't blame Rinaldo for the crime, but I do feel he's a contributor because he's been hiring men who commit such acts." Finally, she found the courage to turn her head and look at the priest.

"For what purpose does your brother hire men?" the monk asked.

"Our family owns an iron smelter. When my father managed the smelter, all the workers were honorable men. Now with my brother in control...." She let words hang.

"You cannot let your brother's deeds become your millstone. In Galatians, it says 'Carry each other's burdens and so you will fulfill the law of Christ,' but no one must shoulder another's burden alone. Now that you have told me of your brother's wanton behavior, the weight of his redemption is no longer yours. It is mine. The Priors and I have taken a vow. I will see that Rinaldo returns to the virtuous path."

Gemma would never question the word of a priest, but her eyes narrowed with doubt as she wondered, Priors? How could a priest change Rinaldo's behavior? Their conversation was interrupted by voices behind them, meaning that the novena had ended and women were exiting the church. The priest rose and headed to the sacristy at the rear of the church and Gemma moved toward her mother, who had detached herself from the throng of women.

"I see that you've met Father Giorgi," her mother said, obviously smitten by the departing young priest. "He's visiting from the Monte Cassino Abbey near Rome. He introduced himself to us after mass yesterday."

"How long will he be with us?" Gemma asked.

"Unfortunately, he'll be here only for a few weeks before moving on to Bologna. I wish he could stay longer. He's so understanding and... charming. What were you talking about with him?"

Gemma deflected the question, saying, "He's wearing an unusual gold and silver ring."

Her mother's voice quickened. "We were just talking about that. One of my friends said it signifies that he is a member of the Priors of Constantine. She said it's a secret society of priests that was formed more than a thousand years past."

"I've never heard of the Priors of Constantine, but it can't be a well-kept secret if the members wear rings to identify themselves and your friend knows about it."

"The society itself is not secret. Its members are dedicated to remedying wrongs and evil. What is secret is how they accomplish their mission."

The two women left the courtyard and headed to the pottery shop. As they walked, Father Giorgio's words echoed in Gemma's mind: "I will see that Rinaldo returns to the virtuous path."

12

PISA, SEPTEMBER 8

When the warehouse supervisor invited him to dinner, Massimo had assumed they would dine at a restaurant in Pisa, until Giuseppe suggested that they meet at a stable where a wagon would be readied for them. Massimo left ample time to walk across the city from his inn to the Piagge Gate. Giuseppe had said that the stable was only a short distance beyond the wall, and indeed, Massimo saw the stable ahead as soon as he passed through the gate.

The only person at the stable when Massimo arrived was a stable boy who had taken a chestnut mare from her stall and was hitching her to a small wagon. Massimo watched the boy put a harness on the horse while he waited for Giuseppe. From behind him, the supervisor's voice called, "We can go as soon as the wagon is ready. It will be worth the short ride. The dinner will be excellent." Giuseppe boarded the wagon and Massimo climbed up next to him.

Giuseppe kept up a continuous patter as they followed the Arno River east, away from Pisa. Massimo guessed that Giuseppe didn't pause in his monologue because he didn't want to entertain any questions from his passenger. The supervisor finally quieted when they passed through the town of Cascina. On the far side of the town, he steered the wagon onto a side road that led to a secluded building at the edge of a thicket of scrub trees.

The building itself looked in need of repair, but the grounds surrounding it were well maintained. Rows of neatly trimmed shrubs flanked a walkway leading to the building's entrance. Nearby, ducks paddled on a pond and occasionally bobbed for pondweed.

Giuseppe led Massimo to the inn's common room, where a lone man sat at the only occupied table. Massimo's initial glimpse of the man dispelled his notion that he would be dining with a common outlaw. The man wore an impeccably styled ivory-colored tunic with pearl buttons. A silver medallion on a thin chain hung around his neck. His hair was pulled back smartly in a horse tail.

Upon seeing the new arrivals, the man poured two glasses of wine. Giuseppe introduced Massimo, saying, "He's the one from Naples."

The man smiled broadly as he gestured toward a chair and said, "I am known *as il Fornitore*."

il Fornitore, the supplier. I wonder what he supplies and to whom, Massimo thought.

A clap of Fornitore's hands summoned a buxom woman carrying a platter of assorted shellfish. "The chef's alternative to traditional antipasti," Fornitore explained. "This selection is a pleasurable change from restaurants in Pisa whose chefs overcook the sea's most delicate creatures until they have the toughness of leather. They are all outstanding, but these are my favorite," he said as he scooped a generous portion of oysters onto his plate.

As soon as the men had taken a share, the server reappeared to replace the nearly empty platter. Fornitore kept the conversation light throughout the pasta and fish courses by recounting Pisa's history from its formation as a Roman colony to its greatness as a major sea power. His voice swelled with pride as he told of the Pisans driving the Saracens from Sardinia and the Muslims from Sicily in the eleventh century. Three bottles of wine stood empty on the sideboard by the time the men had finished the custard dessert course.

The server poured three glasses of grappa and left the bottle close to Fornitore. He took a sip of the potent brandy, leaned back in his chair, turned to Massimo and said, "You are one of the partisans who drove the French from Naples. I want to know how you did that, but first, tell me how the French came to be in Naples." Bitterness crept into his voice as he added, "Did the French buy Naples as Florence bought Pisa?"

Massimo laughed. "No, the French didn't buy Naples. In truth, the invaders weren't from the Kingdom of France but from the neighboring duchy of Lorraine."

Fornitore waved a hand in a dismissive gesture. "Bah. They're all Frenchmen."

"Seven years ago, when Ferrante became king of Naples upon the death of his father, the Duke of Taranto decided it was the opportunity for him to grab power, but he knew that he would need help to be successful. So he invited the Duke of Lorraine to join him. They must have had some agreement for sharing power."

Fornitore raised a hand for emphasis. "Surely King Ferrante had an army."

Massimo took a sip of grappa. "I can only assume that Ferrante's captain-general was an incompetent fool because his army was soundly defeated in its first battle. The king and his bride narrowly escaped with their lives. From then, Ferrante's only support came from partisans in the countryside."

Fornitore's eyes narrowed. "And this I do not understand. How could untrained farmers and laborers stand against the duke's army?"

Massimo smiled as he reviewed in his mind the account he had read of the conflict. He leaned forward, placed his hands on the table, and continued his tale, saying, "At the outset, we had no weapons. It would have been impossible to challenge the duke's forces without help. Thanks be to God, Pope Pius and an Austrian Prince provided us with arms and taught us how to use them."

With bewilderment in his voice, Fornitore asked, "What roused the interest of a prince of Austria in the problems of Naples?"

Massimo spread his hands. "For that, I have no answer," he replied and continued his fabrication. "Even with arms, it would have been madness for us to attack the duke's garrison. We were too few. Instead, we harassed them at every opportunity. I recall vividly, one night while the French were asleep, we raided their encampment and took their horses and supply wagon. We didn't unsheathe even a single sword that night. The following day, our scouts watched the Frenchmen trudge under the hot sun all the way back to Naples.

"Eventually, they could no longer tolerate our intimidation, so they came looking for us. We lured them out of the city and into the hills, where we knew every hiding place. Again and again, we attacked their patrols and their supply wagons. We avoided skirmishes where their large force would have been an advantage. In time, their numbers diminished, and their morale fell until finally, in the town of Troia, we struck the decisive blow that persuaded them to withdraw."

Massimo reached across the table for the bottle of grappa. He refilled his glass and raised it. "I drink to partisans everywhere." The others joined his toast, even Giuseppe, who had been quiet throughout the dinner.

Fornitore rubbed his chin. "You are telling me that you were able to drive out the French invaders because you used deception and fought at a distance from their strongholds?"

Massimo replied, "And we believed in our cause. We knew we could defeat the foreigners."

Fornitore laughed as he said, "You were like insects, like a swarm of *zanzare*. When they swat at you in one place, you nettled them elsewhere." Then abruptly he turned serious. "The French were newcomers who didn't know the territory. Do you believe you would have been successful if the invaders had been entrenched? If they were familiar with the Neapolitan countryside?"

"Perhaps not," Massimo replied. "But invaders never come to know the lands they conquer, as well as those who were born there. The duke tried to rule with his army quartered in garrisons and fortresses. The soldiers never explored the streets and treasures of Naples."

Massimo decided it was time to press Fornitore. "Your words mark you as a man who values history, but I can tell your interest is more than a scholarly pursuit. You didn't invite me to this wonderful dinner for mere casual conversation." Massimo had learned the power of silence from Vittorio. He leaned back, folded his arms across his chest, and watched as Fornitore decided how to respond.

At length, Fornitore replied, "You said that a belief in your success was crucial. There are men in Pisa who wish to once again be free of Florentine oppression. They wish for freedom, but they question whether that day will ever come. For their dream to become real, they need confidence. They need to believe the future is in their hands."

He leaned forward and locked eyes with Massimo. "They need to hear of success from a man who has driven foreign oppressors from his homeland. I invited you here because Giuseppe told me you might be one who can convince the partisans in Pisa that victory is possible. And after hearing your story, I agree with him. My freedom-loving Pisan countrymen need to hear from a hero. They need to hear what you have told me. "

Fornitore's praise caused Massimo to chuckle. "I'm no hero. What I told you will be buried in the pages of history."

"In time, it may be swallowed by history, but now it can be an inspiration."

"It would be deceptive for me to tell your countrymen that belief alone will bring them success. In Naples, we had help from His Holiness Pope Pius and the Austrian Prince. We would not have prevailed without the arms that they supplied."

Fornitore waved a hand dismissively. "Weapons are not an issue for us."

Massimo paused as though considering Fornitore's request that he speak to a group of agitators. At length he said, "It would not be healthy for me to tell Pisans they should take up arms against Florence. Florentines have long memories."

"I'm not asking you to incite Pisans to rise against Florence. I'm only asking that you... to use your words, share with them a page from history."

Again, Massimo paused before giving his acceptance, knowing that the meeting would let him face the rebels. "You speak as though you are their leader, so I assume you will be there as well."

Fornitore laughed. "I am not a leader. As I told you, I merely supply what is needed."

Fornitore reached to refill Massimo's glass, but Massimo held a hand over the glass. "It is getting late, and Giuseppe will expect me to move my share of goods at the warehouse in the morning."

As Giuseppe and Massimo left the inn, Fornitore called to them. "I will make the arrangements."

13

PISA, SEPTEMBER 8

Vittorio was standing outside when Nico arrived at Tre Stelle. "Is there a problem?" Nico asked.

"People," Vittorio replied, and cocked his head toward the trattoria. Nico pushed the door open a crack and a cacophony of voices and laughter escaped from the dining room.

"A family celebration," Vittorio explained. "There's another trattoria on the next block. I can't vouch for the quality of the food, but it's quiet enough for us to hold a conversation."

Nico said, "We can go now. Massimo sent me a note saying that he won't be joining us because he's meeting someone who may have important information."

Vittorio led the way to the eatery he had found. As soon as Nico stepped inside, he sniffed the air and said, "Calamari and garlic. I hope the chef doesn't overcook the calamari. There's nothing worse than calamari cooked until it turns into leather." Vittorio glanced at Nico, bemused, but he said nothing.

As Vittorio had said, the room was quiet. Four elderly men occupied one table at the front. They ate slowly, as though age had sapped their energy, and they spoke little. Nico and Vittorio chose a table at the rear, where they could converse without being overheard.

A server greeted them with a terse "Buonasera." He set a plate of olives and cheese on the table and filled their glasses with an amber-colored wine. He didn't describe the menu. Once the glasses were filled, he returned to the kitchen without a sound, not even a footfall.

Nico, eager to share his news, began speaking before sampling the food or wine. "A courier of the Medici bank was killed while carrying documents to Florence. The documents were taken."

Vittorio raised an eyebrow at the surprising news, took a sip of wine, and asked, "When did this happen?"

"This morning. Soldiers found the courier's body on the road near the town of Cascina. He had been stabbed, possibly by a sword. I went to the bank to speak with the manager, but when I arrived, the piazza was filled with soldiers. I waited until the soldiers left before entering the bank. The manager told me that the courier brought bank records to the main office in Florence every week, and never before had there been a problem."

"Did the manager think that this was meant as a symbolic attack against Florence?"

Nico knew what mattered to the investigator, so he replied factually first. "He said there is no evidence that the robbery and killing were directed against Florence." Then Nico added the hearsay. "But the bank manager has learned that his customers are being pressured to move their accounts to Pisan banks."

"Does the manager know who is applying the pressure?"

"No, but he gave me the name of one client who is being intimidated. Domenico Carlucci, the owner of an importing company. I intend to call on Carlucci tomorrow. I'd welcome your interviewing expertise if you're able to join me."

Vittorio replied, "Tomorrow morning, the sister ship to that of the abducted sailor is scheduled to arrive in Livorno. I want to be there when word of his abduction reaches the arriving crew. Their reactions might be telling. But I can join you in the afternoon.

"Afternoon then." Nico's eyes brightened. "And I have another lead."

Nico's account was interrupted by the server who brought plates of calamari in a garlic and lemon sauce. He set a plate in front of each man, said only "calamari," refilled their wine glasses, and retreated to the kitchen without another word.

Nico's apprehension vanished when he tasted a piece of the fried squid. "It's cooked to perfection," he said happily. "In a garlic and lemon sauce. I should have detected the lemon aroma."

Vittorio, who was less concerned with the food, prompted, "Your other lead?"

"While I was waiting in the piazza for the soldiers to leave, I overheard two men complaining about the presence of the soldiers. One of them, a farmacista, expressed vehemently his belief that Pisa would be better if it were free from Florence and his hope that the day will come soon. When I spoke to him later, after I had spoken with the bank manager, he said there are others in Pisa who share his view and he invited me to meet one of them. He said that every Thursday afternoon the man I should meet brings him plants that he uses in his medications."

Vittorio cocked his head, his face showing doubt. "The farmacista was willing to speak freely with a Florentine about unrest in Pisa?"

"I didn't reveal that I was a Florentine. I managed to use a few words in Pisan dialect. They might not have been enough to convince him that I was a Pisan, but at least he didn't ask whether I was a Florentine."

"You've met with more success than I," Vittorio said. "I haven't found a hint of unrest in Livorno. The men only talk about work and having fun; they aren't interested in worldly matters. However, I did come upon one crime, the beating and abduction of a sailor.

"I've given my attention to this abduction because my eavesdropping in Livorno hasn't revealed any disparaging talk about Florence, and the Livorno Guardia seem to be incompetent. They've made no progress in finding the man who was abducted. Either they have no ability or no interest in solving crimes."

The server returned to clear away the dinner plates. A young girl following him carried plates of brandied apricots topped with dollops of cream. She blushed slightly as she set the plates in front of the two strangers. Nico waited until the girl returned to the kitchen before asking Vittorio, "Could the sailor have had a quarrel with one of his shipmates? Maybe he owes money to one of them."

"If he owed money, they would have threatened him and his wife. They wouldn't have dragged him away. A clash with another sailor might have earned him a beating, but the abduction tells me there's a more serious reason."

"How are you going to find him?"

"The sailor, Stefano, hung with others like himself. Livorno isn't a big town. If I watch and listen, I'll eventually hear something. Criminals like to brag about their offenses. Unfortunately, his ship is en route to Tunisia and won't return for weeks, but its sister ship, the Triton, is due to arrive on Wednesday. I plan to be listening when word of Stefano's abduction reaches the Triton's crew. Their reactions will tell whether the news is a surprise or whether they expected it."

14

LIVORNO, SEPTEMBER 9

Early morning fog hugged the waterfront as it had on previous mornings, but it did not extend into the town. Vittorio leaned against a pylon on the wharf, waiting for the sun to rise high enough to vanquish the mist. The Nereid's sister ship, the Triton, was scheduled to arrive, but it would not attempt a landing while the port was blanketed under thick fog. While he waited, Vittorio watched the two old fishermen on the dock who were having better success than they had the previous day. Their baskets were nearly filled with fish, some still squirming.

A fishing boat moored to the dock bobbed up and down on the swells. When Vittorio had first arrived, he could see only that ship's hull. Now portions of the masts were visible. The fog was lifting, but slowly. Vittorio crossed the road to a nearby trattoria that was a popular breakfast venue with the locals. He sat inside sipping on a mug of warmed wine and watching the fog creeping up the masts. When the main mast yardarm became clearly visible, he headed back to the wharf.

A ghostlike image emerged from the fog as the Triton made its way to port. The ship's pilot steered the vessel deftly to its berth.

Deckhands dropped the sails while others jumped ashore to secure mooring lines. The waterfront quickly came alive with dockworkers unloading cargo and hauling it to the line of wagons that appeared as if by magic. Tax collectors examined every item as it was unloaded, noting its value in their records. When the final crate was unloaded, the tax collectors compared their tallies with the manifest presented by the ship's master. Only when the chief tax officer was satisfied that the two accounts agreed did he allow the wagons to depart for warehouses in Pisa.

With the ship secured, the master released his crew, who were eager to return home to their wives and women friends after weeks at sea. Only two crew-members remained on board to act as watchers. Vittorio had thought he might find a clue to what had happened to Stefano by observing the crewmen of the Triton. If he had spotted factions and rivalries among the crew of the Triton, it could mean that similar confrontations existed on Stefano's ship, but he saw no strife among the seamen.

Chilled by the damp morning air seeping through his cloak, Vittorio returned to the trattoria for another mug of warmed wine. As he sat watching the now deserted waterfront, a small wagon came out of a side street. Its driver climbed down and walked to the edge of the pier nearest to the Triton. He glanced around furtively, but he saw no one since the two fishermen had already filled the baskets and left with their bounty. He whistled, a single tone loud enough to be heard on the ship but not loud enough to attract the attention of anyone that his scan might have missed.

The sound brought the two watchers from the ship's cabin. One raised a hand in response to the driver's signal, then climbed down a rope ladder into the ship's hold. The second man positioned a hoist over the open hatch. The men called to each other as they prepared to raise an object onto the deck. Vittorio considered leaving the trattoria so he could hear their conversation, but he did not want to chance that the men might see him.

Several minutes later, the man on deck pulled on the hoist rope to raise a crate up from the hold. He swung the hoist away from the hatch and let the crate settle onto the deck. The two men lifted the crate and carried it to the wagon. The crate was not large, but Vittorio noticed the men grimace as they struggled with the heavy load. Whatever was in the crate, the two watchers wanted to keep it hidden from their fellow crewmen and the tax collectors. "Smugglers," Vittorio said to himself.

He memorized the faces of the two watchers; however, he could see only the back of the wagon driver. Without a view of the driver's face, anyone else might have found it impossible to identify the driver, but Vittorio noticed two distinctive features: a tear on the right shoulder of the man's cloak and a splatter of green paint on his right boot. During his tenure as a member of the Guardia in Florence, Vittorio had built an enviable reputation by exposing criminals using only minor clues such as these, although he had no expectation that he would stumble upon the driver merely by wandering the streets of Pisa.

When the crate was secured, the watchers returned to the ship, and the wagon set off in the direction of Pisa. Vittorio studied the wagon and noted that its side had been repaired using wood that did not match the original. The patch was distinctive enough that Vittorio believed he might be able to find the wagon if its destination was indeed Pisa and not a distant city. He emptied his mug and stepped into the road to watch the wagon disappear in the distance.

Vittorio turned away from the waterfront and walked to Stefano's house. In two days, he had encountered abduction and now smuggling. Vittorio did not believe in coincidence. Either Livorno was rife with crime or the two acts were related. Stefano's wife's eyes were red when she answered the door. "It's early," she said reflexively, as she moved aside to let Vittorio enter. A single candle illuminated the house's darkened interior with dim light that barely carried to the corner of the room where her infant whimpered in its cradle.

"Has the Guardia made any progress in finding Stefano?" Vittorio asked.

"I don't know. They haven't told me anything," she said, a touch of fear evident in her voice. She gestured toward a chair, inviting Vittorio to sit, but he declined. She continued, "Simona Grassi came to see me yesterday. She's Stefano's cousin. You came here yesterday with her husband Salvadore. He's the manager of the shipping company.'"

"How well do you know Salvadore?"

"I see Simona often, but I rarely see her husband."

Vittorio phrased his next question carefully. "Do you know Salvadore to be a man of integrity?"

Surprised by Vittorio's question, the woman looked at him with a blank expression. Unsure how to respond, she said, "He is a lector of his church."

Her answer told Vittorio nothing, because he had sent more than one devout churchgoer to prison. In his experience, religious patronage did not erase depravity. Vittorio changed direction. "Did Stefano seem disturbed lately? Did he mention anything unusual happening on his ship?"

"He didn't say anything about the ship, but lately his mind seemed to be elsewhere. If I asked him a question, he wouldn't answer. It was like he was thinking about something and didn't hear me." She looked at Vittorio expectantly. When he said nothing further, she asked, "Do you know something? Do you know what happened to my Stefano?"

"Not yet," he replied, "but I will keep looking for him."

From Stefano's house, Vittorio went to the office of Transporto Rapido. He had to know whether the manager, Salvadore Grassi, was involved in the smuggling. "Is he in?" he asked the clerk, who pointed to the manager's office door without looking up from his ledger.

Before Vittorio reached the door, Grassi said, "Come in." When Vittorio entered, Grassi rubbed his temple with both hands. "I heard nothing from the Guardia. I've had dealings with the Guardia captain before, so I went to the Guardia office yesterday to speak with him. When I asked about Stefano, he said 'people disappear all the time.' I reminded him that Stefano didn't disappear, he was abducted, taken from his house with his wife as a witness. The captain didn't seem to care. I don't believe the Guardia is looking into his disappearance at all."

Grassi reached out and picked up the netball from a container on his desk. He squeezed the ball rhythmically as he said, "I've spoken with the men at the warehouse, but most of them don't even know Stefano. I'm not surprised because warehouse workers and the ship's crews rarely interact with each other."

Vittorio didn't want the clerk to overhear his conversation with Grassi. He said, "We need to discuss a private matter. Outside."

Grassi gave Vittorio a puzzled look, but when Vittorio walked out of the building, Grassi followed him to an open clearing where they could not be overheard. Vittorio fixed his eyes on Grassi and said, "Members of the Triton crew are smuggling goods into Livorno." He studied Grassi's reaction for telltales, indicating that the manager already knew about the smuggling operation.

In Vittorio's experience, some guilty men became defensive when confronted, but others evidenced their guilt with small indicators, such as a tensing of muscles or the flutter of an eyelid. He detected only a slight quiver of Grassi's lip, which could have been a reaction to news that his ships were being used for criminal activity. Vittorio decided to take the chance that Grassi was not aware of the smuggling. He described his surveillance of the Triton's arrival and the actions of the two watchers.

"I remember those men," Grassi told Vittorio their names and said, "They joined the Triton's crew last year. They came together looking for work. They claimed they had been deckhands on a cargo ship that sailed between Genoa and Sardinia, and they came to Livorno looking for better pay. I've had no complaints about them from the Triton's captain."

Vittorio asked, "Where can they be found when they're not on the ship?"

Grassi shrugged. "I can't say for certain. There are apartments in

Pisa that rent rooms to transients. Maybe they stay there... I don't know."

He paced across the clearing, turned, and returned to where Vittorio stood. "I could report them to the Guardia," Grassi said, and looked for Vittorio's reaction to that suggestion.

Vittorio grimaced and held up a hand. "From what I know of the Guardia, that would be a wasted effort. You shouldn't do anything yet. Before you tell anyone, I need to learn what they are smuggling and whether any other members of the crew are involved."

After Grassi agreed to Vittorio's proposal, Vittorio voiced a speculation. "If Stefano found out about the smuggling, that could be the reason for his beating and abduction."

Grassi expressed surprise at the suggestion, then took a moment to consider the implication of Vittorio's premise. "The crews of the two ships rarely, if ever, interact with each other. For Stefano to become aware of the smuggling, members of the Nereid's crew would also need to be involved in the smuggling. It seems unlikely that men on both ships would be engaged in smuggling. Do you believe the operation is that widespread?"

"I don't know, but for now, tell no one. I'll let you know when I learn more about the operation." Vittorio turned away and walked along a road that would take him to Pisa, where he would meet Nico. Grassi meandered through the streets of Livorno, muttering to himself, before returning to his office.

15

PISA, SEPTEMBER 9

When Vittorio arrived at Nico's inn, Nico was in the common room telling Finito of Vittorio's prowess during their mission in Bologna. Finito gazed up in awe at the stern-faced investigator and, more than ever, the boy wished for a reason to spend time with the two Florentines. "My uncle doesn't have any chores for me now, so I can come with you. I can guide you to any place in the city," Finito said hopefully.

Nico patted the boy's head and said, "Not this time, my young friend. Maybe later." Finito stared up at the staid investigator standing alongside Nico, then stood and plodded away.

Nico watched the disheartened boy leave, then he turned to Vittorio. "The innkeeper gave me directions to Domenico Carlucci's palazzo. He's the Medici bank customer who received threats and was persuaded to move his account to a Pisan bank. His palazzo isn't far." Chuckling, Nico added, "I'm sure we can find it without Finito's help."

As they walked to the palazzo, Vittorio told Nico about the smuggling operation he had uncovered and his suspicion that the men involved might be the ones who abducted Stefano. "I have no evidence connecting the two crimes, but if Stefano discovered the smugglers and threatened to disclose their operation, that could be the reason for his abduction."

"Are you going to report the smugglers to the Guardia or to Captain Carfi?"

"No... at least not yet. First, I want to learn what cargo is in their crates. The Nereid and the Triton travel between Livorno and Tunisia. Many valuable commodities come from North Africa: artifacts, gold, even exotic animals."

Nico said, "But all you know is that the wagon carrying the crate left Livorno heading toward Pisa. It could be anywhere."

"That's true. Since I don't know the wagon's destination, it's not likely that I can find it, but the shipping company manager said that deckhands often rent rooms in the apartment houses in Pisa. It might be easier to find the sailors than the wagon. Once I locate the place they are staying, I can follow them. Eventually, I'll hear them boasting about their scheme. Sailors spend much of their time ashore in taverns, and when they've had enough to drink, they love to boast about their exploits. They'll brag to anyone who will listen. All I have to do is have an ear close enough to overhear."

"There are rooming houses spread throughout the city," Nico said. "How will you find the right one?"

"I'll just watch each building, one at a time, until I spot the two men."

"That could take days," Nico said.

The serious investigator cracked a rare smile. "Investigations always take time."

Nico stroked his chin. "Do you know the sailors' names?"

"I overheard them talking, so I know their given names."

"Ahh, then I have an idea that might be quicker than watching every room house in the city." His concentration broke and his inspiration was left unsaid when he stopped in front of a gray stone structure and scanned its facade. "This is Palazzo Carlucci." The building was as tall as those alongside it, but much narrower, looking as though its massive neighbors had squeezed it.

"If this is the merchant's home, shouldn't we be calling upon him at his place of business?" Vittorio asked.

"Signor Carlucci has no office. He owns an importing company, but he doesn't take part in its ongoing activities. His sons manage the business."

"Most unusual," Vittorio mused. "Few men would trust enough to give others total control of their affairs, even to their children."

Nico nodded. "Misplaced trust can be costly. At the university, I studied a case where an owner's son gained control of the family business and drove his father out with only the ducats in his coin purse. The father filed charges but lost the case because the magistrate ruled that the son's actions were entirely legal. That case happened in Venice, but I know that Florence also has its share of predatory children, and I wouldn't doubt that Pisa does as well."

A servant responded to Nico's knock. He stood with a stiff military posture, waiting for the callers to state their purpose. Vittorio cocked his head to better hear the faint music drifting out from the palazzo. Nico announced, "Signori Argenti and Colombo to see Signor Carlucci."

"Is he expecting you?"

Nico answered tersely, "No."

From their dress, the servant could tell the men were not vagrants or common laborers. Still, he was unsure whether to admit the two strangers. Nico said, "We are members of the Florentine Security Commission."

Although the servant was unfamiliar with the Florentine Security Commission, the title sounded important. Nico reached for his official letter of introduction, but before he could produce the document, the servant said, "This way," and escorted the men into the palazzo.

They passed through a vestibule to a hallway beyond the reception room. As they continued along the hallway, the music grew louder. The servant entered the next room and stopped inside the doorway. Nico scanned the room. The walls were bare except for a single painting of a seascape on one wall and a mountain scene painting on the opposite wall. Music reverberated off the walls and the high ceiling. At the far end of the room, a man sat in front of an elaborate wooden box, the source of the music. Nico stared, fascinated, watching the man run his fingers across a row of toggles to produce different notes. Flames of the candles in a candelabra on a nearby table seemed to dance to the music.

The servant and the two visitors listened until the man stopped playing. Then the servant announced, "Signore, these men wish to speak with you."

Signor Carlucci withdrew his hands from the instrument and rose. He was tall with a narrow face and long, thin fingers. His long black hair, streaked with gray, reached to his shoulders.

Nico crossed the room to study the instrument. "The sound is lovely. I've never seen one of these...."

"Clavichord," Carlucci completed Nico's thought. "It has a unique timbre because it produces sound by striking the strings rather than plucking them." Carlucci reached down with one hand and played the melody of a popular folk tune. "Playing this clavichord has become my passion, but I'm sure you aren't here to listen to my music."

Nico introduced himself and Vittorio as members of the Florentine Security Commission. Vittorio observed that Nico's mention of the Security Commission elicited no reaction from Carlucci. He continued to watch Carlucci's response as he said, "We understand someone pressured you to move your financial accounts from the Medici bank to a Pisan bank."

"Pressured?" Carlucci echoed. "That's not so. No one pressured me. A colleague put me in mind that Pisa is a community and for our community to prosper, all Pisans must support our local businesses. Who told you I had been pressured?"

"The manager of the Medici bank," Nico replied.

This time, Carlucci did respond. He bit his lip, paused for a moment, then said, "He is mistaken." Another pause, then, "Perhaps the fault is mine. I may not have chosen my words carefully when I spoke with him."

Vittorio noted that Carlucci had tensed. He asked, "Who suggested that you move your accounts to a Pisan bank?"

"My accountant. We meet periodically to review my accounts, and he broached the subject the last time we met."

"We would like to speak with him to understand his reasoning. What is his name?" Nico asked.

"Fonte. His name is Pippo Fonte. I've done business with Pippo for many years. I assure you he didn't pressure me."

"Does he manage all the accounts for your business?" Nico asked.

"He manages my personal accounts. I have no idea who manages the business accounts. My father founded the company. Eventually, control passed to me, and now to my son. Managing an import business takes a toll. I am now free of that burden, free to enjoy my music. I do see financial statements of the company periodically, and from what I've seen, my son is doing exceedingly well." Carlucci laughed. "He's a better steward of the business than I was. He can tell you who tallies the company accounts."

Nico and Vittorio exchanged a look. They could tell that the conversation had made Carlucci uncomfortable, but there could be many reasons for his anxiety; perhaps he was eager to return to his music. Nico thanked Carlucci for receiving them. The servant, who had remained near the room's entrance, escorted the two visitors out of the building. The clavichord strains that followed them were more somber than Carlucci's earlier selections.

Outside, Nico asked, "Do you think Carlucci was being truthful?"

"I believe that what he told us is the truth, but I believe there are things he did not tell us, such as why he was suddenly encouraged to move his account. He has had a long-standing relationship with his accountant, and the fact that his account is at the Medici bank had never surfaced as an issue before. What motivates the accountant to raise it as an issue now?" Vittorio posed rhetorically.

"The only way to answer that question is for us to talk with the accountant," Nico replied. "It's too bad I didn't let Finito join us because he could have led us to the accountant's office. He seems to know everything and everyone in Pisa."

Vittorio abruptly changed the conversation, saying, "Earlier, you claimed to have a way to find the rooming house where the smugglers are staying."

Nico grinned and scanned the shops fronting the piazza. "This way," he said, and headed toward a leather goods shop with Vittorio trailing behind. In the shop, he bought a new coin pouch, transferred all but two silver coins from his pouch to the new one. He explained his scheme to Vittorio. "At each apartment, I'll ask for the smugglers by name. When I find them, I can say that I found this pouch on the wharf in Livorno" — He held out the old pouch containing two silver coins. — "and was told it might belong to one of them. If they claim the pouch is theirs, my only loss would be this old pouch and two coins, but for that price, I will have found the men."

Vittorio slapped Nico on the back. "That's a deception I would expect of a street lout. Did they teach you that at the university?" Shaking his head, Vittorio turned and led Nico to a row of old apartments that he passed each time he came into Pisa from Livorno. At the first building, a caretaker who was repairing a broken stair tread told Nico that the men he sought did not live there. He received similar responses at the next two units. At the fourth building, a caretaker uttered hoarsely, "Upstairs on the left."

The stairs creaked as Nico climbed. With each step, the fetid smell of lingering body odor became stronger. Halfway to the second level, he glimpsed two red rodent eyes peering down at him. The creature held its position until Nico reached the upper level, then it scurried away along the dark hallway. Nico listened at the door on the left but heard nothing. Neither his first knock nor a second, louder knock drew a response. Out in the street, he told Vittorio, "This is the building, but they must be away. They didn't answer my knock."

"Show me," Vittorio said as he advanced toward the building.

Standing outside the smugglers' door, Vittorio withdrew a thin metal blade from his boot. He slid the flexible shiv between the door and the jamb and worked it slowly, sliding it up and down, until the latch released, then he pushed the door open.

"That's a trick I didn't learn at the university," Nico jested as he followed Vittorio into the room.

Without cracking a smile, Vittorio replied, "It's just one of the many skills I've gained by spending time with criminals."

Two beds were set against the side walls of the sparse room and at the foot of each bed was a duffel filled with rumpled clothes. A small desk and a washstand filled the far wall. Papers spread across the desk drew Vittorio's attention. The first sheet he lifted from the desk stated the destinations and departure dates of the ships: Nereid, Triton, and Pallas. The second sheet said, "When you arrive, a wagon will meet you to collect the silver." He showed the paper to Nico.

"Silver," Nico noted, "That's what they're smuggling."

Vittorio carried the paper to the room's only window to study the handwriting's unique characteristics, the slant of the letters, and the peculiar curls at the end of each word. They searched the room, looking through the duffels and under the beds, but found nothing else of interest. Vittorio folded the paper into a small square and clutched it in his hand when they left the room.

"Now that you've found where the smugglers are staying, what will you do next?" Nico asked.

"Your ingenious scheme saved time in finding the smugglers' apartment. Now I have only to watch it and the next time they leave, I'll follow them. Eventually, they'll lead me to the person who controls the smuggling operation." When they stepped into the street, Vittorio turned in the direction that would bring them back to the inn and said, "But first, let's see if your young friend can tell us how to find Carlucci's accountant. It may be too late to find him at his office now, but we can call upon him in the morning."

16

PISA, SEPTEMBER 10

A rhythmic thumping led Nico to the alley alongside the inn, where Finito was throwing a ball against the side of the building and trying to catch the rebound. The uneven stone surface deflected the ball at unpredictable angles, making it nearly impossible to catch. Nico picked up an errant ball that rolled toward him and tossed it to Finito, who snatched it from the air with both hands. A grin spread across the boy's face upon seeing his Florentine friend. "You need a smooth building or a thrower," Nico said. Finito opened his mouth, but before he could speak, Nico, anticipating Finito's request, said, "Maybe later. Now I need your help to find someone." He told Finito the accountant's name and asked, "Can you give me directions to his office?"

"I know him. First, go...." Suddenly, Finito stopped and flashed a mischievous smile. "I forget the names of the streets, so I can't give you directions... but I can take you there."

Nico tousled Finito's hair and said, "Very well, Hermes, lead the way." Finito looked up, puzzled by the name Nico had called him. "To the ancient Greeks, Hermes was a boy who was always playing tricks on the gods," Nico explained.

"Hermes," Finito echoed, not sure whether to be pleased or offended.

Sensing the boy's unease, Nico said, "Hermes wasn't just known as a trickster, he was also known for being clever. You must be familiar with the lyre, the stringed instrument. It was invented by Hermes." Now mollified, Finito danced away playfully, with Nico and Vittorio following.

Finito took a nearly direct path to the piazza in the central business district and pointed to a building directly across from the Medici bank. "That's his office," Finito announced.

"Hermes indeed. He couldn't remember the street that leads to the city's main piazza," Vittorio muttered to himself.

Nico handed the boy a coin. "Go buy a treat at the pasticceria while Signor Colombo and I meet with the accountant."

The storefront had no sign or other marking identifying it as the accountant's office. If it weren't for Finito's record of success in guiding him throughout Pisa, Nico would have been reluctant to enter. Inside, a lone man sat behind a desk with papers neatly arranged across its surface. Nico expected him to be about the same age as his client, Signor Carlucci, but the accountant was much younger. He was well built and stylishly dressed in a pale blue silk tunic. "May I be of assistance?" he said in a resonant voice that gave him a commanding presence.

Light reflecting from the unusual green stone in the man's ring distracted Nico momentarily. He turned slightly to avoid looking at the ring and introduced himself and Vittorio. He did not mention their affiliation with the Florentine Security Commission. "Are you Signor Pippo Fonte?"

The accountant set down the quill he had been holding. "I am Pippo Fonte."

"Signor Domenico Carlucci is a client of yours?" Nico asked.

The accountant gave an almost imperceptible nod. Nico said, "You persuaded him to move his accounts from the Medici bank to a Pisan bank."

Fonte leaned back in his chair, and responded to Nico's allegation by asking, "Why should that be a matter of interest to you? Are you employees of the Medici bank?"

Vittorio replied, "Our purpose is to investigate allegations that discredit the reputation of the Medici bank."

"You must be Florentines," the accountant said in a calm, steady voice.

Nico declared, "This is the Florentine Republic. We are all Florentines."

Fonte folded his arms across his chest and in a defiant voice said, "Those of us who live in this city think of ourselves as Pisans." He waved a hand as though brushing aside the distinction. "Yes, I suggested that Signor Carlucci move his funds to a Pisan bank. I offered similar suggestions to all my clients. For this city to prosper, Pisans must advocate for each other. Do you find that objectionable? Surely those of you who live in Florence favor your neighbors."

Vittorio placed his hands on the desk, leaned down to meet Carlucci's eyes and said, "No one would be concerned if Pisans only acted to support each other, but this city is rife with ominous rumors."

"I cannot answer to all the rumors you may have heard. I can speak only for myself."

Vittorio pressed. "You say that you speak for yourself, but is that so, or does someone else originate the ideas?"

Fonte placed his hands on the desk to match Vittorio's posture. "My beliefs are my own, although I acknowledge that I share them with others. I contend it is you who may be bending the truth. Is your concern truly only the reputation of the Medici bank, or do you have a larger purpose?"

Nico said, "The Florentine Signoria recognizes there is discontent in Pisa and it would like to resolve any problems. We are here for that purpose. Violence serves no one's interest."

The accountant snickered. "The people of Pisa do not see the intentions of the Florentine Signoria. We know only the actions of the Florentine governor. If the Signoria wants to avoid problems, they should begin by recalling him.

"Last year the spring rains did not come," he continued, "and by the heat of July, crops withered in the fields. Our farmers pleaded with the governor to petition the Florentine Signoria for relief from the onerous taxes on vegetables and grain. He had no sympathy for their plight and said it was their duty to pay. You want to resolve problems? Where were you when many of those good men and their families were forced to leave their farms?"

Nico asserted, "You are the second man who has voiced complaints to me about the governor. Trust that Signor Colombo and I will bring your grievances to the Signoria." Further discussion convinced Nico that the accountant sympathized with Pisa's malcontents, but nothing that Fonte said suggested that he supported violence.

17

PISA, SEPTEMBER 10

Massimo spent the afternoon carrying urns of a foul-smelling substance from the warehouse to a barge ready to head upriver. He could not identify the brown slurry, but he did not care enough to ask anyone. He just lugged urns hour after hour in the late summer heat. When the barge was fully loaded, he had picked up enough of the putrid smell that he could barely tolerate himself.

As he left the warehouse, eager to return to his inn and soak in a washtub, a voice called to him. "Fornitore asked me to bring you to the gathering."

Massimo turned to face the speaker, whom he did not recognize as one of the warehouse workers. "Now?" he asked.

"Now," the man replied.

"I need to wash and change clothes." Massimo spread his hands wide. "I smell like…"

"Fresh manure," the man said, completing Massimo's thought. "There's a rain barrel behind the warehouse. You can wash there."

Massimo removed his smock and plunged his arms and head into the water. He was not the first person to use the rain barrel as a wash-basin. Someone had left a length of rough leather hanging over the barrel rim. Massimo used the leather strap to scrape the smell from his arms, hands, and neck.

"You can wear this." The man handed Massimo a smock. It was a snug fit, but it was clean and didn't smell. Massimo picked up the smock he had been wearing, and even at arm's length, the smell was offensive. "Fertilizer," the man said. "You'll never get the smell out." Massimo dropped the smock onto a trash heap.

They walked through the Porta Calcesana city gate to a nearby stable where horses had been readied for them. They rode east on a road paralleling the river. In less than a quarter hour, they turned onto a dirt track that passed through fields that may have been farmland at one time; now they were overgrown with weeds. From the crest of a low hill, Massimo spotted their destination, an old farmhouse surrounded by tethered horses and wagons.

They tied their mounts to a fence and entered the building, where Massimo caught the smell of sweat and body odor from the men packed inside. He tried counting the men, but they were constantly in motion, chatting and greeting each other. He estimated there were approximately thirty, none of whom he recognized. Most were dressed as he was in workmen's clothes.

One man stood out from the others. He wore a tunic, rather than a smock. He had smooth skin with no apparent scars or blemishes, and his hands had no calluses. Upon seeing Massimo, he clapped his hands to draw the attention of the others, whose conversation quickly faded. A few men found chairs; most remained standing. The leader began, "Joining us today is one of the partisans who drove the French invaders from Naples. He is here to tell us how a small band of brave men can drive encroachers from their homeland."

The leader summoned Massimo to the front of the group. He made no introduction and said only, "Tell them."

Except for an occasional fist pumped in the air and spirited hoots, the men remained silent and still as Massimo recounted the tale he had told Fornitore the previous evening. When he finished speaking, he could sense the enthusiasm of the crowd, eager to copy the tactics he had described. The leader clapped him on the shoulder and said simply, "Well done." He too realized that Massimo's talk had motivated the men exactly as he had intended.

Massimo stepped away to melt into the crowd when the man who had escorted him to the farmhouse tapped him on the shoulder. "Your part is done. It's time to take your leave." Massimo looked puzzled. He had hoped to hear the leader speak, expecting that he might reveal their plans for actions against Florence. "The gathering is only for Pisans," the man added.

The escort followed Massimo outside and watched him ride away until he was out of sight over the nearby hill. On the far side of the hill, Massimo tied his horse behind a clump of trees and headed back toward the farmhouse on foot. Waist-high weeds in the field afforded cover to keep him from being seen should anyone come out of the farmhouse. He moved quickly, eager to hear what the leader would say. When he reached the area where the horses were tied, he worked his way around behind the building and found a door that had been left ajar. He pushed it open enough to slip inside the room that had once served as the kitchen. Stepping carefully to prevent the old floor from creaking, Massimo crossed to the far side of the kitchen. From there, he could hear the leader speaking.

"You just heard that in Naples, the partisans did not confront the powerful French army directly. They succeeded by antagonizing their enemy, bruising them with small actions that led to victory. They were not fools. They did not raise swords against the powerful invading army."

A man at the far side of the room began speaking. Massimo pressed his ear against the kitchen door to hear the man's words. "In Naples, they had help from His Holiness and some prince. The new pope is a Venetian. I can't imagine him doing anything that might restore Pisa as a sea power to compete with Venice. Like all the other Venetians, he must be delighted that Pisa is getting crushed under Florence's foot." Several other men grumbled their agreement.

A man at the back of the room shouted, "We keep saying we're going to peel off the Florentines. I'm tired of talk. It's time for us to do something!"

The leader raised a hand. "It's true that we cannot count on aid from the Papal States. In time, we may find other allies, but for others to support our cause, they must see that we are on a path to victory." He pointed to the man at the back of the room. "You are correct. It is time for us to make a move and our first act will be to rid ourselves of the Florentine governor. He..." Just as the leader was about to describe the plan, Massimo heard footsteps in the other room. They grew louder as someone approached the kitchen.

With no place to hide inside, Massimo slipped out the door and ducked down in the weeds behind the house. He left the door open wide enough for him to peer into the room. He watched as a man came into the kitchen, look around, saw the open door, and pushed it closed.

Massimo remained hidden for several minutes before making his way back to the house. He pressed an ear against the door to listen for footsteps or other movement. Hearing none, he pushed the door to ease it open, but it didn't move. *Damn*, he thought, *it must be latched*. He worked his way around to a window on the side of the building and kneeled in the weeds, listening. He could hear a voice which he guessed was the leader speaking, but the cloth window coverings muffled sound. He heard occasional shouts and cheers, but could not make out any words.

When the leader stopped speaking, Massimo knew he should leave because the gathering might be concluding. He moved silently around to the front of the farmhouse to study the horses and wagons, looking for any distinctive markings. Only one, a well-groomed black mare with a fine leather saddle, stood out from the others. Massimo assumed that the mount belonged to the leader.

"Our first act will be to rid ourselves of the Florentine governor," Massimo repeated the leader's words as he hastened over the hill to the clump of trees where his horse was tied. Although he didn't know when the agitators would strike, he had learned one piece of valuable information: the governor would be their initial target. He also knew what the leader looked like, although the man had no distinguishing features other than his ring with its unusual shiny dark green stone, so it would be hard to describe the man to Nico and Vittorio. Massimo pounded his fist against a tree to vent his frustration that he had not learned more.

18

PISA, SEPTEMBER 10

Massimo met Nico at his inn and from there the two men crossed the city together to the Santa Maria della Spina. From the rear of the small Gothic-style church, they could see the city gate where the road from Livorno entered the city. It was the road that Vittorio would be traveling as he came to join them. While they waited, they watched water from the Arno River flowing onto the field alongside the church. Early autumn rains had come early and already the river had swelled over its bank. If the abnormally heavy rains continued into September, the church would be flooded again, as it had been many times before. Brown stains encircled the church, marking the high-water levels from previous inundations.

Massimo turned away from the river and eyed the road. "Two wagons are coming this way, but they're too far for me to tell whether Vittorio is on one of them." He locked his gaze on the approaching spots, and a minute later said, "He's not on the first wagon, but there's too much dust to see the second wagon clearly." When the wagons passed a bend in the road, he got a better view of both vehicles. "He's there. I can see Vittorio in the second wagon."

Inside the Porta a Mare gate, the wagon stopped to discharge

Vittorio. He grimaced as the soggy ground in the water-logged field suctioned his shoes. When he neared Nico and Massimo, Vittorio gestured toward the departing wagon driver. "He's a brick maker. Every day he brings bricks to the masons who are building the wall around Livorno. He said the Medici initiated the construction of the wall so their new villa would be protected. He admitted that other Pisans are angry with Florence, but he's not. He's pleased to have the work, especially since it's being paid for by the Florentine treasury."

Vittorio looked down at his wet shoes. "Can we go somewhere dry before my feet start to rot?"

Massimo pointed to a path that followed along the city wall. "This is higher ground," he said as the three men set off along the path at a leisurely pace.

With excitement in his voice, Nico asked, "Has word reached Livorno yet that the Florentine governor has gone missing? The news has spread quickly throughout Pisa. I heard it from my innkeeper."

Vittorio and Massimo looked surprised. "Was he abducted?" Vittorio asked.

"No one knows for sure. There are conflicting rumors. All we know for certain is that the governor and his wife disappeared from their residence," Nico replied. "I heard that the army will be leading the search for them."

Massimo, who was walking ahead of Nico and Vittorio, stopped and turned around to face the others. "I would bet they were abducted. This afternoon I was taken to a meeting of men who want independence for Pisa. Since I was a stranger, they didn't share their plans with me, but I did overhear their leader say that they planned to target the governor."

"Exactly what did he say?" Vittorio asked.

"The men were all determined to free themselves from Florentine rule and the wanted to act now. Their leader told them that he had a plan and it would begin by targeting the governor. That's all I heard."

"It does sound like he could be responsible," Vittorio declared. "Where can we find the man who made that threat?"

Massimo ran a hand slowly over the bark of the tree next to him as he thought about the meeting. "I'm not sure how to do that. The meeting was held at an abandoned farmhouse outside the city. About thirty men were there, but I didn't recognize any of them. From their clothes and behavior, most seemed to be farmers and laborers.

"Only the leader stood out from the others. He wore a clean, stylish tunic, not a smock. His hands weren't rough, and he didn't use the dialect commonly spoken by the lower classes. He's likely a merchant or a city official. I'd recognize him if I saw him again, but he didn't have any distinguishing characteristics." Massimo paused for a beat, then added, "Except for his ring, which had an unusual green stone."

"Was it a smooth green stone with swirling light and dark colored bands?" Nico asked.

"Yes, how did you know?"

"This afternoon, Vittorio and I met with an accountant who's been advising his clients to move their accounts from the Medici bank to a Pisan bank. He feels strongly that Pisa should be free from Florence. He admitted to impressing his views on others, and his complaints targeted the governor. He wore a ring with a green stone that had light and dark bands like the one you described. He has no regard for Florence, but he didn't seem prone to violence. However, if he is the same person you met with, we might have misjudged him. He may have hidden his aggressive intentions."

"The stone is malachite," Vittorio interjected. "Some people believe malachite has the power to ward off sickness, but I doubt that is why he wears it. He didn't impress me as a superstitious person. Can you describe the man you saw? Did he have a birthmark on the right side of his neck?"

Massimo laughed. "Investigator, I'm always impressed by your observational skills. I only give beautiful women enough attention to notice their birthmarks. I can only say that the man has a strong jaw and piercing eyes. I think his intensity is what makes other men listen to him and follow his leadership."

Nico nodded slowly. "Strong jaw, piercing eyes... that description fits him. We need to pay Signor Fonte another visit."

Nico looked for agreement from Vittorio, who said, "You and Massimo can visit him in the morning. I've been watching the smugglers. Thus far, I've learned nothing, but tomorrow is their last day in port before their ship sails. It's the last chance that they might lead me to the person who is heading the smuggling operation. I don't want to lose the opportunity."

19

PISA, SEPTEMBER 11

An early rain kept all but the most essential workers from venturing into Pisa's normally lively central piazza. Nico and Massimo positioned themselves at one end of a counter in the pasticceria, the first shop to open each morning. From their vantage point, they could see the accountant's office through the shop's small window. Several times they thought they had spotted Signor Fonte, a chore made difficult because everyone looked the same in their hooded cloaks.

"That's him," they said simultaneously as one of the hooded figures unlocked the door to the accountant's modest office.

As they crossed the piazza, Massimo said, "He is the one who led the meeting of disgruntled Pisans at the farmhouse."

Fonte had barely removed his cloak when Nico and Massimo followed him inside. His eyes went wide when he saw Massimo grinning at him. Nico announced, "I spoke with you yesterday, and you already met my associate, Signor Massimo Leoni. We are members of the Florentine Security Commission."

Fonte folded his arms across his chest defiantly and looked directly at Massimo. "So, you are a Florentine. The story you told about being a Neapolitan who drove the French from Naples was *un mare di cazzate*?"

"Not everything I told your men was a load of crap. I wasn't one of the Neapolitan partisans, but other than that, the story was true. The partisans did drive the out the French without a major military battle." Massimo pushed aside a stack of papers and sat on the edge of the accountant's desk. "At that meeting, you told your men that you had a plan to remove the Florentine governor; now he and his wife are missing."

Fonte replied sharply, "I had nothing to do with their disappearance."

Nico stepped forward to be nose-to-nose with the accountant. "Yesterday, you told me that you blame the governor for repressing Pisa, and you told Signor Colombo that you had a plan to remove the governor. How can you expect us to believe that you are not responsible for his disappearance?"

Fonte looked directly at Nico, and in a calm voice, said, "You came to my office claiming that your interest was the Medici bank." He gestured toward Massimo. "And he spoke lies at a meeting of Pisan loyalists. You both spout deceptions and yet you dare to accuse me of being untruthful. My compatriots and I are not the only ones who condemn the governor. Others have spoken out against him using harsher words than mine."

Massimo said, "The meeting you led yesterday had two dozen or more men crowded into that farmhouse. I heard you tell them it was time to act. Even if you yourself didn't abduct the governor, you can't be certain that your words didn't incite the others."

"I've known most of those men since childhood. They may complain loudly, but they're family men, church-going men who wouldn't resort to force."

Turning away from the accountant, Nico said over his shoulder in a firm voice, "Your explanation isn't at all reassuring. You said that you had a plan to remove the governor and now, less than a day later, he and his wife are missing."

Massimo turned toward Nico. "I think we should deliver him to the army. They're leading the hunt to recover the governor, and I know they have ways that will make this one reveal his plot."

Unfazed by Massimo's threat, Fonte moved around behind his desk and sat. In a steady voice, he said, "I have no need to resort to violence. I have only to publicize the truth. The governor is an adulterer. Once I let that be known, I'm confident that the Florentine Signoria will recall him. They will not want to be represented in Pisa by a moral degenerate."

Massimo laughed. "That's a worthless contention. It wouldn't surprise me if half the men in Pisa have mistresses."

The accountant started to say something but held the thought and in a calm voice said, "I didn't say that he has a mistress nor that he beds loose women and prostitutes. He's an adulterer. The object of his passion is a married woman."

Nico weighed the possible reactions should Fonte's assertion be disclosed. "Adultery is a crime... and a sin, but the governor would not be the only man whose soul is stained with that indiscretion. His infidelity might not have the consequences you expect. The Florentine Signoria could easily overlook an accusation that its appointed official is entangled with a Pisan woman, whether she is married or not."

The accountant's lips turned up in a cynical smile. "But his affair is not with a Pisan woman. Twice monthly he travels to Florence claiming that his visits are for government business, while the real reason for his visits is business of the flesh."

Startled by the implication, Nico queried, "His affair is with a Florentine woman?"

"Yes, and not merely any Florentine woman, but a married member of Florence's smug aristocracy. One whose behavior, should it become known, would shame the entirety of Florentine society," came the accountant's immediate reply.

Reluctant to ask the woman's name, Nico asked, "You have proof of this alleged liaison?"

"An aide to the governor who travels with him is willing to testify that he has seen their dalliances."

"His aide is a Pisan," Nico said dismissively. "The testimony of a Pisan servant would hardly cause a ripple in Florence."

Fonte's lips turned up in a cynical smile. "And how will proud Florentines react when the woman's own sister, also a Florentine aristocrat, speaks out to denounce her sibling?" Fonte reached into his desk and withdrew a letter, which he handed to Nico. Nico's mouth dropped open when he read the signature. Without a word, he gave the paper to Massimo.

"Damn!" Massimo exclaimed. He re-read the letter, then said, "This is addressed to her father, the ambassador. How did you get it?"

The accountant brushed away Massimo's query, saying, "I have many sources." He continued, "But now you understand why I have no reason to abduct the governor. I'm confident that when his illicit affair becomes known, the Florentine government will dismiss him."

Nico paced across the small office, then returned to face the accountant. "You said there are others who want the governor removed. Who are they?"

"I hear things, but I can't be sure which stories are credible. Some people stuff their egos by boasting of deeds they have never done. One rumor claims that a group is buying weapons. Is it true? Perhaps," he answered and shrugged.

Nico pressed him. "Tell me the rumor. Who is buying weapons?"

"When you were here yesterday, I told you about farmers who were driven from their homes because they couldn't pay the taxes. I heard the farmers joined together with the goal of securing Pisa's independence, and they intend to do so by force as soon as they acquire weapons. That's all I know."

"If they couldn't pay their taxes, how can they afford to buy weapons?" Massimo asked.

"As destitute farmers they can barely afford to feed their families, but as fighters committed to expel the oppressive Florentines..."
— He held out a hand defensively to imply that he did not origi-

nate the pejorative phrase — "funds might become available to them."

"From whom?" Nico asked.

"Farmers aren't the only ones who find the taxes burdensome. Businessmen do as well, and many can certainly afford to purchase weapons." Again, he held up a hand. "And before you ask, that is my supposition. I have not heard any rumors about businessmen supporting the farmers or buying weapons."

Massimo asked, "If the farmers have a benefactor who can provide them with weapons, what need do they have to abduct the governor?"

Fonte shrugged and replied, "As I told you, I was voicing my conjecture. I do not have the answer you seek."

Frustrated by the lack of useable information, Nico pounded his fist against the wall. "There must be some whom you suspect of abducting the governor," he snapped. "What name came into your mind first when you heard he was missing?"

Without taking a beat to think, the accountant responded, "Settimo. He's a thief, a vicious person, always looking for trouble. He spent time in prison for battering a man with a boat anchor because the man was slow to pay a gambling debt."

"Where can we find this Settimo?" Massimo demanded.

"It's impossible to say. He never stays in one place for long. He has as many hiding places as a cockroach. Even the Guardia can't keep eyes on him. I've never met him, but I've been told he has a Genovese dialect, so he may not spend all of his time in Pisa."

Nico and Massimo left the accountant's office discouraged that they had little more than Settimo's name and description. They had no clue to find him and no sound basis for connecting him to the governor's disappearance. Nico said to himself as much as to Massimo, "Pisa was a peaceful city when we arrived. The only reason for our being here was to investigate one piece of disturbing information, a fragment of conversation, hardly more than speculation, overheard by the cousin of a Signoria member. Since we've been here, the situation has gotten decidedly worse: a bank courier has been killed, the provincial governor and his wife have gone missing, and we've made no progress toward resolving any of these problems. Nor have we found any agitators."

Massimo patted his friend on the shoulder. "You could add to the list of misfortunes that a sailor was abducted in Livorno, and Vittorio believes he's uncovered a band of smugglers." He chuckled. "Maybe if we return to Florence, conditions in Pisa will improve."

20

FLORENCE, SEPTEMBER 11

Bruno Fiorello's lawyer was already seated at the defense table when two Guardia officers escorted Fiorello into the courtroom. He swaggered up the central aisle with the same disdain he had shown in his previous trials. The officers left him with his lawyer and took positions in the gallery at the rear of the chamber where they could keep a careful watch on their charge. The only other person in the gallery was a young Benedictine monk.

Fiorello dropped into a chair beside his lawyer and scanned the raised platform at the front of the room, where seats had been made ready for the three magistrates who would be presiding over the tribunal. "Why are there three chairs?" Fiorello asked.

"This is a capital trial," the lawyer replied dispassionately. "You are being charged with murder. The law stipulates that three magistrates preside in capital cases."

Fiorello looked across the room to where prosecutor Luca Sasso and his notary were reviewing their notes. "He's the same fish head as last time, and you beat him before. I hope this doesn't take long. I need a drink," Fiorello said, not understanding the gravity of his situation. His lawyer merely glared at his witless client.

A cool puff stirred the stale air of the tribunal chamber when the court notary opened the door to the magistrates' chamber. He held the door open until three men had entered and reached their places on the raised platform at the front of the room. The chair creaked as the senior magistrate lowered his bulky frame onto the padded seat. Once he was settled, the notary faced those assembled and boomed, "Quisque attendere! The Santa Maria Novella district court is now convened." The magistrate took his time adjusting the sleeves of his robe. When he was finally comfortable, he looked toward his associates seated alongside him to gain confirmation that they were ready to proceed. Having their approval, he turned to the prosecutor and raised a finger to indicate that he should begin by reading the accusation.

Sasso rose. He scanned the room, shifted his weight from foot to foot, cleared his throat and began with a firm voice. "Honorable magistrates, the Comune of Florence accuses signor Bruno Fiorello, an ironworker residing in the Santa Spirito district, of the crimes of assault and murder."

As Sasso spoke, all eyes of those in the gallery fell on the muscular defendant whose size dwarfed the lawyer beside him at the defense table. His tunic stretching tightly across his broad chest, looking ready to tear open if he inhaled deeply. His hands were balled into fists, his teeth bared like an animal sizing up its prey, and his eyes glared at the prosecutor.

Sasso continued, "One week past, while on his regular patrol, a Guardia officer came upon a man being severely beaten by the defendant, a beating so severe that it resulted in the victim's death. That officer is prepared to give his account of the incident and testify how he apprehended the defendant. Then a second witness, an eyewitness, will testify that he also saw the fatal beating administered by the defendant."

Fiorello turned to his lawyer, who had been fidgeting with a trinket on the table in front of him, seemingly uninterested in the trial proceeding. The lawyer flinched reflexively from Fiorello's sour breath when he leaned close and growled into the lawyer's ear, "Say something! Protest. What are you here for?"

The lawyer turned and gazed at his client with the look one might give an insolent child. "What do you expect me to say? That you didn't do it? No one would believe your word against that of a Guardia officer. Your only hope is to claim self-defense."

"Can't you find a witness? You've found witnesses before."

The lawyer felt shame when forced to admit to himself that he had, on occasion, found peasants willing to perjure themselves in return for enough coin to buy a night of pleasure at their favorite tavern. His only solace came by rationalizing that he had used the ploy only in cases of minor consequence, and this was not a case of minor consequence. The victim deserved retribution. "There are no witnesses," he said flatly.

Sasso motioned to the court clerk who fetched the prosecution's first witness from a nearby anteroom. The Guardia officer marched into the room with his chin held high. He stood tall behind the witness stand and ran his hands over its familiar wood frame. He had stood there many times before testifying against drunks, pickpockets, and thieves he had apprehended in the course of his duties, but this was his first time testifying against a murderer. He began when the prosecutor said, "State your name and your Guardia assignment."

"I am Officer Pasquale Barbarigo. I've been an officer in the Guardia for seven years. Every night I patrol the Santa Maria Novella district. I walk the side streets and alleys looking for muggers, pick-pockets, anyone committing an offense. Any well-dressed man walking alone at night can be a target of the derelicts who roam those streets. Last week alone, three men reported having money purses torn from them by lowlife scoundrels. One of those men..."

The prosecutor interrupted the officer before he could recite other details irrelevant to the case being heard. "Tell the magistrate how you came upon the victim."

"I was approaching an alley when I heard a noise, a pounding sound. Over and over. Like when a butcher chops up a piece of meat.

The alley was dark, so I couldn't see anyone at first. Then I saw that man, the defendant," — he pointed at Fiorello — "kicking at something on the ground. Repeatedly, he pummeled the object with his boot. As I moved closer, I saw the object was a person. He was lying on the ground, and he wasn't moving."

The magistrate interjected, "Has the victim been identified?"

The Guardia officer could have answered the question, but protocol required that he defer to the prosecutor, who responded, "No, the victim has not been identified." The magistrate gave an understanding nod. He knew the city was filled with laborers, derelicts, and transients who had no family members to notice if they went missing. Rarely would those people be identified if they became victims of violence. The magistrate waved a hand, signaling the officer to continue.

"When the defendant saw me, he stopped kicking and moved away. He started walking toward the far end of the alley. I called for him to stop, but instead of stopping, he ran away. I chased after him and he might have gotten away if he didn't trip and fall. He was dazed from hitting his head when he fell. I bound him and dragged him back to where the victim was still lying immobile on the ground. I couldn't rouse him. He was dead.

"I heard a noise and noticed a second man in the alley. He was pressed against a storefront, trying to hide. He said that he saw the whole altercation. I took both men to the local Guardia office." The officer turned toward the prosecutor and smiled broadly, feeling satisfied that he had described the situation exactly as they had reviewed it.

The senior magistrate looked to Fiorello's lawyer, indicating that he should proceed. The lawyer pressed his palms down onto the defense table and used his hands to push himself up to a standing position. He too was smiling, but his was a cunning smile. "When you called for my client to stop, did you identify yourself as a Guardia officer?"

Color drained from the officer's face. "No," he replied hesitantly. "I just called for him to stop."

The lawyer's smile broadened further. "In a dark alley in an area that you described as seething with thieves, you just called for him to stop?"

Sheepishly, the officer answered simply, "Yes. "

The lawyer shifted to face the magistrates. "Esteemed magistrates, if I were passing through a darkened street in an area of our city known to be frequented by muggers and a stranger called for me to stop, I would run in the opposite direction and I am certain that any other man who values his safety would do the same."

The lawyer struggled to show a smug expression as he settled back down onto his chair. He, and everyone else in the courtroom other than Fiorello, knew that his point, while valid, had no bearing on the charge of murder. In contrast, Fiorello slapped his lawyer on the shoulder and said, "Good. You did good with that Guardia swine."

Since the defense lawyer had no further questions, the officer was dismissed, and the clerk brought in the second prosecution witness, a short man with a slight build and a scraggly beard. Sasso instructed, "Say your name and then tell the magistrate what you saw on the night of the beating." The witness gripped the stand tightly, leaning against it as though he could not stand without assistance. He opened his mouth and began speaking, mumbling words that could not be heard clearly. "Start again. Speak louder," the prosecutor admonished.

"I am Giuseppe. I was going through the alley when I heard voices. Two men. One of them was yelling at the other one. It was dark, but I could see them ahead of me. Then suddenly the one who was yelling started hitting the other one."

The prosecutor asked, "Can you identify the man who started the hitting?"

Giuseppe pointed to the defendant. "It was him." Fiorello glared up at the witness.

Sasso said, "Even though it was dark, you are certain the defendant is the person you saw beating the victim?"

"Yes, I am certain. I wasn't very far away from them."

Repeatedly, Fiorello slapped his fists against his muscled thighs as his rage grew. Giuseppe continued, "He kept hitting the other man until the poor man slumped down to the ground, then he started kicking him. At first, the man on the ground pleaded for him to stop, then just moaned, and finally, he said nothing. He didn't move."

"What were you doing when this was happening?" Sasso asked.

"I tried to hide in the doorway of the shoemaker's shop. I was afraid that he" — again the witness pointed to Fiorello — "would start beating me next."

"To be clear," the prosecutor said, "you saw the defendant begin to hit the victim and continue pummeling the victim until he could no longer move or respond. Is that correct?"

The witness lowered his gaze, afraid to meet Fiorello's eyes. "Yes, that's what I saw."

Sasso sat down and the magistrates turned their attention to the defense table. Fiorello's lawyer rose and stroked his chin as though thinking, then asked, "Giuseppe, where were you before you entered the alley?"

"I was around the corner on Via Santa Lucia."

"And what were you doing on Via Santa Lucia?"

"I was with some other men, friends, at a tavern."

"You were in a tavern, so you must have been drinking. Is that so? What were you drinking?"

"We go there after work. We drink beer."

"How much beer did you drink?"

"I don't remember how much."

"Was it more than one or two mugs? Maybe three or four?"

"Maybe three," the witness replied tentatively.

"From where you were hiding in the dark alley, could you be certain that it was the defendant who struck the first blow? Is it possible that the other man threw a punch that you could not see?"

Again, the witness shrugged. "I don't think so, but I guess it's possible."

The lawyer turned to face the magistrates. "This witness can't even remember how much beer he drank, yet he expects us to believe that he can recall what happened in that darkened alley. This witness admits that my client may have been merely trying to protect himself from a vicious attack. I contend that my client was acting in self-defense. Honorable magistrates, I ask that you dismiss the charges against my client." The lawyer slowly settled back down onto his chair.

Sasso recalled his previous witness. The Guardia officer was uneasy when he returned to the witness stand. He slouched forward over the witness stand and directed his puzzled expression to the prosecutor. He had already delivered his prepared testimony and worried about what might be asked of him next. Sasso spoke in a smooth voice to ease the officer's apprehension. "Would you describe the defendant as a big man?"

"Yes."

"Would you say he is bigger and stronger than most of the criminals you have apprehended?"

"Yes."

"Did you have an opportunity to examine the victim, the one who was beaten to death by the defendant?"

As the officer became comfortable with Sasso's questions, his voice grew firm. "Yes, I examined the victim in the alley and again after he was taken to the Guardia office."

"Was the victim as big as the defendant and did he appear to be as strong, as muscular, as the defendant?"

With a scornful tone, the officer replied, "No, he wasn't big. The victim was a little man. He didn't have broad shoulders or muscles like the defendant."

"In your long experience as a Guardia officer, how often have you seen a little man like the victim begin a fight with a big man like the defendant?"

The officer, now grinning broadly, replied firmly, "Only when the small man had a weapon, and the big man did not."

Upon hearing the response, Sasso forced himself to suppress a smile as he asked his final question. "Did either man have a weapon?"

Fiorello didn't wait to hear the officer's reply before growling at his lawyer, "Do something! Stop this dung show!"

Fiorello's voice carried throughout the room, causing the senior magistrate's face to redden. He pounded a fist on his desk and bellowed at the defendant, "Show respect for this tribunal or I'll have you taken back to your prison cell." Fiorello mumbled something audible only to his lawyer.

Sasso repeated his question, "Did either man have a weapon?"

The witness bared his teeth in a broad grin. "No. Neither man had a weapon."

After both lawyers made their final statements, the magistrate announced, "We will consider the material that has been presented and we will render our decision tomorrow."

At the rear of the chamber, the Benedictine monk was deep in thought as he watched the Guardia officers pull Fiorello from his chair and lead him away.

21

FLORENCE, SEPTEMBER 11

All Florentines knew that the Arnolfo tower atop the Palazzo Signoria held the city's first public clock, which had marked time in Florence for more than a hundred years. Everyone also knew that Florence's infamous Stinche prison was the place where convicted criminals served their sentences in dungeon-like cells. However, few Florentines knew that accused criminals awaiting sentencing were held in a tiny cell high up in the Arnolfo Tower.

The young Benedictine monk was one who did know where Bruno Fiorello was confined while three magistrates decided his punishment. The priest climbed to the top level of Palazzo Signoria and approached the guard stationed at the base of the tower. The guard recognized the monk as the priest who had served mass the preceding Sunday. He stood as a gesture of respect and asked, "Father Giorgio, are you here to see the prisoner?"

The priest smiled and spoke in a kind voice. "Yes, if it is permitted. All God's children, even the darkest sinners, deserve to be reassured that God loves them."

The guard retracted a bolt and opened a door at the base of a long flight of stone steps. The men's footfalls echoed throughout the narrow, curving passageway as they climbed. At the top of the stairway, the guard released a latch and opened the heavy metal door of a cell that had no furniture other than a narrow bench. Father Giorgio reeled at the stench of mold and stale urine emanating from the room even before he entered the tiny space. Across from him, Fiorello was gazing out through an opening at the Arno River far below. The guard did not enter the cell. He remained rigidly straight, his bulky frame filling the doorway.

The priest turned back to face the guard. "You can go. I will call you when I'm ready to leave."

"Are you sure you want to be alone with him? He's dangerous. He's accused of killing someone."

"I am sure. I'll be fine."

"Rap on the door when you want to leave." The guard pulled the door closed, latched it, and descended the staircase.

Fiorello eyed the monk. "I don't need no priest," he sneered.

In an assertive voice, the priest said, "I was at your trial, and I saw how the magistrates reacted to the testimony of the witnesses. Tomorrow they will render their verdict and I have no doubt, nor should you, that they will find you guilty of murder and sentence you to be executed."

"My lawyer was a fool. He did nothing…"

The priest raised a hand to interrupt Fiorello. "You are the fool if you cling to that false belief. No lawyer could have erased the truth of your guilt."

Fiorello snorted. "Why are you here? Did you come to mock me? If you came to pray, then say your prayer and leave."

"I came to say there may be a way for you to escape the executioner's blade." Fiorello's eyes narrowed in disbelief. He knew the magistrates would decide his fate, not this priest. Father Giorgio continued, "You work for the Bastine family as did the man you killed, and I believe you were ordered to kill him by Rinaldo Bastine." Fiorello's reaction confirmed the priest's assumption. "If you were willing to testify against Rinaldo Bastine, the prosecutor might be willing to prevail on the magistrates to lighten your sentence and keep you from the executioner."

A long moment passed while Fiorello absorbed the import of the priest's statement. "Signor Bastine is respected. The Bastine family is respected. Who would take my word?"

"True, it is unlikely that anyone would believe your word alone, but there are others who could add credibility to your statement."

～

The priest went directly from the Arnolfo Tower to the office of Luca Sasso. The prosecutor registered surprise at having a priest call upon him at his office. He motioned toward a chair. Father Giorgio introduced himself, then said, "I was present during the trial of Bruno Fiorello earlier today."

"Yes, I remember. It is unusual to see a priest in the courtroom. Rarely do they attend trials, even those for the most serious of crimes." Sasso leaned back in his chair. "Your presence there, and now here, tells me that you have a purpose beyond that of saving Signor Fiorello's soul."

"I have information that will be of interest to you. The person Bruno Fiorello killed was the Bastine family carriage driver."

Sasso's brow wrinkled. "How do you know that? The Guardia has not discovered his identity, and no one has come forward to identify the body."

"Bruno Fiorello told me."

"And you believe him?"

"I had already learned that the driver had gone missing. I believe that any of the servants at the Bastine palazzo will be able to confirm Fiorello's claim."

Sasso nodded slowly. It was certainly conceivable, he reasoned, that two men working for the same family could have a disagreement that turned violent. His assumption was dashed by the priest saying, "Fiorello was ordered by Rinaldo Bastine to kill the driver."

Sasso folded his arms across his chest and said skeptically, "I suppose Fiorello told you that as well?"

"He did, but his words only confirmed what I already suspected."

Images flashed into Sasso's mind of the trial two months past when Fiorello had been charged with assault against a competitor of the Bastine iron smelter. At that time, Sasso had believed that Rinaldo Bastine instigated the beating, but he was unable to prove his assumption. He had also received numerous complaints against Rinaldo Bastine by members of the ironworkers' guild, but they too, lacked sufficient evidence to justify any criminal charges. Sasso echoed Fiorello's assertion: "Rinaldo Bastine is respected. No one will take the word of a criminal against his."

"You should speak with the family's servants and members of the Bastine family. You will find some who can corroborate Fiorello's contention."

"If Rinaldo incited the crime, he should be held accountable, but that wouldn't obviate Fiorello's guilt. The magistrates are already considering Fiorello's fate. They'll render their verdict tomorrow."

"I understand that the information I've given you doesn't negate Fiorello's guilt, but might his testimony against Rinaldo Bastine earn him a reduced sentence?"

Sasso rested his chin on his steepled hands and considered his options. "I could request that the magistrates delay Fiorello's sentencing until I, or the Guardia, can investigate the allegations against Rinaldo Bastine."

As the priest rose to leave, Sasso said, "This is the first time anyone has come to me to urge that the punishment of a killer be reduced."

Father Giorgio smiled. "Guidance given in the scriptures often seems inconsistent, but I see the contradictions as virtues. In James it is written, 'Mercy triumphs over judgement,' and in Colossians it is written, 'The wrongdoer will be paid back for the wrong he has done.' I interpret James as speaking to Fiorello and Colossians as applying to Bastine."

22

LIVORNO, SEPTEMBER 11

A kindly driver gave Nico a ride on his wagon to the seaport at Livorno. His was one of many wagons that carried goods produced in Tuscany to ships destined for Sicily and North Africa. Climbing down from the wagon, Nico spotted Vittorio sitting on a bench at the end of the wharf. The investigator held a fishing rod, its line dangling into the inky water. As Nico drew closer, he realized that fishing was a ruse. Vittorio's true purpose was to surveil the ship Nereid. "Caught anything yet, stranger?" Nico joked when he came within earshot.

Vittorio rose from the bench and gathered in the fishing line, which had no hook at its end. He held the rod out for Nico to see. "This gives me an excuse to sit here so I can watch the ship. The two smugglers are onboard. They spend most of their days here doing repairs and making the ship ready to sail. Tomorrow it will leave for Tunisia." The sun had dipped low enough in the sky that its warmth did not overcome the sudden biting breeze coming off the water that made Vittorio shudder. He pointed to the nearby osteria. "I've been sitting here for hours and the cold air has finally penetrated my cloak. I could do with a cup of warm wine."

In the osteria, sheltered from the ocean breeze, Vittorio

wrapped his fingers around the warm cup and listened to Nico recount the meeting he had with the accountant earlier in the day. "Massimo identified him as the same man who led a group of agitators intent on freeing Pisa from Florentine influence. However, he had a plausible explanation to claim that his group didn't abduct the governor. He showed us compelling proof that the governor is an adulterer who is having an affair with a married Florentine aristocrat. He intends to use the evidence to humiliate the governor publicly, and he argued that if the governor were killed, Florentines would view him as a hero who died in the service of the republic. That isn't what he wants. He wants the governor disgraced, not killed."

Nico paused to take a sip of wine. "He suggested that a group of farmers who were displaced from their land by Florentine taxes are angry enough that they are willing to fight for Pisan independence, and he said there are businessmen willing to fund the farmers."

Vittorio shook his head. "Farmers with swords are more likely to injure each other than to be a serious threat to the Florentine army." He turned to face Nico. "However, were they able to secure the leadership of a mercenary captain with proven experience they would at least become an irritant, especially since they would have sympathetic locals giving them places to hide. Was the accountant implying that farmers had abducted the governor?"

Before answering, Nico signaled the server to refill their wine cups. He wasn't familiar with the wines grown locally, but he enjoyed the house wine that the server poured from a ceramic pitcher. It reminded him of the fruity Trebbiano variety produced at his Uncle Nunzio's vineyard.

After taking a sip from his refilled cup, Nico said, "No, the accountant believes a different group... or person... abducted the governor. He mentioned a man called Settimo, but his suggestion was based solely on Settimo having a criminal history. He had no information that would directly connect Settimo to the governor's disappearance, and he doesn't know how to find Settimo." Nico ran a finger casually around the rim of the wine cup, then added, "So, his suggestion isn't very helpful."

"If it's the only clue that you have, don't be too quick to dismiss it. You've made a few acquaintances here in Pisa. You can ask them if they know how to find Settimo. What's the name of that boy who keeps tagging after you? He claims to know everyone," Vittorio laughed.

"Finito," Nico answered. "I hope his knowledge doesn't extend to Pisa's lowlifes, but maybe his uncle, the innkeeper, knows where to find the city's criminals."

Another ship sailing into the harbor drew the men's attention from the Nereid. They watched the ship moor at the far end of the wharf and its crew move hoists into position to raise pallets from the hold. When the first pallet appeared, Nico guessed, "It looks like iron. Perhaps from the mines on Sardinia. Have you ever been to Sardinia?"

"No," Vittorio replied. "Spain is the only place I've been by ship. My father was an official of the armorers' guild. He traveled on behalf of the guild looking for sources of metals and I accompanied him on one of his voyages to Spain. He visited Sardinia many times, but I never went with him."

"I've never traveled by ship. One day I'd like to visit Sicily," Nico mused.

"You want to follow the route of Odysseus?" Vittorio laughed. "I can tell you from my experience, sea travel isn't always a pleasure. Rough seas can make it miserable. And remember all the misfortunes that befell Odysseus at Sicily, sea monsters and the cyclops."

Suddenly, Vittorio stiffened when the two smugglers appeared on the deck of the ship. "Those are the smugglers," he declared, then he and Nico stared silently at the ship, with Vittorio hoping the smugglers would soon lead him to their boss and Nico pondering how to solve the string of crimes that had recently engulfed Pisa.

"They seem to be looking for something," Nico observed.

"Or someone," Vittorio remarked.

With his concentration riveted on the smugglers' movements, Vittorio did not notice the approaching wagon until it stopped alongside the Nereid. Then he recognized the wagon driver and blurted out, "He's the driver who carted away the smuggled silver."

"What's he doing?" Nico muttered, knowing that Vittorio couldn't possibly have an answer to his question.

They watched one of the smugglers jump from the deck of the ship to the wharf and walk toward the wagon, where he exchanged a few brief words with the wagon driver. The driver handed a paper to the smuggler, who unfolded it, read it, nodded, and went back to the ship. The driver turned and climbed aboard the wagon.

Nico leaned forward, his nose nearly pressed against the window. "He's leaving and didn't take anything. All he did was deliver a note."

"We've got to follow him," Vittorio called over his shoulder to Nico as he bolted to the door. Outside, he saw the driver loosen the reins and encourage his horse to move toward the road that would bring him from Livorno to Pisa.

Vittorio pivoted, feverishly looking into each nearby street. Finally, he spotted a wagon parked on one of the side streets and raced toward it. He burst into the nearest shop, where the apron-clad butcher was chatting with another man. "Is that your wagon?" Vittorio barked. "I need a ride to Pisa."

Both men startled and looked at the intruder as though he had lost his senses. Vittorio reached into his coin purse, pulled out a gold florin, and waved it in the air. "I need to go to Pisa now!"

The florin was more than the wagon driver earned in a month. Dashing toward the door, he snatched the coin from Vittorio's outstretched hand. Vittorio followed the driver into the street and to the wagon, where he pulled himself up onto the seat beside the driver. Nico scrambled into the wagon bed. They pulled away from the shop and when they reached the waterfront, Vittorio pointed to the smuggler's wagon, now a distance ahead, and commanded, "Stay behind him."

When the wagons reached Pisa, they did not enter the city.

Instead, they took a track that followed along the outside of the city wall. They bypassed the nearest city gate, and when they passed a second gate, the driver looked quizzically at Vittorio, who declared, "Keep going. Stay with him." The words had barely escaped Vittorio's mouth when the smuggler's wagon left the path and entered a livery.

Nico and Vittorio jumped down from the wagon and walked toward the livery. The driver turned his wagon around and headed into the city. He smiled as he reached into his coin purse and fingered the gold florin.

Vittorio took a position at the side of the livery and waited until his target emerged on foot, heading toward the Porta Nuova gate. When the man came close, Vittorio grabbed his arm and dragged him behind the building. He clamped one hand over the man's mouth so he couldn't shout for help. The dumbfounded man stiffened but did not struggle. Pressing his mouth next to the man's ear, Vittorio growled, "I need information. If you tell me what I want to know, I won't hurt you. Do you understand?" The man grunted and tried unsuccessfully to move his head enough to nod. "When I take my hand away from your mouth, don't shout. Don't utter a sound. Do you understand?" Again, a grunt.

Vittorio slowly eased his hand away from the man's mouth. "What's your name?"

"Gio."

"Three days past you took a crate of smuggled silver from the ship Nereid at Livorno." Gio's eyes went wide. "Where did you deliver it?" Vittorio demanded.

In a barely audible voice, the man said, "Smuggled? I know nothing about smuggling."

"The two crewmen who delivered the crate to you waited until the other sailors and the tax collectors had gone. They wanted to be sure that no one saw what they were doing. Didn't that seem strange to you? Didn't it occur to you that they were smuggling?"

"I got paid to bring a crate from Livorno to Pisa. I didn't think..."

Vittorio interrupted, "Think now, you fool. Bringing silver into the port without paying taxes is smuggling. It's a crime, and you helped them, so you are as guilty as the two sailors."

Gio shuddered. Raspy words came from his dry mouth. "Are you tax collectors?"

Vittorio ignored the question. "Where did you take the silver?"

"I didn't open the crate. I didn't know it held silver."

"Where did you take it?" Vittorio demanded.

The frightened man pointed toward the road. "Not far ahead is the road to San Giuliano. I delivered the crate to another wagon where the two roads meet."

"Who was driving that wagon?" Vittorio asked.

"A big brute. He carried the crate from my wagon to his by himself. I tried to help, but I could barely lift one end of the crate. He lifted it easily. He never spoke, so I don't know his name. The other man is the only one who said anything."

"What other man? Tell me about him. What did he say? What did he look like?"

"He's the one who opened the crate. He was pleased when he saw what it contained. He paid me for delivering it and said they will need me again when the next ship arrives... the Pallas. He was not big like the brute." His eyes swept over Vittorio. "He was about your size, and well dressed. The brute had greasy hands and wore a dirty smock, but this man and his tunic were clean."

"Did he say his name?"

"No."

"Did he say where they were taking the silver?"

"No."

Vittorio turned away and banged his fist against the livery. "Useless," he muttered to himself.

Nico had never seen the normally staid investigator this upset. He stepped in front of Gio and spoke in a calm voice. "You handed a note to one of the sailors on the Nereid. Who gave you the note?"

"The brute gave it to me. I have a job delivering hides to a tannery, so the brute knows where to find me. He comes to the tannery whenever they want me to fetch a crate from one of the ships or deliver a message."

Nico looked at Vittorio, who merely shook his head. "Go," Nico said and stepped away from Gio, who rushed away.

Vittorio bristled. "I wasted three days watching these men and learned nothing useful."

"Don't fault yourself," Nico said. "We know they'll be smuggling more silver, or something else, when the Pallas arrives. We can alert the Guardia and have them arrest the smugglers."

"I want to find out who organized the smuggling operation. This one knows nothing, and it's likely that the sailors don't know the leader either." Again, Vittorio pounded a fist against the side of the livery. "And don't expect much from the Livorno Guardia. From what I've seen, they're incompetent. I wouldn't be surprised to find that some of them are involved with the smugglers."

As they walked toward the Porta Nuova gate, Nico pondered, "I wonder why they hire Gio to fetch cargo and deliver messages to the ship? The people who hire him have a wagon. There must be a reason why they don't go to Livorno themselves."

Vittorio, who was quietly pondering a different question, said suddenly, "There are so many people involved in this smuggling operation. It's much bigger than I expected." Nico stopped walking and faced his companion. Vittorio continued, "They can't be simply dividing the profit amongst themselves. Silver is a valuable commodity, and they're bringing in a crateful every time a ship comes into port. For what purpose?" The question hung in the air; neither man tried to answer it.

23

FLORENCE, SEPTEMBER 11

At Massimo's urging, the three commissioners met for dinner at Pisa's finest and most popular restaurant. Larger than the trattorias they had frequented since arriving in the city, it had more than a dozen tables in the main dining room, plus others in an adjacent alcove. Seating for dinner had barely begun and already half the tables were occupied. An attentive server placed a jug of wine and three glasses on their table even before the three Florentines had seated themselves.

As he lifted the jug to fill their glasses, Massimo said, "After five days of fish, I need a thick cut of something that walked on land and doesn't flake apart when I bite into it."

Nico said, "I heard one of the servers mention that dinner tonight is *cinghiale.*"

"Ah, wild boar, a good sturdy animal. Not as tasty as buffalo, but a welcome change from fish." Massimo hesitated a moment, then added, "I didn't know there are boar in this area."

"Most likely the cinghiale came from the hills near Florence and was brought here on a river barge," Vittorio said. "If there were boar in this area, this wouldn't be the only restaurant in Pisa serving cinghiale."

As more tables filled, conversations grew louder until they merged into a steady background noise. The constant patter made it impossible for anyone to hear the lute player who performed gallantly in a corner of the room, his music heard by none other than himself. A lull in the chatter when the pasta course was served let Nico hear snippets of talk at two nearby tables. At both tables, the discussion centered on the disappearance of the Provincial Governor. Both groups had men who cursed the governor and wished he would never be found. Only a few men expressed hope that he and his wife would not be harmed.

As they sipped wine, waiting for the main course to be served, Massimo said, "I took a walk through the city on my way to the restaurant. There were soldiers everywhere asking about the governor. Along the river they were searching through warehouses and in the business district they were inquiring at every shop."

Vittorio said, "They have to take steps to show the Pisans that abducting a Florentine government official is unacceptable, but such deployments rarely yield results. Success will come either by laboriously sniffing out clues or having an informer come forward."

The three Florentines leaned close to their table and spoke softly to avoid being overheard. Vittorio, still distraught over his failure to uncover the head of the smuggling operation, told Massimo about the encounter with the smuggler's wagon driver. "All I learned is that the silver was delivered to a well-dressed man with clean hands," he said, then pounded his fist on the table, sending his wine glass hopping into the air and attracting curious looks from nearby patrons.

"You're being too critical. It was your keen observation that uncovered the smuggling operation," Nico said, hoping to mollify his colleague. "And if the ship Pallas brings another shipment of contraband, we can track its delivery to the leaders of the operation."

Vittorio raised his wine glass in a gesture of appreciation. "Your optimism is always welcomed."

"We didn't fare any better," Massimo said. "All we learned from the accountant is his belief that a criminal named Settimo might be responsible for abducting the governor. And his belief is nothing more than a guess. Settimo may be a criminal, but that alone is no reason to hold him responsible for the governor's disappearance."

"I agree," Nico said. "From what the accountant told us, Settimo's crimes were committed for his personal gain."

With one large swallow, Massimo emptied his wine glass. He lifted the jug to refill his glass, found it to be empty, and signaled a server to bring another jug. "Smuggling, abductions, and a bank courier killed. All since we arrived here." He looked at Nico. "You are due to send a report of our progress to Chancellor Scala. What are you going to tell him?"

Nico rubbed his hands together while thinking. "We can confirm the hearsay about agitators in Pisa, which is the reason we were sent here. Indeed, we've found that resentment against Florence and especially the Florentine governor is widespread and strongly felt. We've connected with one group of agitators that intends to have the governor removed by humiliating him." Nico looked to Vittorio and added, "And Vittorio has uncovered a smuggling operation."

Their conversation paused and Massimo's eyes brightened when servers set plates of cinghiale and roast vegetables in funghi sauce in front of each of the hungry commissioners. Conversation resumed with Vittorio saying, "Chancellor Scala will want to know how we intend to recover the governor and his wife."

"I've given that some thought." Nico said. "Chancellor Scala said that if we need help, we can call upon Captain Tano Carfi. He's the commander of the Florentine army contingent here in Pisa. Scala said the captain is honorable and trustworthy." Looking at Massimo, Nico asked, "Do you know Captain Carfi?"

"I've never met him, but everything I've heard about him is favorable."

Nico said, "I think it's time for us to meet with the captain. It may be unlikely that Settimo abducted the governor, but even if there's a small chance that Settimo is responsible, we should tell the captain about him. I'm also eager to learn whether any progress has been made in finding out who attacked the bank courier."

"They could also help apprehend the smugglers," Vittorio said. "I've seen no indication that the Guardia is competent to do it."

"And smuggling is a violation of Florentine tax laws, so the crime falls within the army's jurisdiction," Nico added.

Eventually, the restaurant quieted as some diners began leaving while others, too satiated to engage in vigorous conversation, lingered over glasses of digestivo. Nico sipped a glass of grappa and said, "I was in the piazza on the day when the bank courier was killed. I spoke with a farmacista who was maligning Florence. He told me that someone who is actively working to 'free Pisa from Florentine oppression' will be coming to his shop on Friday. I intend to go to the farmacia to meet that person."

Massimo and Vittorio exchanged glances, then Vittorio said, "Going by yourself is not a good idea. Meeting one of the agitators could be dangerous."

Massimo leaned forward and looked directly at Nico. "Vittorio is correct. You could be putting yourself in danger. If this contact is one of the agitators and he discovers that you are a Florentine, you could meet the same fate as the bank courier."

Nico bit his lip as he absorbed the implication of Massimo's warning. "This could be a crucial contact. I can't dismiss it."

"But you can't go alone. I'll go with you. While you are inside the farmacia, I'll be outside in the piazza, close enough to hear if there is a problem." Massimo grinned and rested a hand on Nico's shoulder. "Your sister made me promise that I'd protect you. She'd never forgive me if anything happened to you."

Nico nodded his approval of Massimo's plan while thinking, *there's little chance of my being in danger in a shop in the central business district.*

24

PISA, SEPTEMBER 12

The three commissioners met at a pasticceria, intending to have breakfast, but each man, in turn, dismissed the idea as soon as he arrived. "Last evening's dinner might carry me for a week," Vittorio declared.

Massimo said, "You've come upon one of our differences, Vittorio. I'm prepared to return for another delicious meal tonight. Perhaps today the menu will feature buffalo." Despite his bravado, even Massimo bypassed the pasticceria's tasty offerings and settled for a mug of ale.

They crossed the river on the Della Fortezza bridge and headed for the structure that housed the Florentine military garrison. Several detachments of soldiers hurried past them, heading toward the center of the city. When they neared the fortress, Nico turned to Massimo and said, "It's an impressive building. I noticed it when I first arrived in Pisa. Have you ever been assigned here?"

"No, I haven't, but I've met other soldiers who spent time here. The fortress is called Cittadella Nuova. It was built about two decades past, so the Florentine army could keep watch over the Pisans. That was another time of unrest in the city. Notice the battlements face toward the city. They aren't positioned to repel attacks from outside the city."

"It must have been an irritant to the Pisans."

"From what I've been told, it was hated then, and it still is."

Nico said, "The Florentine Signoria could have been justified in fearing an uprising, but constructing this massive fortress might not have been the best way to make Pisans feel like welcome citizens of the Florentine Republic."

Two weighty doors at the main entrance stood open to create the impression that visitors were welcome to enter, but soldiers stationed in a guard house alongside the opening intercepted everyone, including the three commissioners, when they reached the building. Nico handed his letter of introduction to a lanky young soldier who read the letter and passed it to his colleague. After the two soldiers conferred briefly, one said, "Wait here," and scurried into the fortress.

Minutes later, he returned with a sergeant who read the letter, inspected the three visitors, and asked, "Are you all members of the Florentine Security Commission?"

"We are," Nico replied. "We would like to meet with Captain Tano Carfi."

"Captain Carfi is very busy," the sergeant replied.

"I'm certain he will want to see us," Nico said resolutely.

The sergeant hesitated only a moment before saying, "Come with me," and leading them into the building and up a flight of stone steps to an office on the second level.

In the office, the captain stood behind his desk, dictating orders to two other officers. The sergeant remained at the doorway until the captain finished the instructions and dismissed the officers. After they left the room, the sergeant announced, "Captain, these men would like to speak with you."

Carfi looked up from the document he was holding and motioned for the visitors to enter. Nico held out the introduction letter and as the captain took it, he said, "I am Nico Argenti," then pointing to Massimo he continued, "and this is..."

Captain Carfi interrupted Nico by raising a hand. Facing Massimo, he announced, "You are Sergeant Massimo Leoni, on temporary assignment with the Florentine Security Commission." Turning his gaze to Vittorio, he continued, "and you, Guardia investigator Vittorio Colombo, also on assignment with the Security Commission. You three men have been roving around Pisa for a week and did not think it fitting to inform me of your presence?"

Nico drew in a long, slow breath. "Captain, we meant no disrespect. Much of our time has been spent becoming acquainted with the city." He explained their mission in Pisa and said, "We didn't reveal our presence for fear that Pisans working here and at the governor's office might have connections to the agitators."

Carfi said, "We do have Pisans working here at the garrison, but we are careful to avoid disclosing information to them. However, I can't say the same for the governor's staff, so I understand your reluctance to have your mission known. What brings you here now?"

"Recently we've become aware of information that might be useful to you," Nico replied.

Carfi motioned his visitors to the conference table. "As you're aware, the governor's disappearance has created a tense situation."

Fixing on the captain's earlier comment, Vittorio asked, "How did you know we've been in Pisa for a week?"

"Not all the men under my command wear uniforms. Some wear peasant clothes, so they can blend in at places frequented by undesirables. Word travels quickly among the rabble when Florentine strangers suddenly appear in the city and begin asking questions." Adding, with a sly smile, "My men became aware of your presence shortly after you arrived in Pisa." He turned his attention to Nico. "You said that you have information that might be useful."

"We met with an accountant who heads a group dedicated to having the governor removed. Massimo was invited to participate at one of the group's meetings."

The captain looked to Massimo, who began by describing his meeting with the man known as Fornitore at an inn near the town of

Cascina. "His words showed him to be well educated. He was well-groomed and wore a stylish tunic with pearl buttons. He arranged for an excellent dinner and the staff at the inn were attentive to his every need."

"He calls himself the supplier. What does he supply?" Carfi asked.

"I don't know, but when I mentioned that rebels need weapons, he dismissed the concern. He said that arms are available from many sources, so perhaps he's an armorer or an arms merchant. He arranged for me to meet with a group of the agitators the next day. When the workday ended, I was escorted from the warehouse to a gathering of angry men at a farmhouse outside the city where their leader, whom we now know as the accountant, said they would be targeting the governor. There were at least thirty men at that gathering."

Carfi tapped a finger on the table. "We've known about the accountant, but we didn't know his group was that large. Thirty men," he repeated and paused a moment while he considered the implications of a group that large before adding, "My men questioned the accountant. He definitely wants the governor removed, but we concluded that his group is not responsible for the abduction."

Nico said, "He showed us evidence that the governor has been having an illicit relationship with a married Florentine aristocrat. He plans to use that knowledge to force the Signoria to recall the governor."

The captain sat up straight, his eyes widened, and he said slowly, emphasizing each word, "That is interesting." He thought about asking the woman's name but instead he asked, "He showed you evidence... solid evidence?"

"A letter from the woman's sister," Nico replied. "He also claims that an aide to the governor is willing to testify about the affair."

Carfi said, "That certainly confirms our belief that his followers had no need to abduct the governor."

Massimo said, "He suggested that a man called Settimo might be the abductor. But that was just supposition. He admits that he has no proof to support his contention."

Carfi said, "Settimo is an insect who dwells with the scum. He's caused trouble before, many times, and that made him one of our first suspects, but my men have confirmed that Settimo hasn't been in Pisa for several days. Last week, he boarded a ship headed for Genoa. He's now a pest gnawing at the Genovese."

"The attack on the Medici bank courier was also a strike against Florentine presence. Is there reason to believe that it and the governor's abduction are related?" Nico asked.

"Possibly. The courier wasn't carrying anything of value and there have not been any robberies reported in that area. So, as you said, the attack appears to have been meant as a slap against a Florentine institution rather than a robbery. The lost documents are merely an inconvenience, an irritant to the bank."

"It was more than that to the dead courier," Massimo said.

"Yes, you are correct. I didn't mean to make light of the killing. Indeed, it is the killing that worries me. If the governor was taken by the same men who killed the courier, then the governor's life is at risk."

"And his wife's," Massimo said.

"Yes, and his wife's," Carfi repeated.

Nico said, "You intimated that the courier was attacked by more than one person."

"We found three sets of hoof prints at the site where the courier was attacked. The cook at the governor's residence said she was locked in the kitchen by one man while others were taking the governor and his wife, so there were at least three men involved in the abduction. Although we have no way of knowing whether the same men committed both crimes."

After a brief silence, Vittorio said, "We have one more piece of information to share, another crime that needs your attention."

The captain leaned forward and looked directly at Vittorio, who continued. "We found that silver is being smuggled into the port of

Livorno. I saw the smugglers unload a crate from the ship Nereid. They waited until the tax collectors had departed and the port became quiet before unloading the cargo. Nico and I interrogated the wagon driver, who received the silver, but the driver could only tell us that he had transferred the crate to another wagon. From his description, it's possible that one of the men on the other wagon is the head of the operation, but the driver didn't know that man's name."

"Damn," Carfi said, and thumped a fist on the conference table. "I've had men posted throughout Pisa, but we've had no indication that there were problems in Livorno, so I hadn't deployed anyone there."

Vittorio said, "We will have an opportunity to apprehend the smugglers tomorrow. I expect the next shipment of contraband to arrive tomorrow on the ship Pallas."

"Sergeant!" Carfi shouted. In an instant, the captain's aide swept into the room. Addressing the sergeant, Carfi said, "These men have discovered a smuggling operation in Livorno. The next shipment of contraband is expected tomorrow." He pointed to Vittorio. "He can give you the details. Work with him to create a plan to stop the smuggling and make it a priority to get the person heading the operation." Vittorio rose and left the room with the sergeant.

"You three have been busy," Carfi said. He looked from Nico to Massimo and asked, "Do you have any other suspicions?"

Nico said that he intended to visit the farmacista who claimed he could introduce Nico to an agitator, and Massimo said he would try to locate the person called Fornitore. "It's possible he might have an insight into who abducted the governor."

The meeting, which began as a testy encounter, ended with the captain and the commissioners agreeing to cooperate and share information.

25

LIVORNO, SEPTEMBER 13

Shortly after midnight, near the Cittadella Nuova fortress, four soldiers cast off on a canal boat. Three men sat in the boat while the fourth man stood, pressing one end of a long wooden pole into the muddy river bottom to propel the boat toward the canal that would take them from Pisa to Livorno. All four men were wrapped in cloaks to shelter them from the cold night air and to hide their uniforms.

Two other soldiers traveled from Pisa to Livorno by wagon in the dim moonlight. The groups rendezvoused at an inn where Vittorio had arranged a room for them. At dawn, Vittorio rapped on their door. One of the soldiers pulled the door open, and Vittorio said, "The Pallas is expected to arrive on the rising tide in about two hours. At the waterfront, not far from the wharf, is a large pile of stones that will be used to extend the wall around the city. The pile is large enough to give you cover. You can take a position behind the stone pile, and from there you'll be able to observe the ship without being seen."

The sergeant who had opened the door asked, "Will you be there with us?"

"I'll be posing as a fisherman at the other end of the wharf. I'll signal you when the smugglers begin unloading the contraband."

An hour later, Vittorio walked to the waterfront, sat at the end of the wharf, leaned back against a post, and dropped his hookless fishing line into the water. The rising sun, still low against his back, cast a long shadow onto the choppy water. He first saw Pallas under full sail near the horizon and watched it as it came near. When it approached the port, crewmen lowered the sails and readied lines to tie the ship to the dock.

On land, wagons from Pisa queued along the waterfront, ready to accept cargo, and tax collectors moved into position to assess fees. The unloading proceeded as Vittorio had expected, the same as when the Nereid had discharged its cargo days earlier. And as before, when the last wagon had been filled and set off on the road toward Pisa, the tax collectors departed, and the waterfront became quiet.

Vittorio let his gaze follow the column of wagons moving away. In the distance, he saw a lone wagon moving in the opposite direction, coming toward Livorno. He watched the wagon until it drew near enough that he could recognize the driver, the same man who had received the crate of silver from the Nereid.

Two crewmen on the ship were busily raising a crate from the ship's hold when the wagon pulled alongside. They hoisted the crate onto their shoulders and carried it from the ship to the waiting wagon. They walked slowly, struggling to keep from dropping their heavy burden. Vittorio waved a hand above his head to signal the soldiers, who jumped out from their hiding place and raced to surround the wagon. With swords drawn and no longer wearing cloaks to disguise their uniforms, the soldiers encircled the crewmen just as they dropped the crate into the wagon bed.

The wagon with the two remaining soldiers rolled out of its concealment in a side street and stopped alongside the smuggler's wagon. The sergeant climbed down from his wagon and eyed the sailors briefly as he moved to the crate. He untied the rope securing the box and lifted the lid to reveal stacks of silver bars. He looked at Vittorio and acknowledged, "As you suspected."

"We didn't know what was in the crate," one of the sailors protested. "We were just unloading cargo."

The sergeant didn't waste time challenging their false claim. He ordered three of his men to take the sailors into custody, then he turned to the driver of the wagon that now held the crate. "Where are you to take this?"

The driver gestured toward Vittorio, who was standing next to the sergeant, and said, "He knows."

The sergeant grabbed the driver's collar and demanded, "Tell me!".

In a quavering voice, the driver responded, "My instructions are to deliver the crate to another wagon. It will be on the road that goes to San Giuliano."

Vittorio confirmed that as the same information the driver had given him previously.

The sergeant instructed three of his men, "Take these smugglers to the fortress and lock them in a cell." To his other men, he said, "Put on your cloaks. We'll ride ahead and find a place to hide near the road junction."

Vittorio waited until the soldiers had departed, then he climbed into the bed of the smuggler's wagon and nestled himself down beside the crate so he could not be seen. When the soldiers' wagon was a distance ahead, he told the driver to proceed.

As before, when they reached Pisa, the driver took the road along the outside of the city wall. They passed two city gates, and as they approached the road to San Giuliano, Vittorio saw another wagon parked beside the road. He surveyed the road ahead looking for the soldiers, but on both sides of the road he saw only marsh with no hiding places.

The driver stopped his wagon behind the other. The man in the waiting wagon climbed down and walked toward Vittorio's wagon. He was big. The term brute that the driver had used fit the man well.

When he reached the rear of the wagon, he noticed Vittorio and snarled, "Huh?"

Vittorio stood, fearful that he would have to face the big man alone. He stepped forward and from the corner of his eye spotted the soldiers' wagon approaching rapidly. They must not have found any hiding places outside the city and had concealed themselves inside one of the city gates.

The soldiers threw off their cloaks, drew their weapons, and jumped from their wagon. The sergeant held his blade against the brute's chest while his men bound his hands and dropped a slip-collar around his neck. The man stood stiffly, but he did not protest.

Vittorio grabbed the sleeve of the driver, who was still sitting on the wagon seat. He pulled the driver toward him until they were face to face. "You said the silver was taken by two men."

"It was. Always before there were two men." The driver pointed. "That one and another one."

Vittorio turned and called to the big man. "Where is your partner?" He received no response.

The sergeant raised his sword tip to the brute's chin so his captive could see the sun glinting from the sharp steel blade. "Where do you take the silver?" Vittorio demanded. Again, the man remained silent.

Vittorio tried again, saying, "Smuggling is a serious crime. Do you want to suffer alone and let your master go free?"

When that query failed to elicit a reply, Vittorio moved forward, but the sergeant raised his hand and said, "A few days in a dark cell with only garbage to eat will loosen his tongue." The brute answered the sergeant's threat by spitting in his direction, which the sergeant avoided by stepping aside deftly.

To his men, the sergeant ordered, "Take him."

Gesturing to the wagon driver, one of the soldiers asked, "What about this one?"

On the driver's behalf, Vittorio said, "He's just a hired wagon driver."

"Let him go," the sergeant declared.

Vittorio sat on the wagon seat beside the sergeant. The soldiers sat in the wagon bed atop the crate of silver, while the collared man walked behind, tethered to the wagon by a rope attached to his slip collar. They took the long road that followed the wall around the entire city until they reached the gate nearest the Cittadella Nuova fortress.

As the soldiers led their captive into the fortress, Vittorio lamented, "Once again, we gathered only an underling. The leader is still out there."

"But this one knows the leader," the sergeant said. "I promise you, in a few days, he will give us a name."

26

PISA, SEPTEMBER 13

Massimo arrived early, as was his custom. He ducked into a shadowed alley to wait for Nico. From his hiding place, he watched Pisans traversing the piazza: men headed to business, women going to market, and children on their way to school. The happy people were unaware that their some neighbors were plotting an insurrection. When he spotted Nico crossing the piazza, Massimo stepped in the sunlight long enough for Nico to see him. Nico raised a single finger in response and continued toward the farmacia, with Massimo a measured distance behind.

The farmacista and another man were conversing quietly when Nico entered the shop. He stopped inside the doorway, but when the shopkeeper saw Nico, he called, "Come. Come here."

Nico moved toward the counter. To his companion, the farmacista said, "This is the one who wants to meet you."

The other man turned around and his eyes swept Nico from head to foot. "Let's go to a place where we can talk. There are others you should meet." Without waiting for Nico to respond, he walked out of the farmacia with Nico trailing behind.

They left the piazza, heading away from the river. They walked for one block, then the man turned into a narrow passage beside a tavern. It took a while for Nico's eyes to adjust to the dim light and when they did, he saw two men ahead, leaning against one of the buildings. In a flat voice, his escort said, "They're expecting us."

As soon as Nico came within an arm's length, the men reached out, grabbed him by the arms, and slammed him against a wall. "What…" he yelped and struggled to free himself, but the two men held him fast.

The leader donned a heavy leather glove. Before saying another word, he struck Nico's face repeatedly, left, then right, again and again, until Nico's vision blurred. The glove lacing tore gashes in Nico's cheeks. Blood dripped from the wounds. "Stupid fool," the leader barked. "You thought you could pass yourself off as a Pisan. Did you think we couldn't tell that you're a Florentine?" He yanked Nico's hair, pulling his head up. "You're too scrawny to be a soldier. Who are you and why are you asking about agitators? Who sent you?"

"No one," Nico replied feebly.

"Liar!" The leader raised his hand to strike again, but his move was ended by Massimo charging into the alley, diving through the air, and driving his shoulder into the leader's ribs. Both men tumbled to the ground with Massimo atop the leader, whose head slammed against the unforgiving ground. Massimo wrested a knife from the leader's belt and pressed the point against the man's throat, only to realize that the fall had rendered the man immobile.

Massimo's sudden attack startled the two men who were holding Nico. One man loosened his grip enough for Nico to pull one arm free. He swung his free arm and hammered his knuckles against the other man's nose. That one screamed in pain as blood sprayed from his nose. He pushed Nico away. Nico tried to strike the other assailant, but after only a few steps, he staggered, his breathing ragged. He leaned against the building for support.

Massimo pushed himself up. Waving the knife in front of him, he advanced toward the two men. They looked at Massimo for only an instant before one turned and ran with the other at his heels.

Massimo rested a steadying hand on Nico's shoulder. "Can you stand?"

"I think so," Nico said weekly.

Massimo made a quick assessment of Nico's wounds. He could do nothing for Nico's eye, already swollen shut, but he could stem the flow of blood from the slashes on Nico's face. He tore his handkerchief in two and pressed the halves against Nico's cheeks. "The cuts aren't deep. Hold these in place until the bleeding stops."

The leader's moan drew Massimo's attention. Using the knife, he cut a cloth strip from the man's tunic and used it to bind his hands. He pulled the dazed man to standing, then pushed him toward the road. "Where are you taking him?" Nico asked.

"To the bank. It's not far and the manager is a Florentine. He can send his assistant to the army garrison. Wait here. I'll come back for you."

"No. I can walk," Nico said as he trudged behind Massimo.

Everyone in the piazza moved aside upon seeing a captive, his hands tied behind his back, being prodded by a knife-wielding man. Massimo's other hand steadied Nico, who staggered along behind his assailant. The clerk and manager stood open-mouthed when Massimo shoved the leader through the doorway into the bank. Massimo pushed his charge into a chair and wagged the knife in front of the man's face. "Stay there. Don't move," he growled.

"Are you going to question him?" Nico asked.

Massimo shook his head. "Questioning him now would be a wasted effort. He won't say anything if he believes that he's not going to be charged. And from what we know of the Guardia, they'd probably just let him go. They'd consider him as one of their own, a Pisan, who got into a brawl with a Florentine. We'd be fortunate if they didn't try to charge you with assaulting him. Our first order is to tend to your injuries."

"Except for these cuts, I'm not hurt," Nico said.

"You're in no condition to make that decision. You were barely able to walk from the alley to the bank."

Nico accepted Massimo's judgement. He lowered himself into a chair and looked up at Massimo. "Captain Carfi can send men to collect this thug." He winced as he turned to face the bank clerk. "Bring me paper and a pen." The clerk stared at Nico but did not move.

"Now!" Massimo commanded. The clerk grabbed a pen from his desk and snatched a sheet of paper from a shelf behind him. He jumped up and handed the items to Nico.

Nico penned a note, folded it, and wrote the captain's name on the outside. He handed the note to the clerk. "Have someone deliver this to Captain Tano Carfi at the Florentine army garrison. It must be given to Captain Carfi directly, no one else."

The bank had no messengers, so if the note were to be delivered, the clerk would have to do it himself. He looked to the manager for approval. The manager waved a hand and mouthed the word go.

Nico watched the clerk depart; then he turned toward the thug seated near him. "My colleague is right. We can't rely on the Guardia to administer justice, but there is another option. You assaulted a government official... me. That's a serious offense, too serious for the local Guardia. Assaulting an official is a crime against the republic, so you can be taken to Florence for trial."

The captive bawled, "You can't do that!"

"Quiet!" Massimo shouted and waved the knife at the man's face.

Nico cringed as he tried to smile and said, "We certainly can do that. It is customary for crimes against the republic to be prosecuted in Florence."

Less than a quarter hour later, four soldiers accompanied Captain Carfi into the bank. His sharp uniform and swagger conveyed his authoritative presence. He glanced at the manager. "I didn't think I'd be returning here so soon." The manager stood open-mouthed but said nothing. Carfi gave a nod of recognition to Massimo before addressing Nico. "Messer Argenti, it has been only a few short hours since I saw you last; yet now you look decidedly worse than you did then."

Nico pointed at the thug. "This one is to blame for my diminished capacity."

The captain shifted his gaze to the captive. "And who is this?"

Nico replied, "He hasn't given us his name, but for now he can be detained on charges of assaulting a member of the Security Commission. When we question him, we will probably find him to be guilty of other crimes as well."

Carfi motioned to one of his men, "Take this scum away." Then to Nico, he said, "We can talk in my office after my medical officer treats your wounds. Are you able to walk? If not, I can send for a carriage."

"I can walk." Nico replied. He and Massimo accompanied the military contingent as it hustled the prisoner across the city. As they walked to the fortress, Nico told the captain about his encounter with the thug. Curious onlookers chatted with those nearby, speculating about what had happened. Some peered at the prisoner to see if they might recognize him. Others focused on the injured man being helped along by his colleague.

They entered the fortress led by one of the soldiers through a tunnel in the underground level to the quarters of the medical officer, a man not much older than Nico. After the medico introduced himself, Nico said, "I recognize that name. Does your father own the bakery in the San Marco district?"

"Yes, he does."

"My sister claims that your father makes the finest sweet rolls in Florence… and I agree with her."

The man beamed with pride. "My colleagues here feel the same. Every time I return from Florence, I bring a sack of father's sweet rolls."

The medico applied a salve to the cuts on Nico's face. "Your injuries are not serious. The bruises on your face are the worst. They look bad now, but they will heal and probably not leave a scar," he said hopefully. "Keep your eye covered until the swelling fades."

Massimo said, "They'd better heal by the time he returns to Florence, or his sister will have me suffering alongside him." The medico eyed Nico, unsure of what to make of Massimo's statement. Nico, looking sheepish, gave a dismissive wave.

After the medico finished treating Nico, a soldier led him and Massimo to Captain Carfi's modest office on the second level. Massimo steadied Nico to help him climb the rough stone steps. Captain Carfi offered his visitors a drink made from apples and sat with them at his conference table.

"What would you like me to do with the prisoner?" Carfi asked.

Massimo replied, "Can you keep him locked up for a day or two? When he realizes that he's not going to be set free, he'll be more willing to talk."

"We can keep him as long as you want."

Nico's brow furrowed as he questioned the legality of detaining the man for an extended period without filing charges. If he were in Florence, he could consult precedents at the law library, but for now, he would accept this as an unusual situation.

Carfi rose from the table, went to a cabinet behind his desk, withdrew a sword, and placed it on the table. "This sword is from a raid conducted by my men six days past. We seized this and eight others like it." He slid the blade across the table toward Nico and Vittorio. "My men don't spend all their time in this fortress. My small team that dresses in workmen's clothes to pass as itinerant laborers has been able to gain the confidence of locals who now speak freely to them. One of my men learned of plans being made for a protest and the location where weapons were being held."

Nico said, "The raid wasn't mentioned in any of the reports sent to the Chancery."

Carfi avoided looking directly at Nico and did not respond to his comment. He said, "We don't want the protestors to know they're being tracked by the military, so we dressed as rogue bandits when we raided the weapons cache at an abandoned farmhouse." With a smirk, he added, "The protestors think their weapons were stolen by a rival band of outlaws or mercenaries."

"There must have been men guarding the weapons," Massimo stated.

"Only two, and they fled when they saw a group of armed men approaching on horseback."

Nico picked up the sword, examined it, and said, "I don't recognize this marking."

"It's a stylized letter N, the mark of the Negroli armory in Milan. A few of the swords had the same mark, others had no markings at all."

After Carfi returned the sword to the cabinet, he said, "The protesters we have been tracking could be the same ones you were sent here to investigate; that's why we should have been informed of your mission from the outset." Nico did not refute the captain's position.

Sounds reverberated constantly through the stone passageways as soldiers moved throughout the fortress. It wasn't until Nico stepped outside and walked along the quiet riverfront after the session with the captain that he observed, "The ringing in my ears has stopped."

Massimo said, "You should rest. I'll leave a note for Vittorio, asking him to meet with us later."

27

PISA, SEPTEMBER 14

Massimo knocked on Nico's door. He heard Nico release the latch, pushed the door open, and ushered Nico to the window. "Come here in the light so I can see how you look. Were you able to sleep, or did the pain keep you awake?"

"I don't know what was in that powder concocted by the medico, but it sent me sleeping in another world. I kept dreaming of giant flying creatures."

At the window, Massimo said, "Turn this way." He moved close to examine Nico's wounds. "Hmmm. The medico's salve closed the cuts, but your cheeks have large purple bruises and there's another one on your neck." He turned Nico to let the morning light illuminate both cheeks and quipped, "With a bit of paint on your forehead, you could march in the *carnevale* parade without need of a mask." In a serious tone, he said, "Your eye still looks bad," and asked, "Are you certain that we should leave for Florence today or would you rather rest for another day?"

Nico stepped away from the window to avoid further examination. "My eye isn't fully open, but I can see with it, and boredom has become more painful than the bruises. I couldn't tolerate another day in this room, and I'm eager to see if our captive will become talkative when he faces the reality of prison in Florence."

Walking from the inn to the Cittadella Nuova army garrison, Massimo remarked, "You are steadier on your feet than you were yesterday. Maybe you're tougher than you look, my friend." Nico ignored his companion's jibe and told the soldier at the gate of their intention to speak with one of the prisoners. The soldier escorted Nico and Massimo to the guard station of the fortress's lower level, where prisoners were confined. "We have three guests today." The guard chuckled as he said, "One speaks no Italian, one is normal size, and one is a giant. Which one are you here for?"

Massimo and Nico exchanged glances, then Massimo replied, "The normal one."

From the guard station, they descended a ramp to an underground level. Openings at ceiling height let air and light into the narrow passageway. Solid earth formed one wall, while the opposite wall consisted of a row of cave-like cells. Nico, who had braced himself for the offensive odor he'd encountered when visiting inmates in other prisons, remarked, "This is the only prison I've visited that doesn't have a sour smell."

The guard responded, "The earthen wall absorbs most odors, but there is the smell of mold when it rains."

"Has the prisoner said anything yet? Has he said his name?" Nico asked.

"None of them have said anything intelligible. The big one just grunts and the normal one just stares at the wall."

The guard had barely finished speaking when a loud wailing came from a cell at the far end of the underground passage. After the lengthy chanting ended, the guard said, "That's the third inmate, the one who doesn't speak Italian. He's quiet most of the time, then suddenly he cries out like that in a foreign language."

"It isn't a foreign language," Nico corrected. "It's a dialect spoken on Sardinia. I didn't understand most of the words, but I did recognize enough of them to know he's begging God to forgive his sin."

Massimo turned to the guard. "What's his offense?"

"He's a stowaway. They found him on a ship that had arrived in Livorno three days past. He jumped from the ship and tried to run away into the town, but two sailors chased after him and when they caught him, they brought him here."

"What will happen to him?" Massimo asked.

"Hiding on a ship to avoid paying for passage is a violation of maritime agreements," Nico explained. "He'll be taken back to the place where he boarded the ship and turned over to the authorities. They'll determine his punishment."

When they reached the cell of the thug who had assaulted Nico, he was sitting on a stone bench, staring at the ceiling. "I was told that someone would be taking him to Florence," the guard said as he unlocked the cell door.

"Yes. He assaulted a government official. That's a crime against the republic, so he'll be taken to Florence to stand trial," Nico responded.

Massimo entered the cell and pulled the thug up from the stone bench. Using a leather strap, Massimo tied the man's hands behind his back and pushed him out of the cell. "It's time for you to go from this prison to another one."

The guard asked, "Would you like another strap so you can bind his feet, or a slip collar with a tether, so he won't try to run away?"

"The restraint on his hands will be sufficient. It would please me if he tried to escape. Then I'd have a reason to pay him back for attacking my friend," Massimo said menacingly.

Two soldiers accompanied Nico and Massimo to a nearby dock where a barge was being loaded with produce destined for Florence. Nico arranged with the barge captain for passage. Massimo sat the prisoner on a crate at the front of the craft while he and Nico found positions at the rear. They watched as lines from the barge were fastened to the harness of the oxen team that would pull the craft upriver. Their prisoner simply stared straight ahead and remained silent.

At the town of Empoli, the barge stopped to unload cargo. The barge crew used the break to take lunch at the inn atop a nearby hill. Local laborers had the tasks of unloading crates and watering the oxen. The busy inn was popular with religious pilgrims from the north en route to the shrine of Saint Francis at Assisi and Saint Peter's Basilica in Rome.

The prisoner stood and gazed up at the inn. He sensed Massimo close behind him and, without turning, spoke his first words, "I haven't eaten at all today."

Massimo had eaten breakfast, but his days in the army had taught him never to pass the chance for a meal. He called to Nico, "It wouldn't be a good idea for us to bring this one to the inn, but they must have some food we can eat here."

Nico said, "I'll go," and climbed the path to the inn in search of food. Massimo addressed his captive. "So, you've shown me that you do know how to speak. What's your name?"

The man turned just enough to glimpse Massimo from the corner of his eye and said, "Nello."

Massimo rubbed his chin. "That wasn't so difficult, was it, Nello? Now, can you tell me who ordered you to assault my friend?"

"For what purpose? Whether I tell you or not, you'll take me to prison."

"Magistrates often look kindly on those who cooperate with investigations."

Nello turned further to glower directly at Massimo, but said nothing before turning away and sitting down on the crate. "Think about it," Massimo counseled.

The seven crates destined for Empoli had already been unloaded when Nico descended the hill from the inn, carrying a jug of wine. Trailing him, a serving girl bore a tray laden with various food items, enough to provide an ample lunch for three men. When Massimo saw them coming, he removed the leather strap from Nello's hands so the man could feed himself. Massimo pressed the strap against the man's throat, and warned, "If you try to run, you'll need more than a medico when you get to Florence."

Hours later, the barge arrived in Florence. Nico summoned two nearby members of the Guardia and instructed them to bring Nello to the Stinche prison. Nico didn't need to show the letter stipulating his authority as a member of the Security Commission because one of the Guardia officers recognized him and greeted him warmly. The two men had known each other since their days as young boys, when both had tried to win the affection of the same neighborhood girl.

Before the officers took Nello away, Massimo grabbed the captive by his collar, pulled him close, and reiterated his earlier advice. "Remember this: magistrates look favorably on offenders who are forthcoming. You do yourself no favor by remaining silent."

~

The Eight of Public Safety consisted of eight administrators who were appointed by the Signoria and given jurisdiction over crimes that affected the overall fabric of Florentine society. Their charter was intentionally ill-defined, thereby giving them the authority to determine which matters fell within their purview. The Eight discharged their responsibilities through a select group of magistrates, notaries, and clerks.

Many years past, the Eight had decided that assaulting a public official was a crime against public safety. Nico went to The Eight's office in the Palazzo della Signoria to file charges against Nello and to schedule his trial. To avoid having to explain his bruises to the men he knew who worked in the palazzo, Nico bypassed the main entrance and entered the building through a little-used rear door.

The veteran clerk in the Eight's office recognized Nico as a member of the Security Commission. He saw Nico's bruises and puffy eye, but he made no comment about the injuries. He merely asked the name of Nico's assailant.

"He would only give his name as Nello. He didn't give his surname."

"That's not unusual. Many miscreants refuse to give any name at all. When that happens, I get to pick names for them." Cackling, he added, "I registered the last uncooperative thug as *bambino Maria*, baby Marie." This time, the clerk wrote "Nello surname unknown," in his register. "Where is he now?"

"Guardia officers are taking him to the Stinche," Nico replied.

The clerk added that information to the register. Then he referred to another document and said, "I can schedule the trial to be held in three days. Is that acceptable?"

Nico agreed to the date, and as he turned to leave, the clerk commented, "I hope Nello suffered worse than you."

Nico turned back and said, "No. I'm sorry to say he didn't. He had the help of two other thugs, so there was little I could do until someone came to my aid. At the first sign of resistance, his associates fled, leaving Nello to face the aftermath of their failure alone."

"Ah, another trait of these petty criminals," the clerk said. "They lack loyalty."

From the office of the Eight, Nico climbed the stone steps leading to the palazzo's top level and the small office allocated to the Security Commission. He had told himself that he should be preparing for Nello's trial, but he knew he was acting out of self-deception to keep his family, especially his sister Alessa, from chastising him for getting wounded. After reconsideration, he admitted to himself that time spent in the office would only delay his reprimand, so halfway up the stairs, he stopped and reversed direction.

When he exited the building through the rear door onto Via del Leoni, Nico was lashed by a strong cold wind funneling through the narrow street. Above, thick clouds had turned the sky cement gray. September weather was unpredictable. One day might recall summer while the next might foretell winter. Fortunately, it was only a short walk to Casa Argenti, the family home where he lived with his sister Alessa and his cousin Donato's family. The house servant welcomed

Nico warmly. Social decorum prevented him from commenting on Nico's physical appearance.

Nico knew that Donato and his wife Joanna would be at the Uccello, prepping the restaurant staff for their dinner duties. "Is Alessa home?" he asked.

"She's in the *studiolo* repairing a quilt," the servant replied.

Rather than delay the inevitable, Nico climbed to the second level and paused outside the study, listening to Alessa singing as she mended the seam of a bed quilt. The studiolo was a small room with bookshelves along two walls, a worktable in the center where Donato attended to the Uccello's business records, and in one corner a comfortably padded chair. Alessa liked the room's cozy, intimate feeling.

When the tune ended, Nico entered and said, "I don't know that song."

Alessa dismissed Nico's comment and, with her back toward him, asked, "Will I be horrified when I look at you? In my dream, your eyes were sealed shut. Someone came to help you, but he was too late." Alessa had a mystical ability to sense when Nico suffered injuries.

Nico leaned down and kissed her lightly on the forehead. "The someone in your dream was Massimo, and he was not too late. He drove away two attackers and captured another."

Alessa set the quilt aside, rose, and turned to face her brother. Before saying a word, she reached out and ran a finger along his cheek, under his injured eye, now encircled by a yellow-green ring. "In my dream, this eye was shut tight... both of them."

Nico elected not to mention the swelling or his temporary vision loss. Instead, he said, "In a few days, the color will be gone."

She managed a weak smile and embraced him. "It is good that you are back home. Is your work in Pisa finished?"

"No. We were sent there to find rebels who are planning an insurrection. Since we arrived, Vittorio uncovered a smuggling operation, the provincial governor was abducted, and we still haven't found the rebel leader. I need to prosecute the man who attacked me, but it's a distraction. His trial will be in three days. After that, I need to return to Pisa."

"Are Massimo and Vittorio still in Pisa?

"Vittorio stayed in Pisa. Massimo came with me to bring our captive to prison."

Alessa brushed her hair from her face and stood taller at the prospect of seeing Massimo before he returned to Pisa. Fearful that a blush might reveal her thoughts, she diverted the conversation. "Bianca came to Florence two days past to show Sandro a sample of the fabric she intends to use for the dress she will model for his painting. I went with her to show the swatch to Sandro. He thought it was perfect."

Nico inhaled sharply, and blurted, "You didn't meet Sandro at Il Pennello, did you?"

Nico's concern caused Alessa to laugh. "Yes, Bianca and I did go to Il Pennello, but we didn't go alone. Bianca's uncle went with us. She never travels anywhere without her protector, although we would have had no problem even if he didn't accompany us. The men in the tavern were surprisingly respectful.

"Bianca expects to finish the dress in about two weeks. If you want to see her the next time she comes to Florence, you need to finish your work in Pisa quickly."

Nico bit his lip and said to himself, "Two weeks."

28

FLORENCE, SEPTEMBER 15

The following morning, Nico returned to The Eight's office to prepare the formal accusation against Nello. When Nico arrived, he saw prosecutor Luca Sasso speaking with an office clerk. When Nico finished preparing his filing, the two lawyers left the building and crossed the piazza to a nearby osteria popular with lawyers and notaries. "I'm surprised to see you in Florence," Sasso said. "I thought you'd be in Pisa searching for the missing governor."

"I should be there, and I intend to return there as soon as possible, but I had to come to Florence to file charges against a thug who assaulted me."

"I was about to ask how you got those bruises. Is the assailant one of the Pisan agitators?"

"He is, but he's merely an underling and he refuses to give us the names of those leading the unrest. He hasn't even given us his full name, but a night in a cell at the Stinche and the prospect of spending many more nights there should convince him to divulge the names of his associates."

A server brought two tankards of beer to the table. Nico took a swig, then changed the topic, saying, "Before I left for Pisa, you felt discouraged about a case you were prosecuting. Did your argument prevail?"

"I lost that case, but it was no surprise because I knew my witnesses were weak. However, the same man, Bruno Fiorello, was back again before a tribunal less than two weeks later. This time he was accused of murder and the witnesses were unimpeachable. One witness is a Guardia officer who apprehended Fiorello in the act of beating his victim."

Nico raised his tankard in tribute. "Congratulations. You said that you'd convict him, eventually."

Instead of lofting his tankard, Sasso raised a hand. "The story doesn't end there. After the trial, while the magistrates were still forming their verdict, a priest came to speak with me. He claimed that the victim was the carriage driver of the Bastine family. That was new information because the Guardia had not yet identified the victim. The priest made an even more extraordinary allegation; he said that Rinaldo Bastine had ordered the killing."

"I've heard of the Bastine family. They own an iron smelter."

"Yes, they do. Rinaldo is the son of the owner. He recently began managing operations at the smelter."

Nico's voice expressed skepticism as he repeated Sasso's words, "A priest accused Rinaldo Bastine of ordering a killing?"

Sasso replied, "Yes. The priest's name is Father Giorgio. He's a Benedictine monk visiting from Rome."

"How could a priest know..." Nico let his question hang. "Surely he didn't violate the sanctity of confession."

Sasso answered indirectly. "Father Giorgio is a member of the Priors of Constantine."

Nico had first heard of the Priors when he returned to Florence after his graduation from the University of Bologna. At a reception hosted by the French ambassador, Nico noticed a bishop wearing the Prior's distinctive gold and silver ring. He described the unique ring to Chancellor Scala, who told him, "The Priors began as a secretive sect in the thirteenth century with a mission of punishing unrepentant sinners. In the preceding two centuries, the sect has grown in number." Nico met the Priors again when they helped him thwart an evil knight who had been threatening a defenseless town. That experience taught him that the Priors have mysterious ways of gaining information and accomplishing their goals.

Sasso continued. "Father Giorgio said Fiorello had told him that Rinaldo Bastine directed him to eliminate the carriage driver. After meeting with the priest, I went to speak with Fiorello myself, and he confirmed what the priest had told me. By then, Fiorello had come to realize that he was about to be convicted of murder and would likely be sentenced to execution. I urged him to testify against Bastine in exchange for a reduced sentence."

"You don't have the authority to adjust sentences," Nico asserted.

"Not by myself, but I knew I could influence the magistrates." Sasso winked. "I had done it before. After meeting with Fiorello, I requested an audience with the senior magistrate and asked him to consider that the witnesses testified only to Fiorello beating his victim. I said there was no direct evidence that Fiorello intended to kill the man. The death might have been a tragic blunder."

Nico laughed, saying, "You clever devil. It is rare for a prosecutor to argue for a reduced sentence. I suppose you recommended that the magistrates find Fiorello guilty of egregious assault rather than murder."

"Exactly. I know that magistrates don't respond well to pressure, so I didn't tell them to issue that verdict. I merely suggested that they consider the possibility. And that's exactly what they did. They sentenced Fiorello to five years in prison.

"The sentence is less than he deserves," Sasso continued, "but a fair compromise if his testimony can help build a case against Rinaldo Bastine. I knew that would take more than Fiorello's testimony to create a solid case, so I tried finding other people who heard Bastine order the killing. I interviewed servants at Palazzo Bastine, but none of them were helpful. Next, I interrogated workers at the iron smelter. One worker said he heard Rinaldo tell Fiorello to 'get rid of the carriage driver.' His statement corroborated what Father Giorgio and Fiorello had told me, but the statement 'get rid of the carriage driver' isn't strong enough to bring murder charges against a man of Rinaldo Bastine's standing."

Sasso rapped his fist on the table. "This is another instance of knowing someone is guilty and not having the proof to gain a conviction."

29

FLORENCE, SEPTEMBER 15

The Stinche prison got its notorious reputation as a dismal lockup in part from its outward appearance. Its plain stone walls, with barred windows and only a single small door, rose three levels above the piazza. Inside, the confinement mirrored Florentine society. At the lowest level, dozens of impoverished inmates crowded into cells with dirt floors and minimal sanitation. Their meals consisted only of food donated by charitable organizations. On the upper levels, wealthy prisoners enjoyed superior accommodations and lavish meals furnished by their relatives.

Nico and Massimo walked the short distance to the prison from the Chancery. No guards were posted outside, so they entered and approached one of the wardens. Nico said, "We're here to see a prisoner who was brought in this morning. His name is Nello."

The warden consulted his register, then pointed to a gathering of visitors. "They are charity workers bringing food to the ward where Nello is held. They can show you where to find him."

As they passed one room, they threaded their way through a group of people, men and women, who were pressed against the bars, conversing with the prisoners. "The wardens are very tolerant of visitors," the charity worker explained. "Wealthy prisoners on the upper levels are even allowed to receive food and other items brought by their servants." His tone suggested that he didn't approve of the policy.

In another room inmates played cards while others sat on the floor leaning against a wall with their eyes closed as though sleeping. This disheveled group had scraggly beards and dirty hands. They had only two visitors, women in peasant clothes. "It's surprisingly quiet," Massimo observed. "Offenders in the confinement area at the army base are constantly voicing complaints about their treatment."

A charity worker responded, saying, "Most of the men in this ward are debtors. Their sentences are short, typically only a month or so. They've resigned themselves to their situation. It only gets loud when there is a fight."

"Does that happen often?" Massimo asked.

"With so many men crowded into each cell, there are fights nearly every day."

Massimo said, "I see only men. Are there any women?"

"The women are in a separate ward," the charity worker replied, then she pointed and said, "The person you want is in that room."

Nico saw Nello sitting alone on a bench and called to him. Nello looked up but neither stood nor replied. Nico said, "Your trial will be in two days."

That news drew Nello's attention. He rose and walked to the front of the cell, facing Nico. "Can I get a lawyer?" he asked in a raspy voice.

"If you can afford one. There are lawyers who prowl the prison looking for clients. You can hire one of them," Nico replied.

"Are you willing to give me the names of your associates?" Nico asked.

Nello glared at Nico. "My friends are waiting for weapons that are expected to arrive soon. You will know their names when they are wielding blades. When that time comes, Florentines will feel the sting of blades made by Florentines." He laughed at the irony.

Massimo stepped forward. "Messer Argenti will be prosecuting your case. He carries the injuries you inflicted, so you would do well not to antagonize him further."

Nello spit at the floor. "What I say is of no consequence. I already know what he will demand at the trial. No words of mine would change that."

Massimo grabbed the cell bars with both hands, pressed his face against them and snarled, "Wrong answer! Messer Argenti can still amend the charges against you. He will advise the magistrate whether you have been cooperative or not, and his words will affect your sentence."

Nello laughed, turned away, and returned to the stone bench.

Massimo stormed away. "Arrogant fool," he muttered to himself.

Outside, Nico said, "Nello claimed that the agitators will be receiving weapons made in Florence."

Massimo, still fuming from his exchange with Nello, said, "He mentioned blades, and there are only three armorers in Florence that make swords. I know them because the army gets weapons from all three. Two of the shops are small. They make mostly armor and custom swords for knights. The third shop is favored by mercenaries who want dependable arms at a reasonable cost."

The three armorers were outside the city walls, where the noise generated by metal working would not disturb city dwellers. Massimo planned a route that would let them visit all three shops. They exited the city through the busy Porta a San Gallo city gate used by travelers headed to Bologna.

They followed a stream bringing a cold flow down from the hills north of the city, and in less than a mile they saw the armorer's shop where the foothills met the flat Florentine plain. It was a small shop that specialized in decorated swords and daggers for ceremonial events. Inside, two men were hammering steel on anvils to shape it into blades. A third man, the shop owner and consul of the armorers' guild, was fitting a leather hilt to a blade.

Upon seeing Nico and Massimo enter the shop, he set the blade down and went to welcome the visitors. He told his men to cease hammering so he could speak with the potential customers. Nico explained that he and Massimo were members of the Security Commission and they had reason to believe that a Florentine armorer was making swords for delivery to Pisa. The owner responded, "None of my customers is from Pisa."

"Do you have any new customers?" Nico asked.

"Only one," the owner replied. He walked to a nearby table and unfolded a cloth covering to reveal a gleaming blade. He lifted the falchion sword, and smiling proudly, he said, "We designed this especially for Count Guidi of Arezzo. It is to be a gift to his son on the young man's twentieth birthday." He turned the sword so they could see the design engraved on the pommel. "This is the Guidi family crest," he explained.

Nico and Massimo complimented the owner on his craftsmanship and left the small shop, convinced that it was not supplying weapons to agitators in Pisa. They followed a road heading south toward the Arno River. The next armory, the largest of three, was located atop a small hill. The metal fabrication shop was a large wooden building set in a clearing. The office was nearby in a separate building near a stand of evergreen trees. Massimo said, "I've been here before to get my sword re-honed. The army has someone who can sharpen blades, but when an edge gets damaged, it needs more than sharpening and for that we take the blade back to the armorer who made it."

The door's creaking, when Massimo pushed it open, alerted the man at the desk that he had visitors. Behind him, light glinted off a variety of armor produced by the shop. The pieces on display weren't new; all exhibited the scars of battle. A protective cuirass plate had countless gouges sustained from an enemy's repeated attempts to drive his sword into the wearer's chest, but none of the hacks had penetrated the strong steel breastplate. Nearby, a pauldron showed the long shallow gash that it received while protecting a knight's shoulder from his opponent's lance.

The owner recognized Massimo immediately. After informing the owner that he had been assigned to the Security Commission, Massimo introduced Nico and explained that they had received information that weapons were being made in a Florentine armory for delivery to a customer in Pisa. "I have no customers in Pisa," the owner replied defensively.

"Do you have any new customers?" Nico asked.

"No, none within the past month." The owner paused to reflect on his recent transactions.

Nico noted the hesitation and prompted, "Is it possible that one of your existing customers is supplying weapons to Pisan militants?"

"No, that can't be," the owner began, then stopped in mid-protest. After a moment, he said, "I did get one unusual order. We get the blanks for our swords and knives from the smelter owned by the Bastine family. I've been doing business with them for many years. When my father started this armory, he began buying blanks from the Bastine smelter. Signor Bastine passed the smelter on to his son Rinaldo, and now I buy blanks from him. Two weeks past, Rinaldo asked me to make swords for him. I thought it strange that he wanted a quantity of arms."

Nico's face lit up at hearing the name Rinaldo Bastine. He asked, "Have you ever made swords for him before?"

"Yes, but only one or two for his personal use or as gifts. Suddenly he was asking for many."

"Did he say why he wanted them?" Massimo asked.

"No, he didn't. He said only that they had to be delivered quickly and at a reasonable price... and he wasn't concerned about quality. To speed the delivery, he cut the processing time at his smelter. That let him get blanks to us quickly; however, the blanks he brought to us were... inferior. I told him swords made from those blanks would be brittle. He knew that, but he didn't care as long as they could be made quickly."

Nico and Massimo exchanged knowing glances, knowing that no reputable dealer would want faulty arms. Nico asked, "When will the order be completed?"

"We already sent one shipment to him, and my men are working on the next one." Before Nico or Massimo could ask another question, the shop owner added, "Rinaldo had another strange request. Normally, we put our insignia on each blade. He asked that there be no markings on the blades." He walked to a nearby table, took one of the blades. He held it out to Nico and said, "We normally put our mark on the guard. See, there is no mark on this one."

Nico turned the blade to examine the underside of the guard. It was polished smooth and lacked the armory's insignia. He passed the blade to Massimo, then asked, "When is your next delivery?"

"Three days from now. Rinaldo's men will come to collect them. I promised to have ten blades ready for them." He looked at Massimo, whom he trusted, and asked, "Should I delay the delivery? I could tell them that there's a problem."

"No. Make the delivery as you had planned," Massimo replied. "We will arrange to have the weapons confiscated before they reach Pisa."

Outside, Massimo said, "You reacted strongly at the mention of Rinaldo Bastine."

"I have a prosecutor friend, Luca Sasso, who has been gathering evidence to prove that Rinaldo Bastine ordered the killing of a Bastine family servant. Thus far, he's been unable to find sufficient proof to file charges."

"A killing," Massimo echoed with surprise. "Do you think the killing and the purchase of weapons are related?"

"I can't be sure. Maybe the two events are a coincidence or maybe the servant learned that Rinaldo was selling arms to Pisan rebels and Rinaldo wanted the man silenced before he could tell anyone."

"I don't believe in coincidences, at least not in coincidences like these," Massimo declared.

"Nor do I," Nico agreed. "I need to tell prosecutor Sasso that Rinaldo Bastine is buying weapons, and we believe he is selling them to the rebels. He might have information that could help to build the case against Bastine."

"While you're doing that, I'll return to Pisa and let Captain Carfi know about the weapons delivery because his men are the ones who will need to intercept the shipment."

30

FLORENCE, SEPTEMBER 16

Luca Sasso looked up from behind the stack of papers on his desk when Nico rapped on his door. "You look glum," Nico observed. "Are you still struggling to find evidence against Rinaldo Bastine?"

"I can't find anyone who heard Bastine order Fiorello to kill the carriage driver." Sasso stood, stretched, and sat on the edge of the desk facing Nico. "My clerk and I tracked down everyone who works at the smelter. Most of them refuse to talk to us. Either they're loyal to Bastine or they fear him. I found only one man who is willing to testify, and all he can say is that he heard Bastine tell Fiorello to get rid of the driver."

Nico said, "The magistrates won't equate that to ordering a killing."

Sasso clenched a fist in frustration. "That's the problem. Fiorello has been working for Bastine long enough to know what his boss means when he says get rid of someone, but to a magistrate, those words are ambiguous."

Nico pulled a chair close to Sasso and said, "I have something to tell you." Puzzled, Sasso dropped onto the chair. Nico waited until Sasso settled onto the seat, then continued, "I've just learned that murder might not be Bastine's only crime." He described his meetings with Nello at Stinche prison and with the armorer.

When Nico finished, Sasso said in a sympathetic tone, "You're in the same position I am. You believe Bastine is guilty of a crime, but you don't have enough evidence to prove it. The armorer can testify that Rinaldo Bastine ordered a shipment of weapons, but he can't say they are destined for rebels in Pisa."

"I don't have enough evidence for a solid case yet, but the proof may come soon when the next shipment of weapons is sent to Pisa. One of my colleagues is arranging for the army to confiscate them. If Bastine's men make the delivery, it will give us a direct link to him." Deep in thought, Nico paced across the small office. Then he turned back to face Sasso. "The person you prosecuted, Fiorello, is one of Bastine's confidants. Did he ever mention anything about weapons?"

"No. I never questioned Fiorello about anything other than the killing, and he is not one to volunteer information. Now that he's in prison and Bastine is still a free man, Fiorello's loyalty might be shaken enough for him to speak openly."

For the second time in as many days, Nico entered Stinche prison. He followed Sasso to the ward on the second level, where Fiorello was confined in a cell with four other men. "Fiorello's lawyer arranged for these accommodations," Sasso explained. "They're better than the dreadful cells on the lower level, but modest compared to those of wealthy inmates. Fiorello must be paying for privileges with his own funds. Certainly Bastine wouldn't continue supporting the man who implicated him in a murder."

Fiorello registered surprise at seeing Sasso. He rose and walked to the front of the cell and looked at the lawyer suspiciously. "You look comfortable," Sasso began. "As comfortable as anyone could be under the circumstances."

Fiorello sneered, "I pay dearly for my amenities. Florence, with all its gold, provides me with nothing."

Not wanting to provoke further hostility, Sasso addressed the reason for his visit. "This is my colleague, Messer Argenti. He has evidence that Rinaldo Bastine is buying weapons for rebels in Pisa. Did you ever hear Rinaldo mention weapons?"

Fiorello suppressed a smile. "The last time you asked me to discredit Rinaldo, you offered something in return. What do you offer now?"

"I had your sentence reduced from execution to a short time in prison, even though your testimony alone cannot convict Bastine. You should be thankful."

"I was thankful," Fiorello said calmly. "Now, if you want something more from me, you can make me thankful again."

Sasso bristled, saying, "You were sentenced to five years for murder. No magistrate is going to lower that sentence further."

Fiorello raised both hands, palms up, in a dismissive gesture. "Then I have nothing to say."

Sasso turned away and said to Nico, "We are wasting time with this ungrateful wretch."

Nico placed a hand on Sasso's shoulder to keep him from leaving. He said to Fiorello, "No magistrate will let you go entirely free, but I can arrange for your sentence to be changed from prison to exile."

Fiorello raised an eyebrow. "How can you do that? Why should I believe you?"

"I know the magistrate," Sasso interjected sharply. "He'll never support that."

Nico responded, "He might not, but the Eight of Public Safety are extremely fearful of arms getting into the hands of Pisan rebels. I'm certain they would revise Fiorello's sentence, and they have the authority to do so. They can assume jurisdiction in any matter that bears on public safety." Although his statement was presumptive, Nico spoke confidently because he knew of another case where the Eight had intervened by offering exile in exchange for information.

Looking at Sasso, Fiorello asked, "Does he speak the truth? Can he be trusted?" Sasso nodded reluctantly, not wanting to lose sway over the criminal he had worked so hard to convict. Fiorello sought confirmation from Nico, "You can arrange for me to leave here?"

Nico said, "If you testify with information that helps convict Rinaldo Bastine, I can have your sentence changed from imprisonment to exile. You would have to leave the Republic of Florence."

"I could go to Siena or Milan as a free man?"

"You could go anywhere, but you can never return."

Fiorello rubbed his chin. He hesitated only a moment, pondering where he would go if he were forced to leave Florence before asking, "What do you want to know?"

"Can you confirm that Rinaldo is shipping weapons to rebels in Pisa?"

"Rinaldo has a contact in Pisa who imports iron from Sardinia. One month past, Rinaldo met with his contact to purchase a new shipment of iron for the smelter. The contact asked whether Rinaldo could obtain weapons from an armory in Florence."

"Rinaldo told you this?" Nico asked.

"Yes, he told me. His vanity won't let him conceal secrets. He was like a gleeful child. He said the weapons were for men who wanted independence and he laughed when he told me that. He said their purpose mattered not. All that mattered to him was that he would be paid in silver hidden from the eyes of tax collectors."

"Who is the contact in Pisa?" Nico asked.

"That I do not know, but one who must know is the supervisor at the smelter. He delivered one wagon load of blades already and returned with the payment in silver. He will be delivering the next shipment of blades soon." Fiorello stepped forward, pressing himself against the bars of his cell. "I've told you what I know. When will I be freed from this hole?"

"As I told you, you will be exiled after you have testified against Rinaldo Bastine."

31

LIVORNO, SEPTEMBER 17

A soft breeze blowing from the east warmed the air, creating the last trace of summer in unpredictable September. The pleasant weather went unnoticed by Vittorio as he made his way along the Livorno waterfront. He had just finished surveilling the arrival of Galatea, a small ship in the fleet of the company that owned the Nereid and the Triton.

The Galatea didn't sail as far as North Africa, so Vittorio hadn't expected the small vessel to be smuggling silver, but he was eager to know whether it carried other contraband from ports in Sicily or Naples. He had watched the crew unload crates of fruit, fresh from the citrus groves of southern Italy. And he had watched tax collectors chatting with each other and wandering aimlessly with little to do while the tax-free cargo moved from the ship to waiting wagons.

Vittorio's interest had piqued after the last crate was unloaded, the wagons drove away, and the tax collectors departed. If the ship held any contraband, that was when it would be removed. Vittorio observed the two sailors who remained on the Galatea as they stowed ropes and swept the deck. They had made no move to extract anything from the ship's hold and no wagon had arrived to accept clandestine cargo. Vittorio surmised that the Galatea's crew was not part of the smuggling operation.

He turned to his second task of the morning, searching for clues to where the abducted governor was being held. He had devoted time each day to visiting shops, taverns, and other gathering places where he might hear a hint that could point to the governor's location. Thus far, his efforts had confirmed only that the men of Livorno universally disliked the governor, although few had condoned the abduction. Vittorio's choice for today was a seedy tavern frequented by old men, where he could sit by himself at a table in a darkened corner of the room with a tankard of beer while observing and listening to the other patrons. His experiences as a Guardia investigator had let him hone the ability of blending in with locals and not being marked as an outsider.

Two excited young boys ran from a side street onto the road along the waterfront. As they passed Vittorio, one boy called out, "They found a body!"

The other boy, his attention on Vittorio, stumbled over an outsized stone and nearly fell. Regaining his balance and grinning happily, he added to his friend's announcement, "In the canal!"

The boys ran toward an old canal that bypassed Pisa and connected Livorno directly to the Arno River. Vittorio changed his direction and followed them. The shallow canal was little used anymore, having been superseded by a wider, deeper waterway that accommodated the new larger barges. Reeds pushing up from the murky water hinted that silt was slowly filling the old canal's neglected channel.

Vittorio and the boys weren't the only ones attracted by the anomalous find. Beyond the newly built city wall, the canal, and the path alongside it, passed through flat marshland that afforded a clear view to Pisa four miles ahead. Midway between the two towns, a group of men stood peering into the water. When Vittorio came close, he saw two members of the Livorno Guardia blocking the path to prevent onlookers from advancing toward the floating object.

"Who is it?" one man voiced to no one in particular. The body floated face down, making it unlikely that anyone could identify it by seeing only the back of a smock. But a bloated hand at the end of an outstretched arm suggested that the shape was a man, probably a laborer or a sailor. Vittorio knew of only one missing person, Stefano, the sailor who had been abducted from his home shortly after Vittorio arrived in Livorno.

The onlookers convinced each other that one of them should be able to identify the person after he was pulled from the water, but the Guardia officers made no effort to extract the body. They only glanced around impatiently as though waiting for someone, perhaps a medico, to take charge of the corpse.

Vittorio snaked his way through the crowd and approached one of the officers. "Why are you not removing the body?" he asked.

The officer held out a stiff arm to keep Vittorio from moving closer and huffed, "We are outside Livorno." He cocked his head toward the floating body. "This is the army's responsibility. We can't be expected to do all their work. Now, move back with the others." The officer's uncaring attitude mirrored that which Vittorio had encountered at Guardia headquarters when he inquired of their progress at finding Stefano or his abductors. They had shown no interest in solving the crime, telling him only that it remained on their list of open cases.

Vittorio had witnessed other corpses recovered from bodies of water. Although flesh decomposed more slowly underwater than in open air, Stefano had disappeared more than a week past, so Vittorio doubted that anyone would be able to identify a body submerged in the canal all that time.

Vittorio scanned the faces of those present and eavesdropped on their conversations for any indications that the abductors might be among those watching the recovery. He found none. As time passed, the crowd's interest in the unknown body waned and several men wandered back to the town. Among those remaining was the cobbler Vittorio had spoken with at the time of Stefano's disappearance.

Vittorio hoped that if Stefano had used the cobbler's services regularly, the man might have known Stefano well enough to identify him. Vittorio moved beside the cobbler and said, "I am Vittorio Colombo. I'm a member of the Florentine Security Commission. I spoke with you when Stefano was abducted."

The cobbler, puzzled at first, grunted "Ahh," upon recalling their discussion.

Vittorio said, "You were acquainted with Stefano. Can you help me to determine whether the body is his?"

Their conversation was interrupted by three soldiers from the army garrison in Pisa arriving in a wagon. The wagon pushed forward, forcing the crowd into a single line at the path's edge. When it stopped in a position alongside the canal, the wagon blocked their view while the soldiers pulled the corpse from the water and wrapped it in cloth. With the face covered, Vittorio thought that any chance of identifying the body was lost until the cobbler leaned close to Vittorio and said, "That's him. That's Stefano. I can tell because I recognize the shoes." Pointing, he added, "See, that's the repair I made."

Vittorio placed a hand on the cobbler's shoulder. "Say nothing. His wife should be notified by a compassionate relative. She shouldn't learn of her husband's fate through gossip."

Vittorio remained at the site until the wagon departed, then he headed to the shipping company office to inform Salvadore Grassi, the company manager and the husband of Stefano's cousin, that Stefano's body had been recovered. When he entered the office and asked to see the manager, the clerk replied, "He's not here. He's gone to Genoa."

The answer surprised Vittorio because Pisa and Genoa were fierce competitors in the shipping trade. "Does the shipping company do business in Genoa?"

"No, we have no business in Genoa. Signor Grassi said the trip was for personal reasons."

"Personal reasons," Vittorio echoed. "Did he say when he will return?"

The clerk, now becoming uncomfortable by Vittorio's questioning, grumbled, "I don't know. He didn't say."

The clerk's reticence made Vittorio more adamant. "It's important that I speak with him," Vittorio said firmly. "His wife may know when he will return. Tell me where to find her."

Although the clerk felt it improper to reveal Signora Grassi's address, he did so to free himself from further interrogation. Using the clerk's directions, Vittorio walked to Salvadore Grassi's apartment on the second level above a candlemaker's shop in the center of town.

A woman, reaching barely as high as Vittorio's shoulder, answered his knock. She pulled the door inward enough for her to see the caller. Her face, perhaps once pretty, showed wrinkles and her hair had gray streaks.

"I am Vittorio Colombo, a member of the Florentine Security Commission. I have news about your cousin Stefano." The woman pulled the door open to allow Vittorio to enter the apartment. "It may be better for you to sit," Vittorio said.

Rather than sit in the reception room, she walked to the kitchen and sat on one of the chairs at the table. She gestured with a hand for Vittorio to sit. Although he normally preferred to stand when questioning subjects, he pulled out a chair and sat facing the woman. "I am sorry to tell you that your cousin Stefano's body has been found."

She crossed herself, then looked up at the ceiling. "Merciful God, may his soul be with You in heaven." She shed no tears. The news was not a surprise. "Where?" she asked.

"He was found in the old canal. Soldiers took his body to the army garrison in Pisa."

She stood, removed the apron she had been wearing, and smoothed her dress. "I must go and tell his wife. The poor woman has no other relatives. She must hear of this tragedy from me, not from a stranger."

Vittorio rose and followed the woman from her apartment. As

they walked to Stefano's house, he said, "I went to the shipping company to tell your husband, but the clerk said he is in Genoa. Do you have relatives in Genoa?

"In Genoa? No, we don't have relatives in Genoa. The clerk is mistaken. Salvadore would have no reason to go to Genoa. He told me he was going to Florence. He said that he had business there. His decision was sudden, and he was upset."

The woman wished to speak with Stefano's wife alone, so Vittorio stepped away when they approached the house. He stayed only long enough to see the door open, and the woman enter the house.

A light rain fell as Vittorio walked to his inn, pondering the conflicting information he had received: the clerk said that Signor Grassi had gone to Genoa, while Grassi's wife said that he had gone to Florence. For what reason had Grassi lied to one of them... or both of them?

32

FLORENCE, SEPTEMBER 17

Nico entered the darkened courtroom. He left the door open and used the dim light filtering in from the corridor to find his way to the prosecution table. He had just reached his seat when he heard rapid footsteps approaching and the court notary swept into the room muttering, "Sorry I'm late."

He circled the room, lighting lanterns that filled the space with their warm glow. The courtroom used by magistrates of the Eight of Public Safety was decidedly smaller than other tribunal chambers in Nico's experience.

The room had only two entrances and no gallery because the Eight did not countenance audiences observing their proceedings. One entrance was used exclusively by the magistrates. The other served all trial participants: lawyers, defendants, and witnesses.

Two prison guards escorted Nello into the room and removed his restraints. He rubbed his chafed wrists and glowered at Nico while taking his seat beside his lawyer. Since the room had no gallery, the guards would be forced to stand during the trial. After Nello sat at the defense table, the guards took positions on opposite sides of the room.

The defense lawyer shuffled his way across the room. By his stooped posture and thinning gray hair, Nico recognized him as one of the lawyers who prowled the prison seeking clients, but Nico didn't recall the man's name.

The notary had just lit the last lantern when the door from the magistrate's chamber opened. The magistrate strode briskly to his seat on the raised platform at the front of the tribunal. Nico registered this too as unusual. Protocols in other courts called for the notary to open the door and announce the magistrate.

The magistrate's creased face and graying hair attested to his long experience. He fixed his gaze on Nico and commanded, "Messer Argenti, read the accusation."

Reading of the accusation was a formality since the magistrate and the defense lawyer already had copies of the document. Nico stood. "Honorable magistrate, on Friday, thirteen September, in the year of our Lord fourteen hundred sixty-five, in the city of Pisa, the defendant, who wishes to be known only by the name Nello, assaulted an official of the Florentine Security Commission."

The accusation was succinct and direct in keeping with the dictums of the Eight. In other tribunals, accusations used more colorful language. They might refer to the defendant as a *vicious criminal* and might state that the victim had sustained *brutal injuries*; however, the Eight frowned on lurid statements.

Nico glanced at the defense table where Nello had leaned forward to rest both elbows on the table. He looked straight ahead with a vacant stare, seemingly indifferent to the charges being leveled against him.

The magistrate verified that Nico's reading conformed to his written copy. Satisfied, he raised a hand to signal that Nico should continue.

"Honorable magistrate, I am the official who was assaulted by the defendant, so I am able to relate the circumstances of the crime."

The magistrate nodded his consent and Nico continued. "I, along with the other members of the Florentine Security Commission, were dispatched to Pisa to investigate rumors reported by a member of the Signoria that agitators in that province were planning unlawful and potentially violent protests. In the course of our investigation, a Pisan *farmacista* arranged for me to meet the defendant who he said could take me to the agitators. The defendant led me from the *farmacia* to a nearby alley where two of his accomplices held me while the defendant struck my head and face with his fists. I suffered injuries and was saved from further harm only by the swift action of a fellow member of the Security Commission.

"With your permission, I would like to read a letter from the medical officer at the Cittadella Nuova army garrison in Pisa who treated my wounds." The magistrate gave a quick wave of his hand. Nico read, "On Friday, thirteen September, Messer Nico Argenti was brought to my office for the treatment of injuries resulting from a beating. Deep cuts on both of his cheeks were bleeding profusely. He also had a large bruise on his neck, his walk was unsteady, and he had blurred vision. I stopped the bleeding; then applied salve to the cuts and the bruise. I gave him a container of salve to take with him so he could apply it at intervals and a powder that he could use to ease the pain." Nico looked up from the paper he had been reading and added, "The letter is signed by Sergeant Marco Pignatelli, Cittadella Nuova medical officer."

Nello's lawyer watched Nico, but he showed no reaction to the reading. Nello poked his lawyer. "Aren't you going to say something?"

The lawyer pulled away from Nello's jab and hissed, "The letter says nothing about you."

The magistrate had no questions or comments, so Nico continued. "Signor Massimo Leoni is another member of the Florentine Security Commission. It was he who freed me from my attackers and apprehended the defendant. He had intended to be present to give his statement, but urgent business of the Security Commission required that he return to Pisa. Before leaving for Pisa, he prepared a statement. With your permission, I will read his statement."

Nello's lawyer stood, but he remained silent until the magistrate gave him permission to speak. "Honorable magistrate, accepting testimony without having the witness appear before the tribunal would make it impossible for the defense to question the witness. That would put the defense at an unacceptable disadvantage. I ask that testimony in absentia be disallowed."

The magistrate leaned forward, placing his hand, palms down, on his table. His brow furrowed as he considered the defense's request. "The defense's plea has merit. I could delay these proceedings until Signor Leoni is available to testify, but in the interest of expediency, I will allow the written testimony to be presented. If questions arise that need answers from Signor Leoni, then we will recess until Signor Leoni returns to Florence." The magistrate looked to both lawyers for any objections to his ruling. When neither man objected, he directed Nico to proceed.

"This document was prepared two days past by Signor Massimo Leoni prior to his departure for Pisa." Nico began reading, "On Friday, thirteen September, I accompanied Messer Nico Argenti to a farmacia in the city of Pisa where he expected to meet with someone who could lead him to a group of lawless agitators. I waited outside the farmacia while Messer Argenti met with the defendant. When the two men left the farmacia, I decided to follow at a discreet distance behind them. The defendant led Messer Argenti to an alley where two of the defendant's cohorts were waiting. They grabbed Messer Argenti and held him while the defendant struck him repeatedly. As soon as I saw the attack, I ran into the alley where I engaged with and apprehended the defendant. His two allies fled."

Nello's lawyer rose, slowly this time. Upon receiving the magistrate's acknowledgement, he said, "It would be unjust to accept that document as testimony. It says that the witness decided to follow my client and Messer Argenti when they left the farmacia, but it does not say why he chose to follow them rather than join them. Without being able to question the witness, we cannot know his reasoning. Acting in a furtive manner suggests that he might have prejudged my client as hostile without cause."

The magistrate motioned for Nico to come forward and said, "Bring me the document." He read the wording carefully, then bit his lip as he pondered how to respond to the objection. Massimo's impression of the defendant did not bear on the assertion that Nico had been attacked; however, legal precedent did allow for questioning witnesses' motives. Frowning, the magistrate announced, "This proceeding is in recess until the witness can appear for questioning." Facing Nico, he ordered, "Advise Signor Leoni that he is to appear before this tribunal in no more than two days' time." Then he rose and stormed brusquely from the courtroom.

After the guards escorted Nello from the room, Nico approached Nello's lawyer. "When Nello was brought to the prison, he had very little money. How could he afford to hire you as his lawyer?"

The lawyer laughed. "Usury may be a crime outside the prison, but inside it is a way of life. He borrowed money from one of the many unscrupulous wealthy inmates."

"He borrowed money to pay your fee? How will he pay it back?"

The lawyer, now grinning broadly, said, "That is not my concern." In a near whisper, he added, "Nello must have an affluent benefactor. He borrowed enough money to pay my fee and to have a message sent to someone in Pisa."

"Was the ploy to delay the trial your idea or Nello's?" Nico asked.

The lawyer dropped his jaw and pressed a hand to his chest, feigning offense. "You do me an injustice calling my objection a ploy. Every good lawyer must exploit all available measures to support his client. Extending the trial does not add to my fee." Again, in a soft voice, he said, "My client is unperturbed by the trial. He feels confident that he will soon be a free man."

Nico walked away slowly, puzzling over what could have been in the message that Nello sent to Pisa and why Nello thought he would soon be free.

33

FLORENCE, SEPTEMBER 17

Nico joined his cousin Donato at a table in a corner of the Uccello dining room. It was a rare quiet time at the restaurant. All but a few of the noontime diners had already departed, and the staff was relaxing briefly before readying themselves for the flood of dinner guests. Donato poured a glass of wine for his cousin and raised his glass in a toast. "Can we drink to your latest victory in the courtroom? Was this your first appearance before the Eight?"

"It was my first time in a tribunal presided over by a magistrate of the Eight, but it's premature to celebrate a victory."

Donato's hand stopped abruptly in midair, nearly spilling liquid from his glass. "How can it not have been a victory? You still bear the bruises Nello gave you. Those alone should have earned a guilty verdict," he said as he lowered his glass slowly to the table.

"The magistrate honored the defense lawyer's petition calling for Massimo to deliver his testimony in person so the defense could have an opportunity to question him. The trial is in recess until Massimo can return to Florence. The magistrate stipulated that Massimo must appear in court within two days, so the Chancery sent a courier to

Pisa to notify Massimo of the magistrate's ruling and ordering him to return to Florence."

"Bah," Donato grumbled. "It sounds like a feeble tactic to postpone the inevitable."

"It probably is a pointless holdup. The magistrate seemed annoyed by the request, but he believed that legal propriety required him to grant the delay." Nico leaned close to keep others in the restaurant from overhearing. "I've become aware of another matter that may draw the attention of the Eight. Two men I've spoken with reported that a respected Florentine businessman is obtaining a large quantity of weapons, and one of them claims that the weapons are being sent to Pisa."

"Into the hands of troublemakers?" Donato asked.

"I think so. There's one person who may be know where the initial shipment was delivered. I intend to..." Nico let himself get distracted by the sound of the restaurant door opening.

A thin man with an off-center nose stepped through the doorway. He stopped and scanned the room. His snug-fitting doublet with brass points on the front and wrist bands showed him to be a man of good taste. His acorn hat sat forward on his head, its brim reaching nearly down to his eyebrows, to hide his receding hairline. Luca Sasso's notary was exactly as Luca had described him. Nico waved a hand to get the man's attention and said to Donato, "He's the notary who went with Luca to question men at the Bastine iron smelter when Luca was building the murder case against Fiorello. He's going to join me in questioning a person who knows about the weapons delivery."

After Nico and the notary left the restaurant, they crossed the city, passed through the Porta al Prato gate, and followed the path beside the Arno River to the Bastine iron smelter. A line of struggling laborers carried crates from the smelter to the nearby dock, while a burly man with a husky voice stood to the side and barked orders at them. "That's him. He's the supervisor," the notary said. "He refused to talk with Messer Sasso when we came here to question the iron workers about the killing."

"Did the supervisor see you? Would he recognize you?"

"Yes, he saw me. He bumped into me when he tried to get away from Messer Sasso, so I'm sure he'll remember me."

"Then it would be best if you stay out of sight."

Nico maneuvered around the line of workers and approached the supervisor from behind. As soon as he came within the man's field of view, he attempted a bluff, saying, "The next shipment of arms for Pisa will be ready tomorrow. Do you remember where to take them?"

The supervisor, his attention still on his men, answered without thinking. "I remember. Of course I remember. To the old farmhouse on Via Calcisona."

"And the person who takes delivery?" Nico pressed.

The supervisor pivoted abruptly to face Nico. "Who are you?" he growled. His meaty hand shot out to grab his inquisitor by the collar, but Nico sidestepped the thrust.

Nico saw no benefit to concealing the truth. "I'm Messer Nico Argenti of the Florentine Security Commission."

"Another lawyer. I don't talk to lawyers." He made an obscene hand gesture, turned away, and barked a command to one of the workers.

Nico tried intimidation to gain a response. "It's a crime to provide arms to lawbreakers. If you are delivering weapons to insurrectionists, you will be prosecuted."

The supervisor eyed Nico with an icy stare and snarled, "Leave here now or I'll have these men remove you."

Nico regretted not having Vittorio with him. On many occasions, he had been impressed by the investigator's talent for persuading subjects to reveal information. Lacking Vittorio's unique skill, Nico turned away and walked to where the notary had secreted himself. "I had no more success with the supervisor than you and Luca. Once he found out that I'm a lawyer, he refused to talk to me."

The notary clapped his hands together. "But I heard you. Your clever approach of catching him unaware was very effective. You learned where the blades are being delivered."

"I was hoping to learn the name of the person who will receive the next shipment," Nico took a deep breath, "but knowing the destination is something. I can pass that information to my colleague, who will be intercepting the delivery when it arrives in Pisa."

"The supervisor isn't the only one who refused to talk with Messer Sasso," the notary said. "None of the men would speak with us, except for him." He pointed at a worker bent low under the strain of the load he carried. "That man. The one with the torn shirt. We found out later that he feels no loyalty to Rinaldo Bastine, because Rinaldo had once made advances to the man's wife."

Nico watched the man lower a large container from his shoulder. "Apparently Rinaldo is never guarded with his words, so it's possible that some of the workers heard about the weapons shipments, but I can't question this one now in the presence of the supervisor."

"I've been monitoring these men because Messer Sasso had asked me to watch the iron workers. I found that after work they often go to *La Piuna Rossa*, the Red Feather. It's a tavern in the Santa Maria Novella district. Perhaps there you can find an opportunity to speak with him alone."

Deciding they could accomplish nothing further at the smelter, Nico and the notary headed back to the city. They had gone only a short distance before they spotted a man and a woman walking toward them. When the pair got close enough to be identified, the notary declared, "That's Father Giorgio."

The priest nodded a greeting to the notary and said to Nico, "You must be Messer Argenti. Messer Sasso told me you had gone to the smelter. May I present Signorina Gemma Bastine, Rinaldo Bastine's sister."

Nico nodded politely and said, "A pleasure to meet you, signorina." Then he waited for the priest to explain why he had been sent by Luca Sasso.

"Messer Sasso told me of your interest in the weapons purchases made by Signor Bastine. Signorina Gemma has something to show you."

"It's this way," Gemma said and headed toward the smelter, with the men following. "My father feels that he's too old to continue with the business. He entrusted the smelter operation to my brother. In my view, it was a misguided decision. Rinaldo changed the business... for the worse. He drove away the loyal family men who worked at the smelter when our father was in control and replaced them with a crew of petty criminals. And Rinaldo's shameful behavior is not confined to these workers. He's becoming a reprobate. On more than one occasion, I caught him violating our women servants."

When she came within sight of the smelter, Gemma turned onto a narrow path that led to a small building partially hidden behind a dense thicket of tall shrubs. "I took no interest in the family business until Father Giorgio told me that my brother might be involved in the murder committed by Signor Fiorello. Lately, I've come to the office when Rinaldo and the supervisor are away. I found records that show Rinaldo is receiving payment for selling weapons."

Gemma unlocked the door to the small shed. "Always in the past, business transactions were settled using bank letters of credit. And now, instead, I found these." She pulled the door open to reveal a stack of silver bars.

Nico advanced into the narrow space to examine the bars. He lifted one and carried it outside into the light. "It has the same markings as the silver being smuggled into Livorno," he announced. His statement had meaning for the notary who knew about the Security Commission's activities in Pisa, but it brought only puzzled expressions from Gemma and the priest.

Gemma looked at Nico with disappointment in her eyes. "Are you saying that my brother is also involved in smuggling?"

Nico replaced the bar and stepped outside. "No, I don't believe so," he assured her quickly. "Rinaldo is probably unaware that his customer obtained the silver from smugglers. From what I've seen, the smugglers are guarding their identities closely. But now I understand what they are doing with their booty. Since they're using the contraband to buy weapons, it is likely that the weapons are being given to the rebels."

"Two criminal groups working together." the notary hypothesized.

"Or one group involved in two crimes," Nico offered.

"What does that mean for my brother?" Gemma asked.

"Settling a business transaction with gold or silver is not unusual, and Rinaldo can't be implicated in smuggling, if he didn't know the source of the silver. A more significant concern is whether Rinaldo knew he was selling weapons intended for Pisan rebels. Did you find any records that name the buyer?"

"There is one document that corresponds to the arms delivery. It mentions payment received, but it doesn't list a name, only the initials SG."

Nico closed his eyes while his mind flashed through the names of everyone he had met in Pisa. At length he said, "I don't know of anyone with those initials."

"If Rinaldo knows the weapons are going to rebels, would that make him guilty of a crime?" Gemma asked.

"Yes, certainly. Providing weapons to rebels is a serious crime," Nico replied.

"And he would be prosecuted?"

"Yes, he would be prosecuted." Nico had been speaking firmly. Now he switched to a soft voice, unsure how Gemma would react. "And I am the one who would file charges against him."

Nico expected that Gemma would be disturbed by his words, but she showed no reaction. She looked at Father Giorgio, who returned her gaze and said, "Your brother has chosen his own path. As it says in Galatians, 'each must carry his own load.' You cannot take Rinaldo as your burden. Only he can account for his sins."

It surprised Nico when she said, "And Rinaldo has many sins to account for."

As the four trekked back to the city, Nico reflected on what he had discovered. At first, he felt disappointment at not having found the name of Rinaldo's customer, but his spirit lifted when he considered what he had learned: the buyer's initials were SG, silver smuggled into Livorno had been used to pay for the weapons, and they were being delivered to an old farmhouse on Via Calcisona, the road that connected Pisa to the village of Navacchio.

34

FLORENCE, SEPTEMBER 18

Nico arrived early at the Eight of Public Safety offices in Palazzo della Signoria. Rather than going directly to the tribunal chamber, he joined Massimo in one of the rooms where witnesses waited before being called to testify. "The next weapons delivery is today. I should be in Pisa with Captain Carfi's men, not here," Massimo fumed.

"I agree," Nico said sympathetically. "But Carfi's men are competent. I'm sure they'll manage to intercept the weapons shipment."

"You have my written testimony. Why is it necessary for me to read it myself? You like to praise the judicial system, but in this case, it's an obstruction." Massimo pounded a fist against the wall.

Nico had no retort to offer in response to his friend's frustration. He could only say, "The proceeding should be quick, then you can be on your way back to Pisa." He left Massimo pacing the small room.

Unlike on the previous day, the courtroom was brightly illuminated when Nico took his seat at the prosecution table. Nello's lawyer avoided looking at Nico as he passed him on his way to the defense table. His aloof behavior hinted that something had changed since the previous trial session. Nico looked to the doorway, expecting two prison guards to escort Nello into the chamber. Instead, one guard came into the room alone. He went directly to the court notary, who was setting paper and writing instruments on the magistrate's table. Nico strained in vain to hear the words exchanged between the guard and the notary. After a brief conversation, the guard took a position standing near the doorway.

When the magistrate entered, the notary met him as he moved toward his table at the front of the chamber. The magistrate stopped in mid-stride while the notary relayed the information he had received from the guard. He shook his head repeatedly as he moved to his position on the dais, ground his teeth together, and announced, "The trial of prisoner Nello is in session." Beaming fiery glares at the lawyer and the guard, he barked, "Where is the defendant?"

The lawyer set his eyes on the guard with a look that said, "This is your responsibility."

The guard cleared his throat. In a quavering voice, he answered, "He has escaped."

It was a shameful but not uncommon occurrence. The constant stream of friends, relatives and service workers flowing in and out of the Stinche prison made it impossible to enforce security. Modest bribes were enough to induce poorly paid guards to aid men like Nello in slipping away by blending into a group of visitors. Inmates incarcerated for gambling, fighting, and other petty crimes served short sentences, so the corrupt guards reasoned that little harm resulted from helping those men end their sentences a bit early. Nico ran a finger over the wound on his cheek, thinking, "This hasn't healed, yet the person who did it is already free."

The magistrate swung his head to face Nello's lawyer. "Did you...."

Before the magistrate could finish his question, the lawyer raised a hand to proclaim his innocence. "Honorable magistrate, I had nothing to do with the escape. I have no idea where my client has gone." It wasn't the first time the lawyer had found himself in that position, although for him it was an enviable outcome. He had already received his fee, and Nello's escape spared him from suffering a certain loss in court by attempting to defend a client who was obviously guilty.

"Do you wish to present testimony or evidence to support your client's defense?"

The lawyer raised both hands, palms upward, in a gesture of resignation. He would have made a token attempt to defend his client had Nello not escaped, but he knew that, under the circumstances, any such attempt would be pointless and would only antagonize the magistrate.

In a voice loud enough to reverberate throughout the chamber, the magistrate announced, "From the evidence already presented, this court finds the defendant guilty." He turned to face his notary and declared, "The Guardia is ordered to apprehend the fugitive and return him to this court for sentencing." He rose and stormed out of the room.

Everyone realized that the order, while proper, was futile. Most likely Nello had fled back to Pisa, away from the jurisdiction of the Florentine Guardia. The magistrate's authority, acting on behalf of Eight of Public Safety, extended to Pisa, but no practical means existed to communicate his order to the Guardia in Pisa. In theory, magistrates could enlist the army to apprehend criminals, but they did so only in extremely rare and serious situations.

As Nello's lawyer passed Nico on his way out of the chamber, Nico detained him by taking hold of his arm. "How did Nello find the means to escape?" Nico asked.

"I wasn't party to his escape," the lawyer snapped. Through a thin smile, he added, "Nello believed that he would not serve a sentence in prison. Yesterday I told you that he had sent a message to Pisa. He claimed that there were those in Pisa who could secure his release. Apparently, his assertions proved true." The lawyer pulled his arm free from Nico's grasp and left the room.

Nico went to the witness room to inform Massimo that he would not be called to testify. He expected to find his impatient colleague still pacing the room. Instead, he found Massimo leaning back in a chair, his arms folded across his chest, his feet up on the table, and his eyes closed. "Earlier you couldn't wait to return to Pisa, and now you've fallen asleep. I'll never understand you." Nico said.

Massimo opened his eyes. "I'm surprised to see you here. I thought that I'd be summoned to the witness stand by the court notary."

"Nello escaped, so the trial is ended. You won't have to testify."

Massimo slapped a hand on the table. "The Stinche leaks like a sieve. It hardly seems worth capturing criminals if the prison can't hold them. I was summoned here from Pisa for nothing."

In an attempt to comfort his friend, Nico said, "If he's returned to Pisa, we might have another chance to apprehend him."

Massimo dropped his feet to the floor, sat up straight, and held a paper out toward Nico. "Nello's escape isn't the only negative turn today. This note from the armorer says that Rinaldo Bastine decided not to take delivery of the blades today. The armorer sent the message to our office and a Chancery courier brought it here. I instructed the courier to have a dispatch sent to Captain Carfi to inform him that the weapons won't be delivered to Pisa today."

After reading the paper, Nico said, "This note doesn't say why Rinaldo stopped the delivery. Did the courier have any more information?"

"No, he didn't. But the armorer might know the reason. We'll have to pay him another visit." Massimo paused briefly while he considered the situation. "Somehow Bastine found out that we were going to intercept the arms shipment. How could he have known that?"

"I may be responsible for that," Nico said sheepishly. "The supervisor at the iron smelter delivered the first shipment of the blades to Pisa, and he expected to make another delivery today. Yesterday, I went to the smelter to question him. He refused to tell me who would receive the blades. All I learned was where he takes them, an old farmhouse on Via Calcisona."

Massimo tried to ease Nico's conscience, saying, "Knowing the location could be helpful to Captain Carfi. Even if the blades aren't delivered today, the farmhouse might be the rebel's hideaway. It could be a key to finding them." He furrowed his brow in thought, then spoke slowly. "Bastine must know the weapons are going to rebels. If he believed they were going to a respectable exporter, he would have had no reason to cancel the shipment."

"I reached the same conclusion, but I have no way of proving it. If I were to accuse Bastine, he could deny any criminal dealings, and the smelter supervisor would surely support that position."

"Can't he be forced to reveal the name of his customer to a magistrate?"

"Unfortunately, no. In prior cases, the guilds have maintained that its members would lose their competitive advantages if they were forced to reveal the names of their suppliers and customers. And the courts have been sympathetic to that argument."

Nico pulled out a chair and sat across from Massimo. He leaned forward and rested his elbows on the table. "I did get two helpful pieces of information from Rinaldo's sister." His lips curled up in a thin smile, knowing that the mention of a woman would draw a reaction from Massimo.

He was not disappointed. "Rinaldo's sister?" Massimo repeated, grinning.

Nico chose to trifle with his friend by not mentioning the circumstances that had brought him together with Gemma Bastine. Using her given name to imply a level of familiarity, Nico said, "By examining the smelter's business records, Gemma learned that the customer for the blades has the initials SG. She also showed me the silver bars that Rinaldo received as payment. They bear the same markings as the silver smuggled into Livorno."

"Gemma?" Massimo parroted. Laughing heartily, he said, "And you're the one who is always accusing me of getting involved with women."

"Come, friend," Nico said as he stood. "Let's get some wine and I'll tell you about my conversation with Gemma and Father Giorgio yesterday at the smelter. Then we can head back to Pisa. I'm eager to know whether the army has made any progress in finding the governor."

35

PISA, SEPTEMBER 19

Nico and Massimo arranged passage on the first barge of the morning, heading downriver from Florence to Pisa. They waited until dockworkers loaded the final crates of wool cloth before boarding the craft. Both men wore heavy cloaks and found places to sit on the lee side of the barge, away from the stiff cold wind hugging the river. They spoke little during the uneventful passage. Crops had already been harvested at the farms along the river's course that would remain a barren brown landscape until Spring.

Hours later, they climbed ashore at Pisa. "Much could have happened here in the four days we've been away," Massimo said as he scanned the warehouses lining the river.

When Nico reached his inn, Finito stopped sweeping, dropped his broom, and rushed to greet his Florentine friend. "I was afraid you weren't coming back."

Nico tousled the youngster's hair. "My business in Florence took longer than I expected, but I told you that I'd return."

Finito peered intently at Nico. "Are you well? Your bruises..."

Nico rubbed a finger down his cheek. "They're almost healed. I'm better, much better than the last time you saw me. I see you've been helping your uncle."

"There is always work to be done at the inn." Finito lowered his voice to a near whisper. "When I'm older, I don't want to be an innkeeper."

Nico laughed. "And what would you like to be if not an innkeeper?"

"I'm not sure... a job where other people do the work and I'm the boss."

Nico laughed. "Everyone shares that wish. Here at the inn, are you the worker and your uncle the boss?"

"My uncle tells me what needs to be done, but there's always enough to keep us both busy. We're both workers." Again, Finito looked intently at Nico. "Your work is exciting. Maybe I could find work like yours."

Nico smiled. "If you consider getting thrashed by a thug exciting, then, yes, at times my work is exciting." He held out a small paper sack. "These are for you. I bought them for you in Florence."

Finito's eyes lit up as he took the package and pulled on the ribbon tie to open it. "They're *canditi*," Nico said. "They're made from oranges grown in Calabria and sugar brought to Venice from the Levant. When I was your age, my favorite treats were from the shop that makes these."

Finito dropped a piece of candied orange into his mouth. "Oh!" he exclaimed. "It's so sweet."

"Maybe when you're older, you can own a shop that makes *dolciumi* like these," Nico teased, then asked, "Have you been taking care of Pisa while I've been away?"

"There is news," Finito said, nearly swallowing the candy. "Signora Governor has been freed."

"You mean the governor's wife? She's been released? What about the governor?"

The boy nodded. "Yes, the governor's wife she was... released.

Everyone is talking about it. I haven't heard anything about the governor."

"Is she unharmed?"

"I don't know. No one tells me anything. I only learn things by listening to people talking to each other. A man who was staying at the inn told my uncle that Signora Gov... I mean the governor's wife, had been freed."

Nico's first thought was to speak with the innkeeper, but he doubted that the man would have more than cursory information. "Soldiers must have found her," Nico speculated aloud.

"Are you going to the fortress to talk with the soldiers? I could show you the best way to get there."

Nico chuckled. "I know how to get to the garrison." Gesturing at the broom on the floor near Finito's feet, he said, "And you have work to do."

Finito looked up at Nico with pleading eyes. "I can finish the sweeping later."

The boy's plea brought to mind the thrill that Nico had felt the first time his father, an army captain, had taken him to the army base near Florence. "You can come with me if your uncle agrees that the sweeping can wait. We can go after I put my duffel in my room."

Finito guided Nico through narrow streets and alleys, a route that would be preferred only by a young boy. En route to the garrison, they collected Massimo, who was also eager to learn details of the governor's wife's release. The guards stationed outside the garrison gave perfunctory nods as Nico and Massimo approached the fortress. They took no issue with the boy accompanying the two men. Finito's eyes went wide as he entered the imposing structure.

They climbed to the second level and waited in the corridor until Captain Carfi finished dealing with two of his officers. After dismissing the officers, Carfi motioned for the visitors to enter his office. He looked tired. His eyes were puffy, his hair had missed its usual careful grooming, and his uniform lacked its usual crisp creases. The extra hours he had spent directing his men in their search for the governor had taken a toll.

Carfi looked askance at the young boy standing between Nico and Massimo. Not wanting to discuss matters in front of the youngster, he called for his aide, "Sergeant, show this boy around the garrison while I meet with these men."

As soon as the sergeant and Finito had left the room, Carfi motioned Nico and Massimo to his conference table. "I received word that there was to be no weapons shipment." It was a statement, but one that called for a response, an explanation.

Massimo began, "During my time in the army, I dealt with the armorers in Florence who make blades. Nico and I questioned them, asking whether they had customers in Pisa. One revealed that he had a customer who was selling weapons to a contact in Pisa."

Nico said, "The person who bought the blades from the armorer owns an iron smelter. I visited the smelter and learned that one delivery of blades had been made already and the smelter owner had been paid in silver, the same silver that's being smuggled into Livorno."

Carfi raised an eyebrow upon hearing that the smuggled silver was being used to buy weapons. Nico continued, "I tried to question the smelter's employees, including the man who delivered the first shipment. He had intended to make another delivery, but it seems that my questioning caused them to change their plans."

"An unfortunate result," Carfi said. "My men were positioned to intercept the delivery."

Nico nodded. "I agree, but I believe the delivery is delayed, not canceled. Greed is one of the smelter owner's many vices. I doubt that he'll forego the chance to extend his silver hoard. At the smelter, I also learned that the delivery was to be made to an old farmhouse on Via Calcisona."

"The road from Pisa to Cascina," the captain muttered to himself, then aloud he said, "I'll send a patrol to inspect all the farms on that road. If any rebels are still there, my men will find them." Carfi stood and walked to a window. He glanced out at the city for a few moments, then turned back to Nico. "Do you have any sense of when the next shipment might come?"

"I have no insight now, but the armorer will tell us when he delivers the blades to the smelter owner. When that happens, a Chancery courier will be dispatched immediately to bring that information to you."

"Good. Good." Carfi rubbed his hands together. He returned to his seat and said, "We will be ready."

Nico changed their topic, saying, "Massimo and I heard that the governor's wife has been released."

"Yesterday morning. A farmer bringing goods to market found her wandering outside the Porta Lucana gate. He didn't know she was Signora Gondi. He thought she was lost or injured, so he took her to a medico. The medico recognized her immediately and sent his son to find a soldier. Even at that early hour, my men were out scouring the city to find Governor Gondi and his wife.

"After the medico determined that she had not been harmed and was only disoriented, my men took her to her residence. I went there to question her. Unfortunately, she couldn't provide any information that would help us find the governor. She said that whenever she was transported, the rebels pushed her into a wagon bed and covered her with a blanket, so she saw nothing. She couldn't say where she and the governor had been held, only that it was a small room with no windows."

"Why did they release her?" Massimo asked.

"To deliver an ultimatum. The rebels gave her a note demanding that the Florentine army withdraw from Pisa by the Feast of Saint Michael, or the Arno River will be colored with the governor's blood."

"The Feast of Saint Michael," Massimo echoed. "That's only ten days from now."

With fire in his eyes, Captain Carfi said, "Ten days or a year, the time matters not. The Florentine army will not withdraw from Pisa. The ultimatum has only made us redouble our efforts to find the governor. An army unit is being sent from Florence to assist my men's search for the governor. We will find him."

After a minute of silence, Nico said, "I would like to speak with Signora Gondi."

Carfi stiffened and inhaled deeply. "You don't need my permission. Go speak with her if you wish. Do you think she will tell you things that she would not tell me?"

Nico, fearful that he had offended the captain, said, "No, certainly not, but she must have been very disturbed when you spoke with her. Perhaps now she is calmer and may remember something that she couldn't recall yesterday."

When Nico and Massimo went to collect Finito, they found the boy fascinated by the sight of soldiers drilling in a practice area. Nico thanked the sergeant for his kindness in entertaining the boy. Outside the garrison, Massimo put a hand on Finito's shoulder and winked at Nico. "Our young friend must need sustenance after his tour of the fortress. I'm sure he can lead us to a pasticceria that serves tasty snacks."

Finito's eyes sparkled until Nico pointed out, "We'll have to be brief. There's an inn that needs sweeping, and we've already kept this hard worker from his duties." Finito led the men at a trot to the nearest pasticceria.

As Finito licked the last remains of a fruit tart from his fingers, Massimo asked, "Did you find your tour of the garrison interesting?"

Before replying, Finito checked his fingers one last time, hoping to find another dollop of raspberry filling. "I never realized how many things soldiers need to learn. I thought that all they needed were swords, and they were ready to fight, but I watched a patrol practicing how to attack a building. They did it again and again. Each time, their leader told his men how they could do it better."

◦

That evening, Massimo and Vittorio were already seated when Nico entered the Tre Stelle trattoria. A half empty jug of wine and a nearly empty cheese platter on their table showed that the two men had arrived much earlier. Massimo spotted Nico, poured the remaining wine into a glass for him, and raised the jug to signal the server for a refill.

Vittorio said, "Massimo told me that your attempt to prosecute Nello was thwarted by his escape from the Stinche."

"The magistrate found Nello guilty from the evidence I presented, but that mattered little since Nello had escaped," Nico said sullenly.

Vittorio pressed his fist down onto the table. "Some of the guards at the Stinche should be in the cells rather than minding them. And the wardens should be dismissed. They know which guards are taking bribes and they do nothing to stop them. I once brought a scoundrel to the Stinche after he had beaten a young woman because she wouldn't submit to his advances. The next day he didn't appear at his trial because his rich banker father had paid one of the guards to let the scum walk out of his cell."

Massimo turned to Vittorio and said, "I suspect there is more to this tale."

"There is. I tracked the abuser to the family's villa in the countryside, dragged him back to the Stinche, and made him tell me the name of the guard who set him free. That guard no longer works at the prison, and whenever I brought criminals to the Stinche after that, the warden was very particular about who he assigned to guard them."

Conversation paused while the server refilled each of the men's wine glasses and set the jug on the table. When she had returned to the kitchen, Massimo said, "I told Vittorio of your discovery that smuggled silver had been used to pay for weapons."

Nico said, "I saw the pile of silver bars with the same marking in a building at an iron smelter. Accounting records at the smelter showed that the weapons sent to Pisa were delivered to someone with the initials SG."

Vittorio, who was about to take a drink of wine, moved his glass away from his lips, set it down, and leaned forward across the table toward Nico. "The manager of the shipping company that operates the ships smuggling contraband, the Triton, the Pallas, and the Nereid, has those initials. His name is Salvadore Grassi."

"But the shipping company is in Livorno, not Pisa," Nico observed.

"And he's probably not the only man in Pisa or Livorno with those initials," Massimo added.

As an experienced investigator, Vittorio was skilled in piecing together fragments of information. He looked from Massimo to Nico and said, "When I tried to speak with Signor Grassi, the shipping company clerk told me he had gone to Genoa. Grassi's wife told me he is in Florence, and neither of them knows the reason for his departure. His sudden unexplained travel doesn't prove him guilty, but it is suspicious."

"You aren't thinking of going to Genoa or Florence to look for him, are you?" Massimo asked.

Vittorio shook his head. "No, but I'm going to pay him another visit as soon as he returns."

The server and a young woman who looked to be the woman's daughter set steaming bowls of octopus soup in front of each man. The young woman returned with a plate of green vegetables and a loaf of crusty bread. While the men ate, Vittorio told them that Stefano's body had been found in a canal. "Days spent in the water had disfigured the body beyond recognition. It was identified only because a cobbler recognized Stefano's shoes."

Massimo said, "Fortuna smiled at you."

"Signora Grassi was Stefano's cousin," Vittorio continued. "I told her about the body so she could be the one to tell Stefano's wife. I didn't want the poor widow to hear about her husband through gossip."

After dinner, while the men enjoyed glasses of grappa, Nico told Vittorio that he intended to interview the governor's wife, Signora

Gondi, the following morning. "She was in distress when Captain Carfi questioned her. Perhaps now she is able to think more clearly." To Massimo, he said, "It might be best if I go alone to question her."

"I agree. Having two men questioning her could be overwhelming."

"I'll come to your inn after I meet with her to let you know if I learn anything."

Massimo summarized, "You're going to speak with the governor's wife, and Vittorio is going to look for Signor Grassi. If the army hasn't searched every building in Pisa by now, I may join one of their patrols."

36

PISA, SEPTEMBER 20

Nico felt it would be proper to wait until mid-morning before calling upon Signora Gondi, so he treated himself to a leisurely breakfast at an osteria across from his inn. The sun was well up in the sky when he turned onto the street that would take him to the governor's residence. When Florentines occupied Pisa sixty years past, they had confiscated the properties of opposition leaders who fled the province. Florence established one of the seized buildings as a residence for its governor. Crestfallen Pisans called it *Casa del dominatore*, House of the dominator.

Two soldiers flanked the door of the governor's residence. Nico handed them a note penned by Captain Carfi stating that they should grant Nico access to the building. The soldier who read the note stood aside while his companion pulled the bell rope to announce the visitor.

The bell still echoed when Signora Gondi's personal maid came to a second-level window and looked out at the men below. "You are supposed to keep people away," she fumed, knowing the soldiers could not hear her complaint through the closed window. She stormed down the stairs, pulled open the door, and glowered at Nico.

"I am Nico Argenti of the Florentine Security Commission," Nico announced. "I wish to speak..."

"The Signora is suffering. She needs to be alone," the maid interrupted. She stood rigidly straight with her arms folded across her chest, waiting for Nico to turn away.

The maid's hostility made Nico wonder whether Massimo's unfailing charm could have been useful in placating the obstinate woman. But instead of charm, Nico opted to appeal to her using reason. "I understand that Signora Gondi has experienced a severe ordeal, but her pain will not end until her husband is returned safely. I am certain she would want to do anything in her power to secure his return as quickly as possible. There may be something she can tell me to help end her dreadful situation. That is why I have come here." Without a word, the maid turned and walked inside, expecting Nico to follow.

They climbed to the casa's third level, which housed the family's private quarters. Nico hesitated briefly, reluctant to enter the signora's bed chamber. He stepped forward at the maid's urging and was relieved to find Signora Gondi in a sitting room, not her bed chamber. The maid stood near the doorway, her hands on her hips, while Nico sat in a chair a respectful distance from the signora. She was a small woman with delicate features. A comb held her hair back, away from her face. She wore a simple brown dress and no jewelry other than a gold wedding band. Her reddened eyes and cheeks, marked with dried tears, showed that she had been crying.

Signora Gondi did not react when Nico introduced himself. "I know this is difficult for you," he said. "Anything you can tell me, no matter how insignificant it may seem, could help us find your husband. Perhaps you have remembered something since you spoke with Captain Carfi. Even a small detail could be important."

The signora looked up but still said nothing. "Tell me about the room where you were kept. What color were the walls?" Nico prompted.

"White," she replied in a voice almost too low to hear. "No, maybe once they were white, but time had turned them gray."

"Was there anything on the walls? Paintings or decorations?"

She closed her eyes to picture the room. "Nothing. There was one patch, a square, lighter than the surrounding wall. A painting may have been there once."

"Did you ever see any of the men?"

"I saw only the one who brought us food. It was always the same man. He never spoke to us. He just opened the door and pushed a tray of food on the floor into the room."

"What did he look like? Would you recognize him if you saw him again?"

"I would know him if I saw him again, but there was nothing special about him. He had brown hair and wore a simple smock, like so many other Pisans."

"You never heard or saw any other men?"

"I never saw any other men, but I did hear them once. Two men were in the next room talking loudly, or maybe arguing with each other."

"Can you recall what they said?"

Again, she closed her eyes and furrowed her brow in thought. "I remember one of them saying, 'I can do nothing more.' The other man said something, but I couldn't tell what he said. Then the first man said, 'I had a member of my family killed to protect us.' They said more, but those were the only words I heard clearly."

I had a member of my family killed. The words struck Nico. Who would do such a thing? He questioned the woman further but gleaned no additional information. When he saw that she was beginning to tire, he thanked her for indulging him and rose to leave. Nico's compassion for her distraught mistress had softened the maid's demeanor. She held a thin smile as Nico moved past her on his way from the room.

Nico recalled Vittorio's account the previous evening. Salvadore Grassi's unexplained departure and his initials matching those of the person who received the weapons shipment had already made Vittorio wary. Grassi was a cousin by marriage to the man who had been killed and dumped in the canal. Was it possible that Grassi was the person overheard by the governor's wife who boasted that he had a member of his family killed? As he stepped out of Casa del dominatore into the piazza, Nico wondered how many people had been killed in Pisa recently. He set off in the direction of the army garrison to pose that question to Captain Carfi.

Guards at the Cittadella Nuova garrison greeted Nico and allowed him to enter the fortress without an escort. He climbed to the second level and followed a corridor to Captain Carfi's office. As he peered into the vacant room, a voice behind him said, "The captain is away with one of the patrols. May I help you?"

Nico turned to face the captain's aide, the sergeant who had given Finito a tour the previous day. A serious expression had replaced the soft look the aide had when he was guiding Finito, so Nico asked directly, "Does the army keep records of men killed in Pisa?"

The aide ushered Nico to the conference table in the captain's office, then asked, "The city or the province?"

Nico thought for a moment. "Not the entire province but the city and the surrounding area... and also Livorno and its surrounding area." He anticipated the next question and added, "In the past month."

Nico expected that the aide would need to consult written documents, but instead the aide said, "Minor crimes are common, but killings are not. In the past month, there have been only two. Earlier this week, a body was recovered from a canal near Livorno."

Before the aide could provide any details, Nico said, "I'm familiar with that incident."

"The other was the body of a sailor that washed up on a beach south of Pisa. It was found by a fisherman. The body had come from a ship. Our medico determined that the death was not an accident; the man had been beaten and thrown overboard." This time, it was the aide who anticipated the next question and said, "Neither crime has been solved yet."

With only two recent killings, there was a strong likelihood that Salvadore Grassi had made the comment heard by the governor's wife and that he had ordered the killing of his wife's cousin.

37

PISA, SEPTEMBER 20

Nico left Captain Carfi's office, eager to tell Vittorio of the circumstantial evidence that Salvadore Grassi had ordered the killing of his wife's cousin. Nico considered a possible rationale for Grassi's action: As a sailor aboard one of the ships involved in smuggling, Stefano might have learned that Grassi was responsible for the smuggling operation and threatened to expose him.

Nico knew that Vittorio and Massimo were accompanying an army patrol searching for the governor in a district near the cathedral. He set out toward the cathedral on a route across the city that took him past his inn. When he came within sight of the inn, Finito ran into the street to intercept him. In an eager voice, the boy said, "A man came to the inn looking for you. I told him that I could find you." Finito held out a folded paper. "He wrote this note and said I should give it to you."

Nico tousled Finito's hair and said, "What would I do without you, my young friend?" The comment brought a beaming smile to the boy's face.

Nico unfolded the sheet and read,

Messer Argenti,

    I have important information for you.

    Pippo Fonte

Fonte, the accountant, Nico mused. What information could he have?

Finito looked up at Nico hopefully. "Will you take me with you?"

"The message is from Signor Fonte. He wishes to speak to me. If you have finished your chores, you can walk with me to his office."

"I've swept the floors and taken the dirty linens to the laundry so I can go with you."

When they reached the central square, Finito went off to look into the shops while Nico called on the accountant. Nico pulled the office door open and saw another man inside meeting with the accountant. He stepped back and eased the door closed, ready to wait outside until the accountant was free, when Fonte noticed him and motioned for him to enter. Fonte dismissed the other man and said to Nico, "You received my message."

Nico waved the paper containing Fonte's note. "It says you have important information."

Fonte leaned forward, resting his elbows on his desk. "The Florentine army has been combing the city, looking for their governor. Every day they trample the privacy of peace-loving Pisans."

Nico stood rigid and placed his hands on his hips. "Did you call me here to tell me something or to make a speech?"

"I came to tell you where to find your governor." Nico stood speechless, waiting for Fonte to continue. "The army patrols are harassing the God-fearing citizens of Pisa needlessly. Governor Gondi is not in Pisa. He is being held north of the city near Mount Castellare."

Nico narrowed his eyes. "How do you know this?"

"As I told you before, I have sources. The leader of the rebels is a man named Salvadore Grassi."

Nico startled upon hearing Grassi's name. His thoughts flashed back to the iron smelter outside Florence, where Gemma Bastine had shown him the smuggled silver and told him that the weapons were being delivered to a person with the initials SG. If Fonte's information was correct, it confirmed that Grassi was using the smuggling operation to buy weapons for the rebels.

Recalling what Vittorio had told him, Nico said, "Signor Grassi is in Genoa or Florence."

Fonte waved a hand dismissively. "He may have been away, but my sources tell me that he is north of the city now, and my sources are never wrong," he boasted. "Grassi is part owner of a tract of land near Mount Castellare. I don't know the exact location of the land, but it is owned jointly by his brother, who should be able to tell you how to find it. The brother's name is Fabbro. He's a blacksmith with a shop near the stable outside the Porta Montaria gate."

"Fabbro... is he also one of the rebels?" Nico asked.

"I'm not certain, but I don't believe so." Fonte leaned back in his chair, suggesting that he had nothing further to add.

In an easy voice, Nico asked, "Why are you telling me this? Why did you not give this information to the army?"

"The army only cares about finding the governor and punishing his abductors." Fonte looked intently at Nico. "When we spoke last, I sensed that you had sympathy for the plight of the Pisan people suffering under the thumb of an authoritarian governor."

Nico paused to weigh the accountant's statement, then said, "Let me verify the information you have given me. Then we can talk further."

When Nico left Fonte's office, Finito was nowhere in sight. The accountant's information needed to be dealt with quickly, so Nico did not search for the boy. Instead, he headed directly toward the cathedral to find Massimo, Vittorio, and an army patrol.

38

PISA, SEPTEMBER 20

The army logistical officer provided horses for the three Florentines who rode with the army patrol to the blacksmith shop. Fabbro was hammering an iron strip when soldiers suddenly filled the street outside his shop. He was not perturbed because army patrols had been roaming the city ceaselessly hunting for the governor. His shop's vantage point near a busy city gate drew two or three questioning patrols each day. *Have you seen any suspicious travelers? Do you have any new customers? Do the nearby shops have any new customers?* That last question made Fabbro struggle to hide his laughter. His attention was consumed by his own work; he had no time to notice activities at other businesses.

Fabbro stopped hammering when Nico and the patrol leader dismounted and approached him. "You and your brother own a tract of land near Mount Castellare," Nico said.

Fabbro nodded, but his expression showed that he found the statement puzzling. Nico had intended to broach their purpose deftly, but the patrol leader stepped in front of him and declared, "We've been told that your brother Salvadore is among the rebels who have abducted the governor."

Fabbro set down his hammer, exhaled heavily, and said, "My brother and I lead separate lives. I know he wants Florentines to leave Pisa, but abducting the governor.... That would be brazen, even for him. He never said anything to me."

"But you do own land together with your brother," the leader said in a caustic voice.

"Salvadore said it was a perfect place to start a vineyard because it's on the south slope of the mountain and the soil is fertile. I've only been there twice." Fabbro pulled a rag from his belt and wiped his forehead. "It was a mistake. I shouldn't have let Salvadore convince me to buy it." He swept his arm in an arc, gesturing to the materials scattered around the shop. "I barely have enough time for all this. I'll never find time to plant grapes."

"Can you tell us how to find the land?" Nico asked.

"I can do better than that." Fabbro went into his shop and returned with a crudely drawn map. "Some of these lines are just wagon tracks through fields of grass," he explained. "You have to look carefully, or you'll miss them."

"One of my men is a skilled tracker," the leader replied.

The men rode north from Pisa alongside an old Roman aqueduct toward the remains of the San Giuliana Terme. The village, popular in Roman times for its thermal baths, had been largely destroyed sixty years past in battles between Pisans and Florentines. They continued parallel to the aqueduct for little more than a mile, then turned onto the wagon road shown on Fabbro's map. A short time later, the scout raised his hand to halt the others, where a narrow path angled sharply from the wagon road. The path, suitable only for horses, headed away from the flat Arno River plain and into the Mount Castellare foothills. Looking at the ground in front of him, the scout said, "The grasses have been trampled flat. The path has been used recently, probably by several riders."

The men formed their mounts into a single column, with the patrol leader directly behind his scout and the three Florentines at the rear behind the soldiers. The path made a sweeping curve alongside a depression that looked to be a seasonal stream. The scout stopped them again at the crest of a small rise. "There," he announced, and pointed to a building in the distance. "I can see one building, but there could be more. It's too far to be sure."

The other riders moved forward and clustered around the scout. "It's all open land," the patrol leader observed. "If we keep following this path, they'll see us coming long before we reach them."

Massimo pointed ahead and to the left. "Those shrubs are the only things that might mask our approach. They could let us get closer without being spotted."

The patrol leader took point and led his men to the left, away from the path. He kept below the crest of the rise so they could not be seen as they moved to a position that put the shrubs between them and the building. Then he led them forward, single file, over the rise and toward the tangle of lilac bushes. The scout urged his mount forward so he could see through the bushes. "There is one large building that looks like a barn and two smaller buildings," he announced. "The barn is old. It's leaning slightly and part of the roof has collapsed. The entrance must be on the far side. I can see six horses, but there could be others hidden by the barn."

The army patrol consisted of seven men. The leader had provided Massimo with a sword, so they numbered eight armed men. Nico and Vittorio were unarmed. "At least six of them," the leader repeated as he assessed the situation. "We could be equally matched or outnumbered."

Massimo winked at him. "In number perhaps, but surely not in skill with a blade."

The leader smiled at Massimo's comment. "True, my men are well trained, but we could be at a disadvantage if we are seen before we reach the barn." He paused to consider his options, then said, "We will split into two groups." He gestured to one group of men. "You three go to the right of the barn and scatter their horses. The rest of you, with me around to the left. Massimo, come with us." Looking at

Nico and Vittorio, both unarmed, he said, "Remain here until we secure the rebels."

Eager to participate in the assault, Nico said, "We can help your men scatter the horses."

"As you wish, but stay to the side." The leader pulled his sword from its sheath, raised it high, and shouted, "Go!"

His men charged forward, brandishing their weapons in the air. They were about halfway to their target when a man, alerted by the pounding of approaching hoofs, peered around the side of the barn. "Soldiers! Soldiers coming!" he shouted and disappeared into the barn to warn his companions.

The rebels' responses confirmed Massimo's expectation that they were neither skilled in using swords nor trained in military tactics. Three men fled. They ran from the barn, rushed to their mounts, and galloped off away from the approaching soldiers.

Another group formed a line outside the barn, hoping to keep the soldiers from entering the building. But their short, stout one-handed swords, popular among huntsmen, offered little opposition to the soldiers whose superior army-issue blades and fast-moving horses stunned the disorganized rebels.

The soldier pulled a dagger from his belt, pressed it against the boy's chest, and said, "Don't make a sound." Nico got to his feet and peered in through the opening. In the dim light, he saw a group of men, perhaps a half-dozen, crowded together at the far end of the barn, facing the locked door. Some had their swords out as though they expected the soldiers to force the door open. None were looking in Nico's direction.

Nico could see that the narrow opening, barely wide enough for the boy, would not accommodate soldiers wearing leather armor and carrying weapons. He gripped the boards on either side of the opening and pulled, hoping that one of them might come free. One board did move slightly as he tugged on it, but it held fast. He released his hold and began running toward the front of the barn. "I'll be back," he called to the soldier who was guarding the boy.

A minute later, Nico returned with Massimo, Vittorio, the patrol leader, and two of his men. Two burly soldiers grasped the loose board and pulled firmly and steadily. Gradually, the old rotted wood splintered away from the pegs holding it in place and the board came loose. They cast it aside and slipped into the barn through the widened opening. The others followed. Moving silently, they took positions behind the five rebels, whose attention was still focused on the door. The patrol leader stepped around the rebels and into their field of view. "Drop your weapons," he commanded. Simultaneously, his men pressed their swords against the necks of the startled rebels.

One man raised his sword and spun to attack the soldier behind him. In the cramped space, he collided with the man next to him, sending his initial thrust wide. Massimo dashed forward, grabbed the man's collar, and simultaneously kicked the back of the man's knees. His legs folded, and he crumpled to the ground. Massimo put a foot on the man's throat and hissed, "Let go of your blade." The man looked up at Massimo with fear in his eyes and slowly uncurled his fingers to let his blade drop to the ground. The other captives, rattled by the incident, muttered and swore, but they surrendered their weapons without further protest.

Vittorio searched the barn, looking for additional weapons and clues to the rebels' mission. In one corner he found a cache of small arms, and in an animal stall he found the provincial governor tied to a chair and with a rag stuffed in his mouth. "They'll pay for this, every one of them!" Governor Gondi shrieked as soon as Vittorio pulled the gag away. Gondi struggled pointlessly against the ropes holding him while demanding, "Get these off me! Untie me!"

He expressed no appreciation for being released as he raced outside to where the soldiers were marshalling the rebels and bellowed at the patrol leader, "Lock them away, every one of them." Looking toward the assembly of rebels, he growled, "You'll never see the outside of a prison cell again. None of you."

"We will take them to CIttadella Nuova, where they'll be incarcerated pending their trials," the leader said, hoping to pacify the irate governor. "Tell me, what happened? What did they do to you?"

"Two brutes." Gondi scanned the captives, then pointed. "Those two. They stormed into my study and pulled me from my desk. They grabbed my arms. I thought they were going to tear me in half. They shoved a filthy rag into my mouth, put a hood on my head, and dragged me into out to a wagon." He gnashed his teeth. "Brutal savages!"

"Where did they take you?" the leader asked.

"I don't know. They put me in a small room with no windows. I couldn't tell where I was. They kept me there for days."

"Was your wife with you?"

Gondi gawked as though he regarded the question as a distraction. "Yes, she was there," he replied, then continued with his story. "Yesterday, they took me from that place and brought me here." He raised a hand to forestall any further questions. "I need a bath and clean clothes. I can ride. Bring me a horse."

The patrol leader had intended to take the governor to the army garrison, but he acceded to Gondi's request and dispatched one of his men to accompany the governor to his residence. As Gondi climbed aboard his mount, Nico said to him, "Your wife was not harmed. She is safe at home." Gondi looked down at Nico with a blank expression, said nothing, and rode off. Massimo stepped beside Nico, put a hand on Nico's shoulder, and said, "That man is an arrogant fool."

After searching the rest of the barn, Vittorio announced, "Grassi is not here." He grabbed one of the rebels by the collar, pulled the man close, and stared into his eyes. "Where is Salvadore Grassi?" he demanded. The man's only response was an evil grin. Vittorio shoved the man away with a force that bounced him off a wall and sent him crashing to the floor.

Massimo moved next to his colleague. "Be easy, my friend. Grassi may have been one of those who escaped."

The soldiers took to their mounts and began shepherding the captives on their long walk to the army garrison. The patrol leader took a position at the rear of the column. He sat tall, his posture reflecting pride that his men had captured the band of rebels without incident.

The three Florentines remained behind to contemplate their next actions. Nico questioned the boy, who had given his name as Elfo, "What were you doing here with these men, Elfo?"

"One of the men who was taken by the soldiers is my uncle. He brought me here. He said that I needed to join him if I want to be a man."

Vittorio stood nearby, eager to ask the boy about Salvadore Grassi, but he held back and let Nico continue his questioning.

"Did he tell you they had planned to capture the provincial governor?" Nico asked.

"No, my uncle said nothing about the governor. He told me that the men were defending Pisa by fighting for its freedom. I didn't find out about the governor until we got here, and I saw him tied with ropes being dragged into the barn. I didn't know who he was until one of the men said that he was the governor."

From the corner of his eye, Nico caught a glimpse of Vittorio clenching and unclenching his fists to relieve his impatience. In deference to his colleague, Nico said to the boy, "This place is owned by a man named Salvadore Grassi. Have you heard that name? Was Signor Grassi here?"

Elfo raised his chin. "Yes, Signor Grassi was here. He was giving orders to the others, but he left earlier with another man."

Vittorio took one step forward toward the boy, but then held his position to let Nico continue. "Did Signor Grassi say why he was leaving?" Nico asked.

"He said that he was going to meet someone who was bringing another shipment of swords. He said he had just received word that they were being delivered."

"Did he say where they were being delivered?"

Elfo thought for a moment, then replied, "No, he didn't say."

"Did you hear him mention Via Calcisona?"

"Via Calcisona? No, he didn't mention that, but the other man, the one who went with him, said something... I think it may have been Via Calicsona. I'm not sure."

"Is that where they were going?"

"I don't know. I just remember hearing the name."

Nico looked at Vittorio, whose hands were no longer balled into fists. Nico had gotten him the information he wanted. Nico turned to Massimo, who also seemed satisfied with the information Elfo had provided. Returning his attention to the boy, Nico said, "You can go. Do you know your way home from here?"

"You aren't taking me with the others?" the boy asked in surprise.

"No. You are free to go." With that, the boy ran down the hillside.

Massimo looked at his two colleagues and proffered, "Via Calcisona?"

Nico and Vittorio nodded. "It's a long road," Nico said. "How will we find where the weapons are being delivered?"

"I have an idea," Massimo said and headed to his mount.

39

PISA, SEPTEMBER 20

The army patrol and its column of captive rebels had not gone far when Massimo caught up with them and approached the patrol leader. "We believe another shipment of weapons is being delivered right now." Massimo relayed the information they had obtained from the boy. "Captain Carfi said that his men had checked all the farmhouses along Via Calcisona."

"That's true," the patrol leader replied. "But they didn't find any weapons cache."

"If there is a new arms shipment, we want to intercept it, but we can't visit every farm along that road. Might the patrols that visited the farms have uncovered anything to help us narrow our search?"

The leader replied, "I wasn't on any of those patrols." He rubbed his chin as he thought. "But my scout accompanied one of those patrols." He called to the scout, who was at the head of the column. He turned his horse and joined the others. "Enrico, these men believe there will be another weapons delivery to Via Calcisona. You've been there. Can you tell them where to look... where the delivery might be made?"

"We searched every farm along that road from Pisa to Cascina.

We found no arms cache, but we did find several places that could have been used by the rebels; abandoned farmhouses and farms where the owners were hostile."

"Go with these men. Show them the places that seemed suspicious," the leader ordered. Then he turned toward Massimo and said, "We need to take these rebels to the garrison, so we cannot go with you, but Enrico is a good man. When we reach the garrison, I'll see that another patrol is sent to assist you."

~

The army scout and the three Florentines crossed to the south bank of the Arno River on an old stone bridge, so old that it could have been built by the Romans. In less than a mile, they reached Via Calcisona. "The road is straight, but in this area, the river course makes large loops. A couple of the farms are tucked into the loops far from the road," the scout explained. He scanned both directions along the road, then pointed. "The nearest farm we should visit is in this direction."

Three wagons passed them on the busy road before they turned from the main road onto a narrower road. After passing through a stand of trees, the scout slowed and gestured toward a building in the distance. "That's one of the farms. The house suffered damage, perhaps from a storm. It's abandoned now."

He dismounted, bent down, and studied the ground. "There are wagon tracks, but the dirt is packed, so I can't tell their age. They could be new, or they could have been made many weeks past." He climbed back onto his horse and led the others forward.

When they reached the house, Vittorio rode around to the back of the house. "There are no wagons here," he announced.

Nico dismounted at the front of the house. "If this is the delivery location, I can't believe the rebels would have left the weapons here unguarded, but since we're here, we should look to be certain." He pushed on the door, but it held fast. "It's stuck or latched on the inside." He braced, then slammed his shoulder against the door. Wood splintered, and the door crashed inward, sending Nico stumbling clumsily into the room. A red squirrel, startled by the noise, looked up at the intruder for an instant, then scampered away into an adjoining room.

Massimo joined Nico and, after a quick search of the house, he concluded, "There's nothing here."

The men left the farm and rode back to the main road, where the scout headed his mount in the direction away from Pisa. As they passed two other farms, he said, "These farms aren't likely the rendezvous." The immense farms stretched far across the flat river valley. Their buildings were set so far from the road that Nico could barely see them. "The next one is a working farm," the scout said. "The last time an army patrol came here, the owner refused to let us into the house. He said we had no right to be on his property."

"What happened?" Nico asked. The question made Massimo laugh. He knew the army would not be deterred by belligerence.

"We searched the house and all the other buildings," the scout said in a clipped voice.

Massimo nodded vigorously. "Only a pea-brain would think he could succeed in a confrontation with the army."

As they rode on in silence, Nico recalled a class when he was a student at the University of Bologna. A Bohemian student had regaled the class by telling how the forces of King George of Podebrady had eliminated a threat by entering homes in the middle of the night and pulling enemies of the crown from their beds. The students applauded the action until an astute professor asked whether the victims had the right to expect a peaceful night's sleep. The professor's suggestion was met with laughter from most class members. The Bohemian student asserted that the royal guard had acted with the authority of the king, and all power rests with the king.

"God is perfect and all-powerful," the professor had responded. "Are royals also perfect such that they should be deemed all-powerful?" The class had ended before the question could be resolved, but the issue had remained with Nico.

The laws of the Florentine Republic, which had a legacy dating back to the Code of Justinian, held that the security of the republic was paramount. No citizen could rightfully object to any action taken in defense of the republic. But is it truly justice, Nico wondered, if an army captain at his own discretion can order that a Florentine citizen be pulled from his bedchamber in the middle of the night — or that every corner of his farm be scoured without his consent?

A farmhouse came into view, ahead on the right. The scout announced, "The owner of this farm has a dog. He's big and looks fierce, but he is not."

"Does the farmer live alone?" Vittorio asked.

"He has a wife and a son. The boy is in his twelfth year. He didn't say a word when we were here last, so he won't be a problem."

They turned onto the road leading to the farm. As they drew near, they saw two wagons parked alongside each other in front of the house, and men transferring items between the wagons. The scout said, "One of those men is the farmer. I don't recognize the others."

Vittorio gritted his teeth and sneered, "One is Salvadore Grassi."

"And the other is the supervisor of Rinaldo Bastine's iron smelter," Nico said. "The weapons must be in his wagon."

Hoofbeats alerted the men, who had been moving swords and silver ingots between the two wagons. Grassi ran to the house with the smelter supervisor at his heels. The farmer stood boldly, blocking the door to the house.

Massimo advanced to the house, stopped directly in front of the farmer, and grabbed the obstinate man by the shoulders and shoved him aside. The farmer balled his hands into fists and raised them defiantly. Massimo touched a hand to the hilt of his sword still encased in its scabbard. "Stand aside and no harm will come to you or your family. We are here for the arms dealers."

With the obstacle removed, Vittorio raced into the house. To his left, the farmer's wife and son huddled close to each other, afraid to move. Seeing Vittorio's determination, the smelter supervisor quickly stepped aside. Vittorio barely noticed the others, his attention focused solely on Salvadore Grassi, who was fleeing through a narrow pantry.

Vittorio charged into the small space, his arm outstretched, ready to seize the fleeing man. In one swift move, Grassi pulled a dagger from his belt, turned, and lashed out at his pursuer. Grassi's elbow hit a shelf, which deflected his thrust, but his aim held true enough for the tip of his thin blade to slice into Vittorio's forearm. Both men froze momentarily as they watched a red stain spread along the sleeve of Vittorio's tunic.

As Grassi turned to run, he threw the dagger at Vittorio. The flat of the blade hit Vittorio in the chest, bounced off, and clattered harmlessly to the floor. Vittorio snatched a ceramic crock from a shelf and hurled it at the fleeing man. The crock struck Grassi's head with a force that sent him vibrating side-to-side like a reed in the wind.

Nico, who had entered the house through the kitchen, blocked the other end of the pantry. He stepped forward and took hold of Grassi, pivoted the dazed man around, and pushed him toward Vittorio. Vittorio grasped Grassi's tunic, dragged him from the pantry, and pressed him against a wall next to the smelter supervisor.

The farmer eyed Vittorio's wound and turned to his wife. "He's injured. Get some bandages," he said sharply. The woman, who had been standing in the far corner of the room and shaking with fear, darted from the room. Moments later she returned with a bundle of clean rags and wrapped Vittorio's arm.

When she finished, the scout said to Vittorio, "That bandage will stem the bleeding, but come to the garrison. Our medico can give you something to aid the healing."

Massimo placed a hand on the scout's shoulder. "You led us to capture the rebel leader and the man who's been supplying him with weapons. You're sure to earn a commendation when you bring these two anarchists, and their wagons filled with weapons and silver, to the garrison."

Massimo's praise turned the young soldier's face red. "You were the ones... I didn't..."

Nico reinforced Massimo's compliment, saying, "We never would have found them without you."

As they ushered the captives outside, the scout gestured to the farmer and asked, "What about him?"

"He has a family, and he owns this farm, so he won't flee. He can be dealt with later," Nico replied.

Massimo, Vittorio, and Salvadore Grassi climbed aboard one of the wagons and headed toward the garrison at Pisa. Nico, the scout, and the smelter supervisor followed in the second wagon. Shortly after they left the farm, the supervisor found the courage to protest. "I didn't know that man was a rebel. And I didn't sell the weapons. I was just told to deliver them."

Nico swung around to face the complainer. In a bitter voice, he said, "Remember me? When we spoke at the smelter, I told you that it's a crime to provide arms to lawbreakers. I warned you that if you delivered weapons to insurrectionists, you would be prosecuted. You should have listened to me."

The supervisor slumped down in the wagon bed and fell silent. They had gone only a short distance before Nico turned around again to face the supervisor. "You are just a little chick. Some chicks find they can help themselves by testifying against the rooster." He was confident the supervisor could puzzle out the significance of his cryptic statement.

The scout kept his eyes forward as he guided the wagon along Via Calcisona. *Who is the rooster?* he wondered.

40

PISA, SEPTEMBER 21

As Nico strolled along the Arno River, he gazed across the river at an unusual octagonal church, its appearance more like that of a Middle Eastern mosque than a Christian church. He had been in Pisa more than two weeks, but had rarely had time to appreciate the city's sights. Nico and Massimo had planned to meet later to call on accountant Pippo Fonte, but since Nico had awakened early, he decided to use the time to explore the city. Shortly after arriving in Pisa, one of his hectic treks across the city had taken him past a jewelry shop alongside the river. On that occasion, he had no time to visit the shop, but he had promised himself that he would return later to find a gift for Bianca. Finally he had an opportunity to visit the shop. A cherubic man with white hair and a sizeable paunch greeted Nico when he entered. "How may I help you, signore?" he asked in a strong Pisan dialect.

"I'm looking for a gift for a friend," Nico replied as he scanned the silver rings and bracelets arrayed on a shelf behind the shopkeeper.

The man stepped aside to give Nico a better view. His lips curled up in a smile. "Each piece is a unique design crafted by my son, who is the finest silversmith in Pisa. He's a master member of the Metal-workers' Guild."

The man selected an elaborate bracelet from the shelf and held it so Nico could examine it closely. "Just look at the exquisite detail in this piece."

"It is beautiful," Nico agreed, "but I'm looking for a piece that will remind my friend of Pisa whenever she looks at it."

A woman who had been working at a bench in the corner of the shop came forward. She held out a necklace with a delicately curved white pendant suspended on a braided cord. Nico took the unusual milky-white pendant. "The double twisting curves represent two people joined together forever," the woman said proudly.

Nico turned the piece over in his hand. "It's lovely," he said as he traced a finger over the pendant's graceful curves. "It looks and feels like polished glass. What is the material? Is it glass or stone?"

"Neither. It is whalebone," she answered, her thin smile broadening. "Whales live in the sea off the coast of Pisa. Every month or so, when I'm at the fish market, a bone looks up at me and tells me that it wants to be carved." From her bench, she retrieved a carving in the shape of a little boy. "Usually, I carve them into statues, like this one. But the one you are holding didn't want to become a statue. It told me that it wanted to serve a special purpose."

Nico left the shop clutching the carefully wrapped pendant. Maybe someday he would take Bianca to Pisa and introduce her to the woman who had created the striking necklace.

Now, worried that he might be late for his meeting with Massimo, he hurried along the riverfront to the Ponte di Mezzo bridge, where they had planned to meet. Massimo was engrossed in watching an obviously inexperienced steersman fighting against the turbulent water to keep his heavily laden barge from crashing into the river-bank. Nico joined Massimo, and as they watched the craft, Massimo asked, "Is our friend Vittorio recovering from his wound?"

"The army provided a room for Vittorio to stay at the garrison overnight, so the medico could tend to his wound."

"Ah, then he's being well cared for."

On their way to accountant Fonte's office, Nico wondered aloud, "Each of the rebels captured yesterday already had a sword. So why was Grassi taking delivery of a second shipment of weapons?"

"I can think of two possibilities," Massimo offered. "Either the weapons are for another band of rebels, or Grassi intends to recruit more men to his cause. Signor Fonte has good information sources; perhaps he can tell us."

When they reached the central piazza, they noticed a man exiting Fonte's office. It took a moment before they recognized the figure. "It's Nello!" Nico shouted. Massimo shot across the piazza in pursuit of the fugitive, with Nico close behind. Suddenly, Nico stopped, turned, and ran toward Fonte's office.

Inside, he found the accountant collapsed on the floor. Nico's cries of "Fonte! Signor Fonte!" elicited no response. Nico leaned close to the battered man to listen for breathing. Rapid and shallow. Fonte's tunic had been torn open as though someone had tried ripping it from his body. He had no open cuts, but red and purple marked the many bruises on his head and chest.

Nico ran outside and accosted the first man he saw in the piazza and boomed, "A man is hurt! I need a medico! Where is the nearest medico?"

The stunned stranger raised an arm and pointed. Nico grabbed the man's outstretched arm and pulled him along. "Show me! Where is he?"

Forced into a run by Nico's tugging, the man led Nico out of the piazza. They had gone less than a block when the man pointed to a building and said, "There."

Nico charged into the physician's office, startling the physician, a patient whose leg was being bandaged, and the physician's apprentice. "A man has been beaten. He's unconscious. He needs help... immediately," Nico implored.

The patient, a bull-necked man with the muscular build of a

laborer, was the first to respond. Looking at the physician, he said, "Go. I can finish wrapping my leg."

The physician, uncertain at first whether to leave his patient, nodded to acknowledge the patient's consent, took a satchel from his desk, and said to Nico, "Show me." Nico hurried the physician and his apprentice to the accountant's office. The physician made a cursory examination of the unresponsive Fonte, looked up at his apprentice and said, "I can't treat him here. He needs to be taken to the hospital. Go fetch a wagon."

Nico wrote a note for Massimo and fastened it to the door of Fonte's office. Then he followed the wagon carrying the accountant to the Hospital of Santa Chiara. Founded more than two centuries past by Pope Alexander, Santa Chiara was Pisa's largest and oldest hospital.

Nico waited in an anteroom while the physician and the hospital staff treated Signor Fonte. He sat alone for more than an hour before Massimo entered the room and asked, "What happened?"

Nico described how he had found the accountant beaten and unconscious. "I'm still waiting to hear about his condition. What about Nello? Did you catch him?"

"Yes, I caught him." With a devilish look in his eye, Massimo added, "I had hoped that he would resist me; unfortunately, he didn't. I gave him over to a group of soldiers. They're taking him to a prison cell at Cittadella Nuova. I told them that Nello is a convicted criminal who escaped from the Stinche prison in Florence. They assured me that he won't escape their custody."

Nico and Massimo waited another hour before an Augustinian monk informed them that Signor Fonte was awake and they could see him. Fonte's bruises were covered with salve. Its gray hue matched his complexion, drained of color by the trauma of his attack. In a feeble voice, he explained that Nello had been furious with him for revealing the location where the governor had been held. "He called me a coward and a traitor. Over and over, he repeated that epithet as he kept pummeling me. He didn't give me a chance to defend my position. I tried to tell him that I want Governor Gondi gone as much as he does, but he wouldn't listen. He just kept shouting and hitting me. Eventually, everything went black until I found myself here. I can't move without pain, but the medico said I suffered no permanent injury and I'll recover in a few days."

Massimo said, "Nello will pay for what he did to you. We spotted him as he was leaving your office. While Nico found a medico who took you to the hospital, I chased after Nello. He didn't get far before I caught him and turned him over to an army patrol."

Nico told Fonte about the governor's rescue and the capture of those who were holding him hostage. "There were no injuries. The rebels surrendered without a fight. A boy who was with the rebels told us that the rebel leader, Salvadore Grassi, had gone to receive a shipment of weapons. We moved quickly and were able to capture him and the weapons."

Fonte listened keenly but said nothing. Nico continued, "Since all the rebels who were captured had weapons, we don't understand why Grassi would be receiving another delivery of weapons. Grassi has refused to say. He's refused to say anything. Do you know if there is another band of rebels?"

Fonte took several shallow breaths before answering. "There is no other rebel band. Those holding the governor believed that their bold action would inspire others to join them... that their numbers would grow." Fonte winced as he continued. "While there is no other organized band, there are rogues who act on their own. Nello is one of them."

Nico could tell that Signor Fonte was growing tired, but he had one more issue to broach with the accountant. "When we spoke last, you showed me evidence of Governor Gondi's infidelity. If you are willing to give me the letter that accuses Gondi of having an affair, I will see that it is delivered to the proper officials in Florence, and I will plead your case with them that Gondi be replaced. It would be a false hope for you to believe that the Florentine Signoria can be persuaded to withdraw from Pisa, but I'm certain the Signoria wants its administration to be fair and just."

"I'll deliver the letter to you when I'm able to leave here," Fonte replied, and closed his eyes.

41

FLORENCE, SEPTEMBER 22

Sun streaming through the large south-facing windows gave the conference room a warm, cheerful feeling. Nico, Vittorio, and Massimo were already seated around the table when Chancellor Scala arrived. A tall wiry man, whom Nico recognized as the vendor from a nearby produce shop, followed Scala into the room and set a tray of dried fruit and assorted cheeses on the table. Gesturing toward the food tray, Scala said, "This amenity is to acknowledge your many successes in Pisa."

From the items on the tray, Scala selected a dried fig and a slice of pecorino cheese. He seated himself next to Massimo and said, "The dispatches sent to me by Messer Argenti suggest that we have much to discuss, but before we begin, have you recovered from your injury, Signor Colombo?"

Vittorio pulled back the sleeve of his tunic to expose his wound. "As you can see, all that remains is a small scar. The cut was deep, so it could have been a problem were it not for the skill of the army medico who treated it. I credit him for my rapid healing."

Scala said, "I understand it was the rebel leader, Signor Grassi, who inflicted the wound."

"Yes. It was a foolish move. He was outnumbered and drew his dagger in desperation. He and his cohorts are now being held at the army garrison in Pisa."

Scala turned to Nico. "Will you be the prosecutor in Signor Grassi's trial?"

"I haven't decided, and I'd welcome your advice. Grassi could be charged with insurrection, supplying weapons to rebels, and smuggling."

Massimo said, "It's also likely that he ordered the killing of his wife's cousin."

Nico nodded. "Yes, we believe he is guilty of that crime as well, but at present, we have only Signora Gondi's statement to support that charge. When she was being held captive, she heard a man say that he had one of his relatives killed. Circumstantial evidence suggests that it was Grassi who made the statement. Unfortunately, Signora Gondi only heard the words spoken by someone in another room; she didn't actually see Grassi admit his culpability. If other witnesses, or the killers themselves, can be found, this could become another serious charge against Grassi, but Signora Gondi's testimony alone isn't sufficient to make a case."

Nico continued, "Vittorio, Massimo, and I are principles who will be witnesses to the insurrection, weapons, and smuggling charges, so it may be preferable to have someone else as the prosecutor."

"Do you have someone in mind?" Scala asked.

"Luca Sasso is a capable prosecutor."

Scala rubbed his chin as he recalled the man Nico had recommended. "Has Messer Sasso ever appeared before a tribunal of the Eight of Public Safety?"

"No," Nico replied simply, unsure whether to press his suggestion further.

"Let me review his record before we make a decision," Scala said and moved to a different topic. "The man who sold the weapons to the Pisans, Rinaldo Bastine, can a case be made that he knew his buyers were insurrectionists?"

"The weapons were delivered by the supervisor of Bastine's iron smelter. He claims that Bastine was aware that the weapons were going to rebels. He's being held in a cell at the army garrison in Pisa, and he's unhappy with his accommodations," Massimo said with sarcasm heavy in his voice. "He'd like to return to his family and his comfortable home in Florence."

Massimo's phrasing brought bursts of laughter from Nico and Vittorio. "Bah," Vittorio snorted. "All prisoners want to return to a comfortable life. He should have thought of that before he agreed to do Bastine's bidding,"

"He may be among the few fortunate ones," Massimo said. "Nico offered him a way to expedite his release."

Nico clarified his position, saying, "To shorten his prison sentence, he's agreed to testify against Bastine. He's willing to attest that Bastine told him the weapons were destined for Pisan loyalists who wanted to gain independence from Florence. He's also given me the names of two other workers at the smelter who heard Bastine say the weapons were going to rebels. I haven't spoken with either of the workers yet, but I'm confident I can convince them to testify against Bastine."

Vittorio quipped, "In the short time since his graduation, our lawyer has nurtured secrets of persuasion that he wasn't taught at the university."

Scala showed a thin smile. "Every successful lawyer learns those techniques eventually, and the best learn more quickly than the others. Are you intending to prosecute Signor Bastine?" he asked.

"I'm looking forward to it," Nico replied. Aside from the crime of providing weapons to insurrectionists, Nico had another reason for wanting to see Rinaldo Bastine punished. He chose not to mention what Gemma Bastine had told him regarding her brother's behavior toward women servants, but he took comfort knowing that if Rinaldo were sent to prison, the servants would be freed from abuse.

Nico took advantage of a lull in the conversation while Scala selected a dried apricot from the food tray. "There is another matter," he said tentatively and paused to gauge Scala's reaction. When Scala looked at him curiously and said nothing, Nico continued, "Among Pisans, there is nearly universal dislike and distrust of Governor Gondi. During our time in Pisa, we've heard many examples of how he has treated Pisans wrongfully. Those instances don't justify his abduction, but they do make us question whether Signor Gondi is a suitable person to represent Florence."

Scala nodded. "I've heard accusations of improper conduct by Governor Gondi, but none that rise to a level that would demand his recall."

Nico handed Scala the letter given to him by accountant Pippo Fonte. Scala's jaw dropped as he read. With incredulity in his voice, Scala probed, "Tessa wrote this? The ambassador's daughter? She is accusing her sister of having an adulterous affair with Governor Gondi?"

"Yes," Nico replied. "And the governor's aide supports the assertions stated in that letter. If it becomes widely known that the Florentine Signoria appoints men of such shameful character to represent our republic..." He let that thought hang a moment, then said, "I believe we should inform the Signoria of this situation."

Scala read the letter again. "If we were to bring this matter to the Signoria, they would deliberate. Without firm pressure to drive a resolution, that's what the Signoria does, it deliberates. Governor Gondi's cousin is a member of the Signoria, and he would undoubtedly make the deliberations interminable." Scala's expression turned from serious to a smile. "I'm in no position to press the Signoria for a quick resolution, but there is someone who can... the archbishop. He won't tolerate having Florence represented by a notorious adulterer, and he has the power to force the Signoria to take swift action. I'll arrange a meeting with the archbishop."

∾

Luca Sasso was leaving his favorite trattoria when Nico joined him in the piazza. Luca greeted his colleague and placed an arm on Nico's shoulder. "Ah, Nico, you've returned to Florence. Is your business in Pisa finished?"

"My business in Pisa may be at an end, but it leaves a matter for us to discuss. Can we meet in your office?"

Surprised by Nico's answer, Luca shot a sideways glance at his friend. "Certainly," he replied, his curiosity stoked.

As soon as they had seated themselves at the table in Luca's office, Nico asked, "How full is your docket? Do you have any pressing cases?"

In a blasé voice, Luca replied, "There are two cases looming. One case involves a man who was cited for public drunkenness. I've sent him away several times in the past. Each time, he serves a short stint in a cell and then resumes his destructive ways as soon as he's released. He's not the only one with that problem. It's too bad those people, the ones with the same affliction, don't join together to help each other.

"My other case is a carpenter who's been accused of selling shoddy products. That case appeared on my docket, but I intend to transfer it to the Carpenters' Guild. They've proven themselves capable of disciplining their members."

Luca leaned forward toward Nico, who was seated across the table. Looking directly at Nico, and said, "Enough of these obtuse questions, my friend. Tell me, what's prompting them?"

"Vittorio, Massimo, and I successfully uncovered an organized group of rebels in Pisa. Their leader is a man named Salvadore Grassi. In addition to being the rebel leader, he's involved in several other crimes. Currently, he is being held at the army garrison in Pisa. I suggested to Chancellor Scala that you be the one to prosecute Signor Grassi." Nico steepled his hands on the table and waited for Luca's reaction.

Luca straightened. He pressed his back firmly against his chair and his palms hard against the tabletop, so hard that his knuckles turned white. "Me? Why me? You captured him, and rebellion is a security issue. You are the Security Commission's lawyer, so shouldn't you be the one to prosecute him?"

"Since I was involved in Grassi's capture, I will be one of the witnesses against him, so it would be best to have someone else as prosecutor." Nico paused a moment before adding, "And there is another reason. Grassi isn't the only one who committed a crime. Rinaldo Bastine is the person who sold the weapons to the rebels."

"I'm not surprised to hear that Bastine is involved," Luca interjected. "You know my longstanding history with him."

"I made a promise to Bastine's sister Gemma and to the priest, Father Giorgio, that I would see that Rinaldo is made to account for his many crimes. And I can't effectively prosecute both Grassi and Bastine."

"Hmmm," Luca murmured as he thought further about Nico's proposal. "I've never appeared before an Eight of Public Safety tribunal. Is Chancellor Scala agreeable to having me prosecute Grassi?"

"Certainly," Nico said. "The Chancellor is familiar with your record." Then he chuckled. "I've only appeared before an Eight tribunal once. We can muddle our way through their procedures together."

Luca ran a hand slowly through his hair. "Tell me about Grassi."

"My colleagues on the Security Commission and I caught him accepting the weapons. You can call us as witnesses, as well as the army scout who accompanied us. Grassi was paying for the weapons with smuggled silver."

"Smuggled silver?" Luca echoed.

"Yes, Grassi is... or was, the supervisor of a shipping company. He used the ships to smuggle silver from North Africa so he could pay for the weapons. Vittorio can give you details about the smuggling operation. He can give you the names of the ships and identify the sailors who were involved. Vittorio collaborated with an army patrol to capture one of Grassi's underlings, who had been transporting the silver. The scoundrel has refused to talk despite being in a cell at the army garrison for more than a week. He seems to believe that someone, probably Grassi, would arrange for his release. I suspect that he'll become talkative when he learns that Grassi is roosting in a nearby cell."

"Have charges been brought against the sailors for their part in the smuggling?"

"No. We can discuss them after Grassi is convicted. Captain Carfi, he's the commandant at the army garrison in Pisa, has men monitoring the ships. They're prepared to seize any future contraband."

Luca had moved to his desk to make notes as Nico continued speaking.

Nico said, "The rebels abducted Governor Gondi and his wife. Since Grassi was the rebel leader, he was certainly involved in the abduction. I haven't interrogated any of the rebels, but some of them will probably be willing to testify regarding Grassi's role in exchange for a lessening of the charges against them. The Eight of Public Safety considers the abduction of an emissary of the republic to be a serious offense. They will want Grassi charged for that crime."

"From what you are telling me, I could spend my entire career prosecuting this one individual," Luca said with a smirk. "Surely, that must be the extent of his transgressions."

"There is some evidence that Grassi ordered the killing of one of his relatives, but the evidence is insufficient to charge Grassi with that crime. I suggest that you not pursue that charge unless other evidence comes to light."

Luca threw up his hands. "Rebellion, smuggling, abduction, killing. Could there possibly be anything else?"

Nico thought for a moment, then laughed as he said, "Grassi tried to escape and, while attempting to flee, he stabbed Vittorio with a knife, so you could also charge him with assaulting a government official."

Turning serious, Nico said, "Now that you know the full scope of Grassi's crimes, are you willing to serve as prosecutor?"

"Absolutely. It will be a welcome change from the mundane cases I've prosecuted recently." Luca said firmly, then added, "But you can expect that I may call on you for advice."

42

FLORENCE, SEPTEMBER 24

Nico and Massimo arrived at the Uccello at the same time. Nico escorted his colleague to one of the private rooms where a large table had been readied for guests. A server carrying two bottles of Chianti followed them. As he set the bottles on the table, he said, "Donato is busy with customers. He'll join you as soon as he can detach himself."

Massimo scanned the table. "There are five settings. Who else will be joining us?"

Nico replied, "Bianca, Alessa, and Donato, if he can get free. His customers enjoy sharing stories with him. Some of their stories are banal, but others are fascinating. Regardless, Donato feels that he owes everyone the courtesy of listening."

Nico noticed Massimo's eyes light up upon hearing that Nico's sister Alessa would be joining them, but rather than joshing his friend, he turned serious. "Luca Sasso has agreed to prosecute Salvadore Grassi. Luca is delighted to have an opportunity for something other than his usual cases, which he referred to as mundane. I'm sure he'll enjoy the challenge because it will be a complicated trial given all the laws that Grassi has violated."

"Will Luca file charges against all of Grassi's infractions?"

"I reviewed Grassi's role in each of the crimes with Luca, but the decision of which to pursue rests with him. Providing weapons to rebels and abducting the governor are major offenses and, in my judgement, there is ample evidence to obtain convictions on these charges. With little effort, Luca should be able to find enough evidence for a smuggling conviction, although smuggling is a lesser offense. Ordering the killing of his wife's cousin is a major crime, but thus far, there is only minimal evidence against Grassi. I advised him to defer action on that charge, but, as I said, the decision is his."

"With Luca prosecuting Grassi, you'll be able to devote your energy to Rinaldo Bastine," Massimo pointed out.

"Yes, I'm eager to declaw that beast. I filed charges against him yesterday. There was an open date next week on the tribunal's calendar, so I requested that as a trial date, although Bastine's lawyer may ask for an extension if he wants more time to prepare his defense."

"Does one week give you enough time?" Massimo asked.

"I could be ready by tomorrow," Nico said confidently. "Alberto, the supervisor of the iron smelter, gave me the names of two of the iron workers who heard Rinaldo admit that he knew the weapons were going to rebels. Both men are named Guido." Nico chuckled. "One is a bull-chested man. They call him Guidono, big Guido. They say he can lift twice his weight in iron slugs. The other one is Guidino, little Guido. He's a wisp of a man who tends the furnace because he's too small to tote iron bars.

"I met with both Guidos this morning. When they understood that Rinaldo would no longer manage the smelter if he were convicted, they readily agreed to testify. Both men had been hired by Rinaldo, but they said he is so mean spirited that it's impossible to remain loyal to him. Alberto, the supervisor, is the third witness who heard Rinaldo admit his crime. With three witnesses prepared to testify against him, a conviction is all but certain. Soldiers should be transporting Alberto to Florence today."

"He was brought here from the army garrison in Pisa yesterday,"

Massimo corrected. "I stayed in my quarters at the army camp last night. Before I left the camp this morning, I passed the stockade and saw both Alberto and Salvadore Grassi. They are being held in isolation from each other and from other prisoners. I gave the guards permission to let Alberto's wife visit him." Massimo held up a folded sheet. "He asked me to deliver this note to his wife. When I bring the note to her, I would like to tell her whether he will be charged with a crime. Have you decided whether to charge him with delivering the weapons?"

"Since he'll be testifying against Rinaldo, and he gave me the names of the two Guidos as other witnesses, he merits consideration. Rinaldo is the scourge who contaminates those around him. He deserves a long prison sentence, but I don't believe that justice demands Alberto's punishment."

A server entered the room and approached Nico. "Forgive me for interrupting Messer Argenti. A member of the clergy wishes to speak with you."

"Father Giorgio?" Massimo speculated.

"It must be," Nico agreed. To the server, he said, "Send him here." As the server turned to leave, Nico added, "And have a place set so the priest can join us for dinner."

Nico and Massimo rose to greet the priest. "I'm pleased to see you, Father," Nico said, "although it's been my experience that visiting priests are often bearers of inauspicious news."

Father Giorgio held up a hand dismissively and chuckled. "Ah, yes. It troubles me that some people welcome our visits little more than they would welcome the angel of death."

Nico poured wine for the priest, who held the glass aloft to study its color before taking a sip. "An especially smooth Chianti," he observed. He took another sip, then set the glass down before responding to Nico's comment. "I bring information that may be of interest to you. You can judge whether it is favorable or ominous news. Yesterday, Rinaldo Bastine received a copy of the charges against him. I assume you are the one who filed the charges."

Nodding, Nico said, "I am."

"Initially, Rinaldo set the paper aside as though ignoring it would make the charges vanish, but gradually his irritation mounted. He began muttering to himself and then started yelling at the servants for no reason. When his father asked what was troubling him, Rinaldo said, 'It is not a matter for you, old man,' and he stormed from the room."

"Where you there? Did you witness Rinaldo's actions?" Massimo asked.

"No. I'm recounting what his sister Gemma told me. She feared for the safety of the women servants, so she took them to a friend's villa near Fiesole. I tried to persuade her to leave as well, but she would not. She feels that she must remain at home to care for her mother and father."

"Do you believe she is in danger?" Nico asked.

"No. I know the family's chef to be an honorable man. He will see that Gemma is not harmed."

The men continued discussing Rinaldo's behavior until their attention was captured by Nico's sister Alessa bouncing into the room, followed by Bianca. Alessa immediately discarded her cloak, but Bianca kept herself wrapped in a long mantello. "Behold, Flora, the goddess of flowers and Spring," Alessa announced, and with a flourish, she whisked the mantello from Bianca's shoulders to reveal a flowing white gown printed with images of springtime flowers.

Bianca pivoted, and the fabric spun as though floating on air. The men's mouths dropped open, and they remained speechless until Alessa prompted them. "Say something!"

Nico leaned forward to examine the colorful designs. "I've never seen a dress like that, painted all over with flowers."

Bianca flashed a proud smile. "They're not painted, they're printed. The color is dyed into the cloth." Then, immediately, she realized it wasn't the technique that astonished the men, it was the design. Women's dresses were made from single color fabrics. They might be embroidered or decorated with jeweled stones, but they weren't covered all over with images. Bianca's flowered gown was outside the fashion realm.

Massimo said, "Outstanding. If I were to conjure a vision of the goddess Flora, she would be you, and that is exactly what she would be wearing."

Father Giorgio shook his head, totally confused by the episode, until Nico explained. "Bianca has her own business in Siena, where she designs unique dresses for fashionable women. My artist friend Sandro Botticelli asked her to create a dress to symbolize the goddess Flora. At Lorenzo de' Medici's urging, Sandro is making a painting he calls 'Primavera.' Bianca agreed to pose wearing that gown as inspiration for the painting."

Nico looked up at Bianca and asked, "Has Sandro seen the dress?"

"Not yet. He'll see it tomorrow when I have the first session posing for him."

Nico's brow furrowed. "At his loft in the Santa Novella district?" he asked. Bianca nodded. Nico took her hand. "I don't think it's safe for a proper woman to wander through the Santa Novella district." *Nor might it be safe for you to be alone with Sandro in his loft,* Nico said to himself.

"She won't be alone," Alessa said. "I'll go with her, and we won't be wandering through the streets. Sandro gave us directions to his loft."

It may be an injustice to my good friend, but I'm not reassured by the prospect of two women I care for being in Sandro's loft, Nico thought.

Massimo sensed Nico's concern, which he saw as an opportunity to spend time with Alessa. He turned to Alessa and said, "I haven't seen Sandro recently. May I accompany you?" She answered with a warm smile.

43

FLORENCE, SEPTEMBER 30

Rinaldo Bastine trial -day one

Other men hustling through Florence's central piazza had their cloaks pulled tight to ward off the cool morning chill, but not Nico Argenti. Warmed by the opportunity to bring Rinaldo Bastine to justice, Nico ignored the cold. He moved at a quicker than usual pace and his nose sensed only the city's pleasant aromas. If there were occasional raindrops, he managed to avoid them.

Inside the Palazzo della Signoria, a crowd filled the corridor leading to the Eight of Public Safety's tribunal chamber. "Why can't we be admitted?" one man snarled at the Guardia members who secured the chamber entrance.

"Other tribunals allow observers in a gallery. Why not this one?" complained another man.

"The Eight do not permit non-participants to attend their tribunals," a Guardia officer replied, but his explanation did not mollify the protesters.

A notary standing behind the officers recognized Nico and beckoned him forward. "No one has been charged with abetting an insurrection in many years, so this trial is drawing much public attention," the notary said as he escorted Nico into the trial chamber. "People have trouble accepting that the Eight refuse to have their proceedings disrupted by unruly audiences."

Nico moved across the room, past the prosecution table where he would be seated during the trial, and exited through a side door to the area where witnesses would be closeted in small rooms awaiting their turns to testify. Armorer Prospero da Aniella and his Chancery clerk escort were ensconced in one room. Alberto Palumbo paced nervously in a second room. His minder had little success in trying to calm the anxious iron smelter supervisor.

The third room was unoccupied. Bruno Fiorello and the two guards bringing him from the Stinche prison had not yet arrived. Since Nico had spoken with the two guards the previous day, he was confident that Fiorello would be ready when the trial began. Only three rooms were designated especially for witnesses, but the notary assured Nico that Guidino and Guidono, the two remaining witnesses, had arrived and were settled in rooms elsewhere in the building.

Nico sat at the prosecution table reviewing his notes when Luca Sasso joined him. Luca wanted to observe an Eight of Public Safety tribunal to become familiar with the magistrates before he appeared in their court to prosecute Salvadore Grassi, so Nico had invited Luca, rather than a notary, to serve as his adjutant. "Do you expect Rinaldo to appear," Luca asked, "or do you think he has fled the country?"

"He's too arrogant to believe that he could be convicted, so he won't flee," Nico responded. "I've tried to keep the names of my witnesses private, but Rinaldo's lawyer has informants everywhere, so he probably knows the strength of the case against his client. But even knowing that, the lawyer won't advise Rinaldo to leave Florence because that would mean the lawyer wouldn't be able to collect his fee."

Noise from the crowd outside, still upset at being barred from entering, filled the chamber as the door opened to admit Rinaldo

Bastine and his lawyer. Rinaldo cast an icy stare at Nico as he walked to the defense table. In contrast to his own thick portfolio, Nico noticed that the lawyer, a short, wiry man, carried only a thin writing tablet. The lawyer startled upon seeing Luca Sasso sitting at the prosecution table. "You've gone against him before. What do you expect?" Nico asked Luca.

"He's far from being the most honorable of men. I swear there've been instances where he's won cases with derelicts who were persuaded to testify for the payment of a few coins... but this is a high-profile case, so I doubt he'll try that sham here. He also has an uncanny ability to find legal exceptions. I suspect that will be his approach in this trial: using trivial details to influence the magistrates."

A door at the front of the room opened. Three magistrates in formal black robes with broad red sashes signifying their superior status entered and took their positions on the dais at the front of the room. Tribunals conducted by the Eight lacked the formality observed in other courts. The senior magistrate, seated between his two colleagues, surveyed the room and, seeing that the prosecution and defense were prepared, said, "Messer Argenti, you may begin."

After a quick glance toward the defense table, Nico rose, faced the magistrates, and asserted, "Honorable magistrates, the Republic of Florence accuses Signor Rinaldo Bastine of committing the crime of treason by the act of supplying weapons to men in the province of Pisa whose avowed purpose was to foster insurrection against the republic. Witnesses will testify that Signor Bastine did so knowingly."

Nico signaled the court clerk, who fetched the first witness. "State your name."

"Prospero da Aniella."

"Signor da Aniella, describe your occupation."

"I am a member of the Arte dei Corazzai e Spadai, the Armorers and Swordsmiths Guild," the witness replied, his confidence growing in response to Nico's calm voice. "I am the owner of the company that has built the finest quality arms ever since its founding by my great-grandfather. We are proud suppliers to the Florentine army, who have used our weapons to defend the Republic of Florence for nearly a century."

"Do you supply arms to customers other than the Florentine army?" Nico asked.

"Yes. Our customers also include private individuals and armies of other countries... all allies of Florence," he added quickly.

"Is the defendant, Signor Rinaldo Bastine, one of your customers?"

"Yes."

"Describe your most recent relationship with Signor Bastine."

"Approximately three weeks past, Signor Bastine came to my shop to place an order for ten blades. He had no preference for the style of blade as long as they could be delivered quickly. He said quality was not important because the blades would be used by men who were untrained and inexperienced."

"Did he tell you who would be receiving the blades?"

"No, he did not."

Nico looked down at his notes and touched a finger to an item on the page. "Did Signor Bastine have any request regarding the marking of the blades?"

Da Aniella's mouth dropped open upon realizing he had forgotten to mention the markings as he and Nico had discussed. "We are proud of our products, so we always mark them with our company's insignia, but Signor Bastine requested that the blades have no markings." He looked at the magistrates with a soulful expression and added, "He was the customer, so we complied with the strange request."

The magistrates had no questions for Signor da Aniella, so Nico dismissed him. While they waited for the second witness to appear, Rinaldo looked for reassurance to his lawyer, who whispered, "His testimony means little. All it proves is that you purchased arms and there is no crime in that. The comment about wanting no markings on the blades is an incidental detail that does not prove criminal intent."

The side door opened, and two prison guards escorted a beaming Bruno Fiorello to the witness stand. At the sight of Fiorello, Rinaldo leaned close to his lawyer and huffed, "Look at him with that smug expression. At one time, he would do anything I asked, and now he's here to speak against me. The miserable scum."

The lawyer had seen this situation before and counseled his client, "Don't fret about him. He's a convicted criminal, so his testimony won't sway the magistrates' decision. They know Fiorello will say anything because the prosecutor bought his appearance with the offer of a reduced sentence."

Nico asked Fiorello to state his name and his relationship to Rinaldo Bastine. In a booming voice, Fiorello stated emphatically, "I am Signor Bruno Fiorello. I used to work for the defendant. He trusted me to do whatever he asked without question, and I never failed him."

"What was your role in the delivery of weapons to Pisa?" Nico asked.

"I had no part in that," Fiorello replied. "Anyone could make deliveries. He didn't need a man of my talent for that menial task."

Nico scanned his notes to verify that Fiorello's response corresponded to his pretrial statements. "So, you were not involved in the delivery of arms to men in Pisa," Nico repeated. "But were you aware that the defendant was engaged in shipping arms to rebels in Pisa?"

"Yes, I heard him boasting about it to the workers at the smelter. It's typical of him. He boasts to everyone about his accomplishments and complains to all about his troubles."

"Tell us exactly what you heard."

"He said that he had a contact in Pisa who wanted arms from an armorer in Florence and that the arms were going to men who wanted their independence. Signor Bastine said that he was delighted to receive silver bars as payment because the bars were hidden from the eyes of tax collectors."

Satisfied with Fiorello's responses, Nico indicated that he had no more questions of that witness. Addressing Rinaldo Bastine's lawyer, the senior magistrate asked, "Do you intend to recall this witness when the defense presents its case?"

When the lawyer indicated that he did not intend to cross examine Fiorello, the senior magistrate summoned the two prison guards to his table. "Signor Fiorello has fulfilled his commitment to testify. Therefore, as previously agreed, by order of this court, Signor Fiorello's sentence is hereby revised from confinement at the Stinche prison to exile. He has informed the court that he intends to leave the Republic of Florence and travel to Genoa. You are instructed to escort him to the port of Livorno and see that he boards a ship destined for Genoa."

Again, Bastine's lawyer sought to reassure his client. "Did you hear what Fiorello said? He said the weapons were for men who want their independence. There is no crime in wanting independence. He did not allege you were aware that the men intended to violate the law. Tomorrow, when we present our defense, I will use those facts to discredit his testimony."

At the prosecution table, Luca Sasso turned to Nico. "I can't justify in my own mind that exile is a sufficient punishment for someone guilty of murder."

"I have misgivings as well," Nico responded, "but his testimony is helping to convict Bastine, who also bears responsibility for the murder." Nico tapped Sasso on the shoulder as he added, "At least Fiorello is now Genoa's problem."

In keeping with the Eight of Public Safety's bent for efficiency, the court notary had already gone to fetch Nico's next witness. He entered the chamber followed by Alberto Palumbo, the iron works supervisor. Rinaldo knew that the supervisor had been apprehended and imprisoned in Pisa, but he didn't know that Palumbo had been brought to Florence to testify against his boss. "Judas!" he bawled loud enough to draw the attention of the three magistrates.

"Quiet!" the senior magistrate reprimanded. "One more outburst and you will be removed from this chamber."

In response to Nico's questions, Signor Palumbo introduced himself and described his job as the supervisor at Rinaldo's iron smelter. "Are the person who delivered the weapons to Pisa?" Nico asked.

Palumbo twisted sideways in the witness stand to avoid looking at his former employer. Beads of sweat formed on his forehead as he said, "Yes. Signor Bastine told me to deliver the weapons to a Signor Grassi in Pisa, and to receive silver bars as payment. I made two deliveries. The first delivery went without any problems, but while I was making the second delivery, Signor Grassi and I were captured and taken to the army garrison at Pisa."

"When you made the deliveries, did you know that Signor Grassi represented a rebel group?"

Palumbo looked at the floor and twisted his hands in agitation. "When I returned with the silver after making the first delivery, Signor Bastine took one of the bars and pranced around the smelter like he was a parade horse." Upon glancing at his notes, Nico realized Palumbo had deviated from his prepared script. He shot Palumbo a look, but the witness ignored Nico's admonishment and continued. "He fondled that silver bar like it was a woman's breast."

Bastine's lawyer jumped up. "Honorable magistrates, this scandalous characterization is unconscionable."

The senior magistrate raised a hand to squelch the lawyer, then pointed a finger at the witness. "Signor Palumbo, you will confine your testimony to the facts as you know them and refrain from expressing opinions and stating analogies."

Palumbo dipped his head submissively and wiped the line of sweat from above his eyes. To reset Palumbo's thinking, Nico rephrased his earlier question. "Did Signor Bastine mention that the arms were going to a rebel group?"

"Yes, he boasted... can I say boasted?" The senior magistrate nodded.

"Signor Bastine boasted that the weapons had gone to a group of rebels in Pisa and that his contact, Signor Grassi, expected they would need more as their numbers grew. I am not the only one who heard him say this."

For emphasis, Nico asked, "Are you certain he said 'rebels'?"

"Yes, that is what he said, a group of rebels."

Pleased with the testimony, Nico dismissed Palumbo. Bastine's lawyer placed a hand on his client's arm. "There is no reason for concern. It will be your word against his."

Nico ended his presentation by calling his remaining witnesses, the two Guidos, who worked at the smelter, Guidono and Guidino. The witness stand creaked under his weight when hefty Guidono leaned against it to testify that Rinaldo Bastine had proudly displayed the silver he received from Pisan rebels as payment for a shipment of weapons. Guidino followed and echoed his workmate's testimony.

"They're only laborers. They don't know what they heard," Bastine breathed into his lawyer's ear.

The lawyer leaned away from his client. "You should have learned to control your mouth. If Palumbo were the only witness, it would be your word against his. But with these two also speaking out against you..."

The senior magistrate confirmed that Nico had no other witnesses. He glanced at his two colleagues, and with their agreement, he announced, "This tribunal is recessed until tomorrow, at which time the defense will present its case."

Nico and Luca Sasso remained until the others had left the courtroom. Sasso said, "That went exactly as you had planned."

"Except for Palumbo's colorful description of Rinaldo's attraction to the silver," Nico laughed.

"Do you have a clue to what form the defense will take?" Sasso asked.

Nico spread his hands wide.

∽

Rinaldo Bastine trial - day two

Unlike the previous day, no men blocked the entrance of the tribunal chamber when Nico arrived. As he made his way to the prosecution table, he saw Bastine's lawyer sitting alone at the defense table. Generally, defendants and their lawyers arrived together, but Bastine must have been delayed. Luca Sasso's legal commitments kept him from joining Nico on the trial's final day; however, Luca had made Nico promise to bring him the news of the outcome as soon as the proceeding ended.

When the bells of the nearby Santa Maria del Fiore cathedral sounded the hour, the court notary conferred briefly with Bastine's lawyer before exiting the room through the side door that led to the magistrates' quarters. Moments later, he returned, followed by the three magistrates. As soon as his fellow jurors had taken their seats, the senior magistrate addressed Bastine's lawyer. "Why is the defendant not present?"

The lawyer rose slowly. "Honorable magistrate, I cannot say. I have not seen Signor Bastine this morning, but I am prepared to proceed with the defense."

The three magistrates consulted with each other for several minutes. Finally, the senior magistrate announced, "It is unusual to continue without the defendant present," he gestured to his right, "but my esteemed colleague has informed us that it is not unprecedented. You may present the defense."

The lawyer picked up his notes and scanned them for a moment before beginning. "Honorable magistrates, yesterday you heard from several prosecution witnesses. I ask that you examine substance and motivation for their testimony. The prosecution's first witness, Signor da Aniella, the armorer, stated that my client purchased arms from him. But the purchase of arms is not a crime. Many of us have purchased arms for ceremonial purposes or to be given as gifts.

"The second witness, Signor Fiorello" — the lawyer affected a snicker with his mention of Fiorello's name — "is a convicted criminal who testified in exchange for having his prison sentence commuted. Can we doubt that he would say anything to gain his freedom? I ask that his testimony be dismissed as being untrustworthy."

Before the lawyer could continue his presentation, a loud creak of the door at the rear of the chamber swinging open drew everyone's attention. Vittorio and Massimo marched into the room, holding Rinaldo Bastine between them. They propelled him forward to the defense table and pushed him down onto a chair. Massimo winked at Nico as he and Vittorio went to take positions against the wall where the two prison guards had stood the previous day. The lawyer froze open-mouthed, unsure whether to continue until the senior magistrate dismissed the interruption and said, "You may proceed."

The flustered lawyer took a minute to review his notes, coughed to clear his throat, and said, "Signor Palumbo admitted that he delivered arms to a man named Signor Grassi. If this were true, and if Signor Grassi were a rebel as the witness claims, then why is Signor Palumbo not being charged with a crime? The court docket shows that no charges have been filed against Signor Palumbo. We can only conclude that either his statements are untrue, or he too, has received a consideration in exchange for his testimony. Thus, we must conclude that there are serious reasons to doubt the veracity of the prosecution witnesses."

The lawyer set down the paper he had been holding and took another sheet from his portfolio. "Signor Rinaldo Bastine is a highly regarded member of our republic, a respected member of the Arte dei Chiavaiuoli guild, and a steadfast supporter of the Church." The lawyer felt sure the magistrates would not know that only rarely could Rinaldo be found under the roof of his parish church. He signaled the court notary to escort a witness into the chamber.

After the man settled into the witness stand, the lawyer said, "State your name and your relationship to Signor Bastine."

The man puffed out his chest. "I am Bernabo Baldovinetti, a consul of the Arte dei Fabbri" — the blacksmiths guild — "as was my father before me and his father before him. Members of my family have crafted the finest metal works since the birth of our republic. Throughout my tenure as chief of our family business, I have purchased iron blanks from Signor Rinaldo's iron smelter."

"In all your dealings with Signor Bastine, has he displayed the traits you would expect from an honorable man, a loyal citizen of the Florentine republic?"

Baldovinetti glanced at the defendant briefly; then he turned to face the magistrates. "Signor Bastine has always fulfilled our business agreements. I have never had a reason to question his business competence." Baldovinetti's response skirted the issues of honesty and loyalty. He laughed as he added, "Although I wish his prices were lower." He quieted abruptly when he saw that no one else joined in his laughter.

Nico had expected that Bastine's lawyer would call a string of other witnesses to testify to his client's character, but there were no others. Bastine's irritated expression suggested that he had a similar expectation. But instead of calling another witness, the lawyer retrieved two sheets from his portfolio and began to deliver his closing statement. "Honorable magistrates, you have heard that Signor Rinaldo Bastine has a long history as a distinguished businessman. Never has his, or his family's impeccable reputation been questioned... until now, by witnesses, who have shown themselves to be unsavory criminals. In the interest of justice, I ask that you dismiss the charges against Signor Rinaldo Bastine."

As the lawyer slowly lowered himself into his seat, Bastine grabbed his arm and pulled him down. "Is that the best you could do?" he snarled. "For all the florins I've paid you over the years, I expect better." Bastine gestured toward the magistrates, saying, "Maybe I should have been paying them instead of you."

The senior magistrate summoned the court notary and instructed him, "Tell the Guardia officers to prevent anyone from leaving the chamber." After the notary hurried away to inform the guards who were stationed outside, the magistrate announced, "This tribunal will remain in session while my colleagues and I confer. Do not attempt to leave the chamber."

The three magistrates filed out the side door to their quarters. Little time passed before Bastine began rapping his fingers on the defense table. Minutes later, he rose, walked to the side of the room, and pounded his fist against the wall. "What are they doing?" he ranted. If his lawyer did hear the query, he chose not to respond as he fussed with the papers in front of him.

Massimo, who had been standing at the side of the room, wandered to the prosecution table, and bent to ask Nico, "Is it customary for everyone to be kept in the courtroom while the jurors deliberate?"

Nico chuckled. "No, it's not customary at all. It would never happen in another tribunal, but the Eight aren't bound by tradition."

"They've been in their quarters for more than a few minutes. Does that mean they're unable to agree on a verdict?"

"I don't think that's the case. If they disagreed, they would recess the trial while they deliberate. I suspect they agree on the verdict and are taking their time to consider the sentence."

Nearly half an hour passed before the magistrates returned and took their positions on the dais. "It is the verdict of this tribunal," the senior magistrate announced, "that the defendant, Signor Rinaldo Bastine, is guilty of the crime of abetting an insurrection against the Republic of Florence. The Guardia officers are to take the defendant to the Arnolfo tower, where he is to be confined until his sentence is pronounced. This session is adjourned."

Bastine jumped up, his face flush red, pointing wildly at the magistrates. "You can't do that. There's no proof. They're all liars. All of them." Guardia officers grabbed the ranting defendant and hauled him from the courtroom.

Massimo and Vittorio joined Nico at the prosecution table. "Where did you find him?" Nico asked.

"He was at his bank asking for a letter of credit," Vittorio replied.

Nico said, "So... he would have fled if you hadn't stopped him. Did he get the letter of credit?"

Massimo grinned, "Not only did he not get the letter, Vittorio told the bank clerk that Rinaldo's access to the account was suspended by order of the Florentine Security Commission."

To Vittorio, Nico said, "We don't have the authority to suspend bank accounts."

Vittorio beamed. "The clerk didn't know that."

44

FLORENCE, SEPTEMBER 30

A fragrant aroma greeted Nico when he returned to Casa Argenti for his midday meal. On the stairs leading to the kitchen on the second level, he heard his sister singing a tune she had recently learned from one of the neighborhood women. When Alessa was younger, she sang and hummed simple tunes in her native Darija language that she spoke as a child in Morocco. Over the years, the refrains from her youth had given way to Italian folk songs plus an occasional ditty learned from an itinerant French jongleur.

Nico found Alessa in the kitchen, standing in front of the stone fireplace stirring a kettle. "It smells great," he said. "Is it one of your own recipes?"

"Yes, it is," Alessa replied, sounding pleased. "The warm woody scent is from turmeric. Spices are most potent when they are fresh, and my favorite vendor at the central market just received a new shipment of turmeric from Tunisia."

Alessa tasted her brew and smacked her lips in approval. "Joanna and Donato should be here soon. They're eager to hear the outcome of the trial." She had barely mentioned Donato's name when he and his wife strode into the room. Alessa ladled portions from the kettle into bowls and set them on the table.

Dipping a spoon into the thick liquid, Nico asked, "Is it soup?

"It began as soup," Alessa laughed, "but I must have added too many vegetables, because now it's more like a stew. What would you call it if you served it at the Uccello, Donato?"

Donato stirred his bowl, took a quick taste, and said, "You know I love the earthy flavors of your Moroccan dishes, but this isn't fare that patrons would expect at the Uccello."

"Then maybe I should open a Moroccan restaurant to serve Florence's adventurous diners," Alessa joked as she fetched a loaf of bread from the side table.

"If you can find any adventurous diners in this city," Donato responded.

"Tell us about the trial, Nico. Did Signor Bastine have a worthy defense? Was he found guilty?" Joanna asked.

"His defense was neither worthy nor convincing. The magistrates deliberated for less than half an hour before delivering a guilty verdict, but they didn't announce his sentence."

"Are they having trouble deciding on the length of his prison sentence?" Joanna wondered.

"In this case, the magistrates have more to consider than the length of a prison term. Signor Bastine was convicted of abetting an insurrection. That's a major crime, as severe, or even more severe, than murder. He could be sentenced to execution, exile, or a prison term."

Alessa grumbled, "Exile? I can't understand why Florence believes it is proper to exile dangerous criminals. If a man is exiled, he can go live somewhere else as a free man. That's not punishment. To my thinking, Hudad law provides real justice. It says that a man who revolts against the leader can be stoned to death."

"I'm not sure that I see public stoning as a fitting means of execution," Nico said, "although I do agree exile isn't a harsh enough punishment for crimes of murder or inciting an insurrection." He hesitated a moment before adding, "But that's our law."

"How long do you expect will it take for the magistrates to reach agreement on Bastine's sentence?" Joanna asked.

"It could be later today, but certainly by tomorrow," Nico replied.

"Will someone notify you when they reach a decision?" Donato asked.

Nico grinned. "Yes, and as soon as the sentence is announced, I'm leaving for Siena. It will be at least two weeks until Signor Grassi's trial, so Chancellor Scala arranged for me to have a six-day holiday, and I'm planning to spend it with Bianca, in the town of Chiusi at her cousin's villa."

Joanna said, "If I'm correct, Chiusi was an Etruscan city."

"Yes, it was one of the league of twelve Etruscan cities. A Chancery clerk, who was born in Chiusi, told me there are tunnels made by the Etruscans under the town, and nearby there is a tomb with Etruscan paintings made a thousand years past. He also said that there's a beautiful lake outside the town."

Joanna smiled at Nico's eagerness to spend time with the woman he loved, no matter where it might be.

When they had finished eating, Nico stuffed the remaining bread and a chunk of cheese into his duffel to eat on his journey to Siena. As he pulled the cords to close his duffel, Alessa handed him a folded paper. "This note is for Bianca, from Sandro."

"What does it say?" Nico asked.

"I didn't read the note, but Sandro told me that Lorenzo de Medici saw his painting, the one for which Bianca posed in the gown she designed. Sandro said the young de Medici lavished praise on the painting and thought that when it is finished, the Palazzo Medici ballroom would be an ideal place to display it."

Nico countered, "Sandro also gave me a preview of his work in progress, and I think a public exhibition would be a more fitting venue, so everyone can admire it."

EPILOGUE
CHIUSI, OCTOBER 5

On the shore of Lake Chiusi, Nico and Bianca sat on the trunk of a fallen tree watching a frog jumping through mud at the water's edge. The low afternoon sun behind them stretched their shadows out onto the water, making patterns on the lake's undulating surface. Nico's eyes were suddenly drawn upward by the flight of three large birds passing overhead.

"Herons," Bianca stated. "They're beautiful. When I was young, my cousin and I would sit for hours watching their migrations. I remember one afternoon when we counted thirty of them."

They tracked the flock until it became hidden from view by a tall stand of trees at the south end of the lake. "Another reminder of time passing," Nico said dolefully. "Summer seemed to disappear without notice and now it's already October. It feels like we just arrived here in Chiusi; yet tomorrow I must return to Florence."

"And I have to return to Siena," Bianca said as she took Nico's hand. "Do you know how Vittorio and Massimo planned to spend their time away from work?"

"Vittorio is spending his in Arezzo. He spent his last holiday there as well, but he never mentioned his reason for going there. Perhaps he has relatives or a friend in Arezzo. Vittorio is a very private person."

"And Massimo?"

Nico grinned. "Massimo didn't say where he would spend his time, but I'm certain he will be enjoying the companionship of a woman."

"Your sister, Alessa?" Bianca speculated.

"Alessa is smitten with Massimo, and he might like to return her affection, but I sense he controls his feelings toward her because she's my sister. He's an honorable man. If he's ever ready to focus on just one woman, I'd be pleased if it were Alessa."

Bianca stood. "We should walk back to the villa. My cousin is preparing a special dinner for our last day in Chiusi. Brustico is a variety of fish in this lake that's been grilled and served with locally grown white beans since the time of the Etruscans. My cousin makes her own variation that is even more delicious than the original recipe."

As they came within sight of the villa, Bianca asked, "Will there be another mission taking you away as soon as you return to Florence?"

"There were no reports of impending crises when I was last in the city, but there's always the possibility that a new problem has arisen during my absence." Nico walked several paces in silence, then added, "I graduated from the university expecting to begin a law practice that would keep me in Florence, but my assignment to the Security Commission has taken my life in a different direction. However, it does give me the satisfaction of knowing that Rinaldo Bastine will spend years in prison." Nico wrapped an arm around Bianca's waist and pulled her close. "The work is exciting and meaningful, but it saddens me when the assignment keeps us apart."

ABOUT THE AUTHOR

Ken Tentarelli is a frequent visitor to Italy. In travels from the Alps to the southern coast of Sicily he developed a love for its history and its people. He has studied Italian culture and language in Rome and Perugia. At home he has taught courses in Italian history spanning time from the Etruscans to the Renaissance. When not traveling, Ken and his wife live in New Hampshire.

∾

What was life like at a Renaissance university?

Get your FREE download of *Nico's Story*, a recounting of Nico's path through the University of Bologna by signing up for our newsletter at https://www.KenTentarelli.com/nicos-story

ALSO BY KEN TENTARELLI

The Laureate: Mystery in Renaissance Italy

(Nico Argenti series book 1)

When Nico Argenti returns from the university, he is drawn into the turmoil gripping his beloved city of Florence.

The Advisor: Intrigue in Tuscany

(Nico Argenti series book 2)

Nico uses his legal training to help a small mountain town threatened by a vindictive knight.

Assignment Milan

(Nico Argenti series book 3)

Nico races to uncover the plot targeting the Florentine Republic when a Florentine banker goes missing in Milan.

Conspiracy in Bologna

(Nico Argenti series book 4)

Nico is dispatched to Bologna to thwart a vengeful renegade and rogue mercenaries.

Ingram Content Group UK Ltd.
Milton Keynes UK
UKHW011946270323
419267UK00019B/447/J